Few contemporary novels have touched the hearts of critics and authors with the emotional power of Elizabeth Berg's stunning bestseller

NEVER CHANGE

"Berg inhabits each of [her characters] as though she's known them since she wrote in their high school yearbooks and has kept her promise to keep in touch. . . . Heavy on the meaning of life and death, NEVER CHANGE is sad, yes, but it's funny, too—a Berg trademark. . . . Berg shows that life is most beautiful in the moments that come and pass away again, a lesson often learned long after high school."

—*The Atlanta Journal-Constitution*

"A superb novel about the persistence of desire and the perils of commitment."

—*Milwaukee Journal Sentinel*

"Filled with sadness and laughter, hope and despair, death and rebirth, NEVER CHANGE invites us to believe in the possibilities of second chances. It is a must-read for the romantic heart that lies in all of us."

—*Winston-Salem Journal* (NC)

"An engaging read that forces us to question who we are and who we want others to think we are. . . . An emotional story of memory, longing, and the confines of social roles."

—*Denver Rocky Mountain News*

ALSO BY ELIZABETH BERG

Open House
Until the Real Thing Comes Along
What We Keep
Joy School
The Pull of the Moon
Range of Motion
Talk Before Sleep
Durable Goods

NEVER
CHANGE

ELIZABETH BERG

WSP

WASHINGTON SQUARE PRESS
PUBLISHED BY POCKET BOOKS

New York London Toronto Sydney Singapore

A Washington Square Press Publication of
POCKET BOOKS, a division of Simon & Schuster, Inc.
1230 Avenue of the Americas, New York, NY 10020

Copyright © 2001 by Elizabeth Berg

Originally published in hardcover in 2001 by Pocket Books

Library of Congress Cataloging-in-Publication Data

Berg, Elizabeth.
    Never change / Elizabeth Berg.
        p. cm.
    ISBN 0-7434-1133-1
    1. Brain—Tumors—Patients—Fiction. 2. Middle aged women—Fiction.
3. Visiting nurses—Fiction. 4. Terminally ill—Fiction. 5. Single women—Fiction.
I. Title.

PS3552.E6996 N48 2001
813'.54—dc21   00-069874

First Washington Square Press trade paperback printing May 2002

10 9 8 7 6 5 4 3 2 1

WASHINGTON SQUARE PRESS and colophon are registered trademarks of
Simon & Schuster, Inc.

For information regarding special discounts for bulk purchases,
please contact Simon & Schuster Special Sales at 1-800-456-6798
or business@simonandschuster.com

Cover photo © Christine Rodin

Printed in the U.S.A.

This book is dedicated to the memory of John Kirk Farrar. He called himself Johnny K. I called him Johnny K. of the Milky Way. I guess that's where he really does live now. More or less.

Once, I was writing an article about what things make the best Christmas presents. So I called John and asked him, "What's the best present you've ever been given?" He thought for a while, and then he said, "You know how cats sometimes run sideways?" I said yes. He said, "That's one."

That's how he was. That's why I miss him. So many do.

ACKNOWLEDGMENTS

Well, of course I want to thank my agent, Lisa Bankoff, who handles my business affairs with such grace and integrity. And style. Many thanks as well to her assistant, Patrick Price, who gets things done, and done well. He is a man who can be trusted, no small thing.

I also want to thank my editor, Emily Bestler, for believing in this book and for stepping up to the plate in cowgirl boots to prove it. Thanks too to her assistant, Kip Hakala, for the many favors he does for me and for making our business dealings such *fun*. Whenever he calls, I feel like something good has just come on TV.

I am fortunate to have two daughters, Julie and Jennifer, who enrich my life beyond all measure. And I have the love of a good man, Bill Young, to provide a foundation I cannot be without. His affection is returned.

My dog, Toblance Floyd Ripken, king of the golden retrievers, deserves his own paragraph for the way he is a constant source of comfort and joy. Here you go, Toby.

This book could not have been written without the spiritual instruction I received at the hands of the many patients I cared for when I worked as a registered nurse. I thanked them then and I thank them again now. I thank them most of all.

The world breaks everyone and afterwards many are strong at the broken places.

—ERNEST HEMINGWAY
from *A Farewell to Arms*

PROLOGUE

The Tuesday before it happened was a perfect summer day. Driving through town on my way home, I saw two young girls holding hands as they tried to cross a street against the light. They would start to cross, then stop; start again, stop. Finally, all the traffic sighed and halted; and the girls bolted to the other side of the street and began to laugh and push each other, exhilarated by their survival.

Next I saw an old woman sitting at a bus stop, eating an ice cream cone with the neat precision of a cat. She wore a yellow print house-dress and white, orthopedic-style sandals, and her purse sat on the bench a slight distance from her, as though it were her companion. One leg was crossed over the other, and her foot swung rhythmically. She stared straight ahead, seemingly lost in memories.

I passed a very small child walking delicately along a stone wall, holding onto her mother's hand. It was a graceful pas de deux; love lay strung along the length of their joined extremities, love and pleasure. And heartbreaking certainty.

I drove by two boys about eleven years old, riding the hell out of their bicycles as young boys do, their real manhood still so frustratingly far off. You could see their sweet toughness in the straining cords of their necks. Each kept passing the other, shouting roughly, shouting insults; but each always looked back to make sure the other was coming.

Two blocks from home, I went past the library and I knew I could go into the children's room and sit in a chair and watch, enjoying every damp curl, every dimpled elbow, every throaty question, every pair of eyes turned upward toward a parent—the wholeness of that trust! I could press my own hands over the children's small prints on the walls of the hamster cage, trying to see what they saw, as they saw it. I could turn the pages of a book that one of them had looked at, then left behind. The question: Why was this not taken?

Yes, and I could stay for pajama story hour, as I often had, and watch the children who gathered on the carpet with their matted, sleep-scented stuffed animals. I could enjoy the children's unashamed eagerness—yanking their thumbs out of their mouths and rising up on their knees to see the pictures, resting their hands unselfconsciously on those ahead of them so that they would not lose their balance.

I suppose I might then have gone upstairs to the reference room, pulled down a weighty text, and searched for some wondrous fact I had never known. I might once again have sat at a wooden table, my own purse on the chair beside me, waiting for words to offer their touchless embrace.

I did not do these things. I headed home, toward what I had come to believe was my destiny.

Y ou know people like me. I'm the one who sat on a folding chair out in the hall with a cigar box on my lap, selling tickets to the prom, but never going—even though in the late sixties only nerds went to proms. But I would have gone. I would have happily gone; I would have been so happy. I wanted the phone call with the rough voice asking "Would you . . . ?" I wanted to finger row after row of pastel dresses in silks and chiffons—their sweetheart necks, their wide ribbon ties. I wanted to have some shoes dyed; I thought it was a miracle they could do it. I wanted to put a wrist corsage in my refrigerator, lock the bathroom door, and bathe in perfumed water with rollers in my hair and the transistor at the edge of the sink blaring "Sugar Pie, Honey Bunch." I wanted to allow an hour for the application of all my new Maybelline, suffer the flash-bulbs of my parents' eager camera, stay out all night, and eat breakfast before I came home, bleary-eyed and in the know.

I didn't get asked. I never once got asked. Not to proms, not to lesser dances, not to movies, not to parties, not for shopping with the girls.

I would get talked to, though. I mean beyond the "Hi!"s in the hall, beyond the preoccupied chatter in the lunchroom. I got talked to a lot. They would call me on the phone, the pretty girls. They would

3

call and talk to me about things that were serious: their parents' alco-
holism. Their hidden scoliosis. Their possible pregnancies. They
talked to me because I knew how to listen, and I gave good advice. I
didn't have a lot of personal experience, but I knew things, because I
read and I watched. That is what there was for me. Those girls talked
to me—and a boy, once, too—because they knew I would never betray
them. Of course they betrayed me constantly. But they didn't really
mean to. Probably they didn't know. They didn't think about it that
much.

I'm the one everybody liked, Myra Lipinski, *oh yeah, Myra, she's
nice*, the one that everybody liked and no one wanted to be with.
The odd shape. The socks, those socks—well, her parents had
accents. The face, unfortunate, with its too small eyes, its too wide
mouth. The hair mousy brown, too thin and straight, greasy after half
a day, no matter what. Even as a five-year-old: the aunt and uncle
who once came to visit, sitting with my mother at the kitchen table,
chatting quietly in Polish, and smiling over at me. "What are they
saying?" I asked my mother, coming over to stretch myself out across
her lap and shyly smiling back at them. "What are they saying about
me?" And my mother finally breaking into English to tell me, "They
say you look like . . . your father. And now we are not anymore talking about *you*." I lay still in her lap, contemplating the yellow-and-
orange pattern of her apron and forbidding myself my thumb, until
she crossed her legs and dislodged me.

So. I sold the tickets and I decorated the gym and I helped win the
volleyball games and I sang a good alto in the choir and I lent my
notes to anyone who asked; and if people wanted to copy from my
test paper, I let them do that, too. I did not become bitter. I don't
know why. Maybe I didn't think I had the right.

After graduation, I stayed here in Ashton, venturing no further
than the twenty-two miles necessary to get to Boston College,
where I earned my BSN. I went to nursing school because I knew it
would be a way for people to love me. And for me to love them,
too. This happens in illness. The sad plates of armor separate; the
light comes in.

At first, I worked in the intensive care unit. I wanted the challenge and the prestige of working in the hardest place. You're eating lunch in the cafeteria, wearing your scrubs, your high-tech stethoscope around your neck, a hemostat clipped onto you somewhere, tourniquets tied onto it. You know a long list of lab values cold; you could intubate if you had to; you can rate heart murmurs and evaluate lung status and draw blood and start IVs better than most of the attending physicians. You see a burst of ventricular tachycardia race across a monitor screen and you save the patient and let the doctor know about it when you get around to it. You can give a lot of drugs that nurses on other floors can't. You can decide when to get certain kinds of tests performed. When you call down to any other department in the hospital and say, "This is ICU," they pay attention. You come first. When you say *stat*, it gets done *stat*.

So you're eating lunch and a code is called over the loudspeaker, and you get up and run back to the unit. It's likely you'll be needed, no matter where in the hospital the arrest occurred. The other people in the cafeteria watch you leave your bowl of soup sitting there, and they nod at you as you pass by. In the army of nurses, you wear four stars.

The pay is pretty good, too, especially for a single woman with no obligations—only child with no children, parents dead. I bought a little two-bedroom house a couple of blocks from the center of town. I bought a Porsche Carrera 911, too. Black, tan leather interior. Incredible sound system. The boys look when I pull up next to them; then look away. I beat them off the line, every time.

The problem with intensive care is that the patients usually can't speak. They're on respirators. Or they're unconscious. Or they have such messed up chemistry that they're confused. Or they stay just until they're stabilized, and then they're out of there and another train wreck comes in. That's what the bad cases are called: train wrecks. It doesn't mean what it sounds like. What it means is: right now, I can't get close to you, you're halfway to death. And anyway, I don't have time.

So there's no opportunity, in the unit, to sit at the side of the bed and shoot the breeze with patients. To get to know them. To admire pictures of their children, to style their hair, to slowly help them eat. Not that many of them eat. Tubes. I know a nurse who works in the unit precisely be*cause* the patients don't eat. "I didn't go to four years of nursing school to load mashed potatoes onto a fork," she says. But I like feeding people. It doesn't feel demeaning. It feels like high privilege.

The best day I had in the unit came when we had a boarder, someone who couldn't get put onto the floor where she belonged; it was full. She ate. She sat up in a chair. She was oriented to time, place, and person. She dug in her purse for lipstick after her bath. The unit was light that day; she was my only patient. She told me she had a crush on her doctor—no surprise, everyone had a crush on Dr. LaGuardia, with his dark, South American looks—so I told her I'd curl her hair, and she'd look beautiful when he came to visit her. We used 4 x 4 gauze pads to make rag rollers, and she did look beautiful when he came. I stopped him outside her cubicle, told him to be sure he noticed her hairdo. He's a good guy, Dr. LaGuardia. He walked in the room and stopped dead in his tracks. "Where was the beauty contest?" he asked, in the accent you could feel in your knees. "Where's the trophy?" Then he told her she could transfer to her floor now, there was a bed available; and twenty minutes later I was taking care of a gray-faced man with multisystem failure.

I stayed working in the unit for a long time. I mixed drugs, counted drops, monitored machines, resuscitated people who arrested, then resuscitated them again when they arrested half an hour later. I rarely had enough time to talk to their distraught family members. I had to walk away from their sad, worried clusters; I had to go and milk chest tubes while they wept and talked in church-quiet voices.

Oftentimes, I worked in my dreams. I heard the beep-beep of the IV telling me the infusion was completed, the rhythmic sighs of the ventilator, the dull bong of the alarm on the heart monitor. I changed dressings in my sleep, emptied urine and bile and drainage from wounds into toilets, sent polyps and kidney stones and spinal fluid to the pathology lab. I tested feces for blood, tested urine for blood, tested vomit for blood, kept track of each ounce that went into a patient and each ounce that came out, monitored levels of consciousness, listened to lungs, to hearts, to various levels of activity in the four quadrants of the abdomen. I awakened after those nights feeling exhausted, feeling like I'd just put in eight hours at the hospital after having just put in eight hours at the hospital. Or nine. Or sixteen.

These days I work for a Boston agency called Protemp, as a visiting nurse. When I was hired, I asked for easy patients; I was tired of high acuity levels. Now that I've been there for ten years, I don't think I could hear a heart murmur if it were as loud as sandpaper on sandpaper. But I'm happy. And when I sleep now, I am back to dreaming only gauzy mysteries.

I have some clients I see daily: Rose Banovitz, who lives in a seedy area on Commonwealth Avenue and needs her morning dose of insulin, and who often sings to me in her high, quivery voice. Fitz Walters lives in Chinatown and needs me to check his blood pressure and his wildly erratic heartbeat in order to determine his dose of Nitropaste. He goes to strip clubs every night, Fitz, though he is blind. The Schwartzes live in the heart of Brookline and need weekly visits to supervise their medications and to keep them from killing each other. Another once-a-weeker, a black woman in Dorchester appropriately named Marvelous, I will keep on seeing even after I'm no longer paid to help her with her colostomy. I also see one DeWitt Washington, because nobody else will put up with the combination of his personality and his neighborhood in Roxbury. I have to go every afternoon and change the dressing on his gunshot wound.

I give eyedrops daily to a rich woman in Back Bay, Ann Peters, who can't see to do it herself and whose family can't be bothered. And since last week, I've been going to Allston to see a fifteen-year-old girl named Grace to help her with the baby she just had. I gave her my home number, and she leaves me messages at least once a day. Things like, "Okay. His shit looks exactly like scrambled eggs. No way is this normal. All I do is fuck up, and he don't even cry. Can you call me? Sorry for the swears, can you please call?"

You know the boy who once called me in high school? That was Chip Reardon. He called because he knew I had been talking to his girlfriend, Diann Briedenbach. They were having trouble. He wanted advice, some inside information. He felt comfortable asking me—we'd had a lot of classes together and he knew how carefully I observed things. Once, in fact, after an essay of mine had been read aloud in English, he stopped me after class to compliment me on my perceptiveness. I treasured that small event, carried the memory of it home from school like a wrapped gift. I even decided, foolishly, that had the bell not rung, that conversation might have led to something more. I remember getting home and looking at myself in my parents' full-length mirror, wondering if I'd finally worn something right, something that would make a boy like him really see a girl like me. I'd worn the same outfit a week later, down to the same color tie to hold my hair back, but of course nothing happened.

Anyway, when he called that night I told him only that he shouldn't worry, Diann loved him, I knew that for certain. He thanked me, though it seemed to me that his relief was not so great. But then I decided I was only making that up, trying to make him less invested in her than he really was. After we hung up, I put my fingers to the place his voice had come from.

As there is one of me in every high school, there is one of Chip Reardon, too. Other end of the spectrum. Every girl's dream boy. The handsome star athlete with a good head on his shoulders, too. And a genuinely nice guy. Everyone fighting over him for college.

He went west. That's what he said, to keep from bragging about Stanford—nobody from Ashton High had ever gotten in there. But now he's back here. I know because I got a message from my agency, asking if I could possibly fit in another client. A man called Chip Reardon. Fifty-one years old. Brain tumor, end stage, apparently; not too much to do. Probably home to die—he'd only need comfort measures.

I called my agency back. I said, yes, I could take another patient. They told me it would be daily visits at first, starting tomorrow. Then they told me where his parents, with whom he would be staying, lived. It was in the south part of town, a newer, wealthy area that is in marked contrast to the rest of this mostly blue-collar area. It's too far to walk to the hardware store from there, to the library or the bakery or the common; but it is close to open areas of farm lands, with their lovely stone walls, their rolling hills and peaceful populations of sheep and cows. I wrote down his nice address and his terrible diagnosis, entered it next to the 2:00 P.M. slot for Wednesday. And you know something bad? You know something bad about me? When I wrote that, I felt happy. I thought only one thing. I thought, Good. Now I can have him.

Not that you should think I haven't had my moments. I have had my moments. Some. Moments. You know, the blind date with the guy whose face at first turns in on itself when he sees what *he* got. But particularly after age forty-five, one can make do. One adult female can offer a certain kind of comfort to one adult male. And although they didn't usually stay the night—only two ever stayed the night—I was glad for that. After my rare interludes, I actually prefer a sandwich alone at my own kitchen table. I know I'm better off sitting under the fluorescent light in my bathrobe, alternating bites of pickle with my ham and cheese, turning the pages of the Chambers catalog and finding the one thing I'll let myself order—that's much better than the smiley conversations I endure when they stay. The awkward partings in the morning, the indignity of picking the guy's hair from my sink when I know I'll never see him again. Better to eat the sandwich and then look to see if any *Mary Tyler Moores* are on where Mary still lives in the old apartment. The only thing wrong with that show is that they acted like Rhoda was unattractive.

People think women like me should settle. That we should not aspire to certain things. Well, I had a crush on Chip Reardon, too, just like all the other girls. I had a full-time longing that went beyond the brief fantasy I enjoyed that day after English class. I saw him kissing me. I was not a different person when I imagined this; I saw him kissing *me*. I was aware that if most kids knew that, they'd snort their disapproval. They wanted me to have a crush on the guy equivalent of me. But of course I didn't. No one did. I didn't want Thomas Osterhout, him with his horrible posture and his stick-out Adam's apple and dandruff dusting the shoulders of black knit shirts tucked into his high-waisted pants—I didn't want him any more than he wanted me. Probably Thomas kissed Diann in his dreams, rode her around in his battered Gremlin while all the jocks stared, their fists shoved into their pockets.

Mostly, I have a dog. Don't laugh. Take a look at marriages that have survived a long time and see if it's the dog or the spouse that offers a better package to either partner. The dog can't call the internist for you; he can't accompany you out to dinner or to a show. But he will lie by you the whole time you're sick, and he will listen to every word you say and offer nothing back but acceptance. My dog, Frank is his name, is an eighty-five-pound golden mix, selected from the suffering souls at the dog pound. He sat quietly in the corner of his concrete cell, asking for nothing. When I stopped in front of his dank space, he walked up to me and sat down. Looked up. Held my gaze and waited.

"This one," I told the overworked attendant.

Frank walked out into the office on the leash I'd brought with me, lifted his leg apologetically against the desk where I filled out the necessary forms, and never again had an accident.

Usually, he sleeps smack up against the side of my bed, quiet as a shadow, except on the nights he has dreams—then he whines through his nose in a way that sounds like a story. Other nights, he senses a need and he jumps up to stretch out next to me. He lies on his side, his back to me. I put my arm around his middle, push up next to him, note with pleasure the salty earth smell of his paws.

It's enough, work and Frank. Or at least it has been, until now.

On Wednesday morning I wake up thinking, *What?* And then I remember. I go into the bathroom, look at myself in the mirror. Well, clear skin, I have that, I've always had that. Straight teeth. I stare a little longer, then go stand on the scale. I could lose weight; that's always been pretty easy for me. Five pounds, no problem, I can lose five pounds in a week. I put my lipstick on carefully. I could get some good mascara, too.

I stop for coffee on my way to Rose's. My favorite Dunkin' Donuts is just at the end of my block. It's always open, owned by a three-generation Russian family that barely speaks a word of English, but they are all remarkably friendly. Once when I was having trouble sleeping, I walked down there in the middle of the night in my pajamas (sweatpants and T-shirt, who could tell?) and I shot the breeze with the mother, Katrina, who works nights with her husband—the grandmother works mornings, the daughter evenings. The husband was in the back making glazed donuts and the wife sat down with me and had a cup of cocoa. We didn't talk a lot, but our eye contact was comforting. Katrina did say, "Where is you dog?" and I told her Frank was sleeping. He was, too. He wouldn't get up.

This morning, the shop is crowded, but I see that the grand-mother has two girls helping her. I open the car door, say, "Stay,

Frank," and then remember he's not with me. I don't bring him when I have to admit someone—filling out all the forms takes at least an hour. And of course you don't want to bring your dog until you've asked the patient if it's all right. Rose Banovitz is afraid of dogs, but all my other patients really like him. I told my agency they should put Frank on the payroll. Once, they did: At Christmas time, they cut a check for him. "Pay to the order of Frank Dog," it said, and the amount was five million dollars. It's in his scrapbook.

When I get to Rose's, I see that a few of the lights are out in her hallway; it's hard for me to see when I make my way down to her apartment. The cooked cabbage smell of the place seems even stronger in the dimness. I wonder how long it will take for someone to replace the bulbs. Last time, it took five months. When the lights were finally back on, it felt like Las Vegas, walking down that hall-way. I'm sure the cockroaches were very upset.

It's not always that the landlord doesn't respond to the tenants' requests; sometimes the tenants don't know they can ask. Or they don't know how to. Or they don't think it's so bad, not having hall lights. At least they have electricity in their apartments. Heat. A lock on the door. Their very own toilet. And you can't take on every-thing yourself, although in the beginning I tried. You only end up on the phone all day long. You don't get your own work done. At some point, you have to make a decision: Do I want to run for office, or do I want to take care of these patients?

Rose is in her slip when she answers the door, her nylons rolled to her knees, one blue plastic slipper on. "Oh," she says, and starts wav-ing her hands excitedly. "You see, it's my nurse!"

"Good morning!" I come in, close the door.

She starts to cry a little.

"How you doing, Rose?" I pat her shoulder.

"I have no *milk*," she says.

I sit at the foot of her iron bed: carefully made, covered with a for-merly white chenille bedspread missing half its tufts. "You don't have any milk, huh?" I rummage in my bag for her chart.

"No. And no orange juice!" She sits beside me. Her thin hair is up in a bun, about three thousand bobby pins at work back there, and a black hair net over it. Still, strands of gray slip and fall, and these she tucks behind her ears.

"Did your home health aide come yesterday? Was Tiffany here?"

"No. She didn't come."

"Oh, Rose. You're supposed to call the agency when that happens—they'll send someone else. Remember? The number is on your refrigerator."

"Oh. Yes. I forgot. I forgot!"

"Okay, it's all right." I look at my watch. I can call the home health aide and listen to a lot of bullshit, or I can call my agency and listen to a lot of bullshit, or I can take care of this problem myself and save a whole lot of time.

I put my bag down on the floor, zip it closed again. "Here's what we'll do, Rose. We need to work together, okay? I'm going to run to the little convenience store, the one right on the corner. I'll get you some milk and some orange juice. Do you have bread?"

"Um hum, I have bread. Do you want some?"

That's how most of these patients are. They'll give you anything.

"No, thank you. I'm just seeing what *you* need. How about fruit? Do you have any fruit?"

She looks longingly into my face and begins to sing "When Irish Eyes Are Smiling."

"Okay, Rose, I'm going to go to the store now. I'll be right back. I'll bring you some food, and then I'll give you your insulin. While I'm gone, you get dressed. Can you do that?"

"I'll get dressed. The bus for day care, I know. I'll be ready."

I check my watch, walk quickly back down the hall, thinking I'll be late for DeWitt—I have to see Ann Peters and Fitz Walters before him. I'd call DeWitt—he's the one patient who really gets mad if you're not on time—but the last time I tried to let him know I'd be fifteen minutes late, I ended up being half an hour late because I spent so long standing at a pay phone listening to him carry on about my incompetence. "You fired!" he finally said. His grand finale. And I

said, "No, DeWitt, I am not fired; I am simply late." "Same thing!" he
yelled, and hung up. And I went over and did his dressing anyway,
and my punishment was that he did not speak to me.

By the time I bring Rose's groceries back, she's sitting at the little
metal table in her kitchen wearing her favorite black dress. It's a good
forty years old, crepe, semiformal, with a once daring neckline now
made modest by Rose wearing a man's T-shirt beneath it. There is a
rhinestone bouquet pinned at the shoulder, all the stones gone cloudy
with age. Her battered black shoes are double-knotted, and she wears
school-girl white socks with them. She has drawn on long, black eyebrows and applied a smear of her ancient coral-colored lipstick to her
lower lip. Her open purse rests in her lap: inside, I see a balled-up
hankie, a red plastic coin purse, and her apartment keys on a string.
She used to always carry a framed picture of her mother, but the glass
got scratched; so now she leaves it sitting on her dresser. Once I
picked up that photo and stared into the clear eyes of Rose's long
dead mother, wondering if she could ever have imagined that this was
how her baby girl would end up.

I put the groceries on the table, fold up the brown paper bag and
then store it at the side of Rose's refrigerator, as she likes me to do.
Her supply of bags—plastic and paper, large size and small—is becoming overwhelming. "You could probably get rid of a few of these bags,"
I say.

"Oh, no," she says. "I need them."

"Maybe not so many, though."

"I *need* them."

She also has a bunch of rubber bands that she keeps in a kitchen
drawer. That's all that's in that drawer—a gigantic nest of rubber
bands. Sometimes I stand outside Rose's building and look up at all
the windows, and I think, *Whose apartment is the craziest?* When I call
Tiffany tonight to yell at her about not showing up, I'll tell her to
quietly get rid of a good third of those bags. After a while, you think
about fire hazards.

"All set, Rose," I say. "Let me give you your shot; then after a little while you can have some breakfast."

She stands, stretches mightily, then shuffles over to her bed. She has a routine: She sits and squeezes her eyes shut, hands gripping her knees. Holds her breath, as though she were getting some whopping dose of penicillin rather than this mosquito bite of insulin. I inject her left thigh quickly, then tell her, "All done."

"*This* time I didn't even feel it!" she says, as she does every time.

"Right," I say. And then, "Hey. Guess what I got us."

"I saw. Milk and orange juice. And bananas."

"No, not the groceries. Something else."

"What?" She can't decide whether to be suspicious or thrilled— too many times she's been offered a bad deal like it's a gift.

"Would you say you're a gambling type, Rose?"

She smiles, looks down into her lap. "I don't know."

I pull two scratch-away betting cards from my jeans pocket. "Know what these are?"

"Coupons!"

"Nope. They're betting cards. You scrape off the covering to see what numbers you have. You can win money."

"From that card? You can get money?"

"Right. Your numbers just have to beat the dealer's."

"Oh. I pick one million."

"No, Rose, you already have numbers. They give them to you, right on the card. We just have to look and see what they are."

I hand her a card, and she peers closely at it. "I don't see any numbers."

"You have to take the covering off of them, remember?" I scratch at my card. "Look here. In this case, I got a seven and the dealer got a nine. So I lose."

She looks at me, stricken.

"It's okay. I have three more chances. But let's see what you got."

Together, we scratch away at Rose's card. The bottom set of numbers shows the dealer with four and Rose with five. "You won!" I tell her. "See? You won five bucks!"

She laughs, claps her hands.

I uncover the rest of my numbers. "Uh-oh. I lost. But Rose, you won! See how lucky you are?"

She nods happily. "What can I buy?"

I look around her wreck of an apartment. Suddenly, the balloon deflates. "Well . . ."

"A new dish towel?" she asks.

"Yes!" I say. "Yes, I can get you a new dish towel."

"And I'll embroider it." She opens the bottom drawer of her dresser and pulls out a large flowered tin. She lifts the lid, shows me skeins of brightly colored floss crammed inside. "This was my mother's, you know." She picks up a handful of colors, closes her eyes, holds them against her cheek.

"Oh, that will be beautiful, Rose. That will be a wonderful thing to do."

"Yes, that will be a wonderful thing to do."

"But right now, you really need to eat breakfast. Your driver will be here soon."

She nods, stretches out the baggy sleeve of her T-shirt to wipe her nose.

"Can you make yourself some peanut butter toast and eat a banana? And drink some milk and orange juice, too?"

"Yes, I will."

I leave her standing over the toaster, peering down into it. She has to make sure the roaches are out before she puts the bread in.

Back in the car, I check my watch. I'm a good forty minutes behind. Then I remember where I'm going at two.

I look in the rearview mirror, smooth down the cowlick at the side of my head. Then I try to remember the last time I saw Chip Reardon.

It wasn't at graduation—the day before, he'd broken an ankle in three places in a touch football game, and he couldn't come. I remember he got a standing ovation anyway when they called his name.

So it must have been the last day of high school when I last saw him. June 8, 1968. Chip and I had English together, sixth period. Diann was in that class, too. We all sat in the back—Diann in front of Chip, me across from him. On that day, near the end of the last class, the teacher was reading us some T. S. Eliot, droning on and on, just killing time before the bell.

Chip took Diann's purse off the back of her chair. It was a big black leather thing, full of intriguing smaller pouches. He started examining everything. I remember thinking how lucky she was that he was so interested in her. And I remember being surprised that she felt no need to hide anything from him—she knew he'd taken her purse; she'd barely turned around. He looked at every picture in her wallet, started to open a note some friend had written to her, then didn't. It impressed me that he would respect her privacy in this way when he was so boldly going through everything else. And it wasn't for my benefit, either—as usual, he had no idea I was watching him. He uncapped the two pens he found, scribbled a few lines with each. He found her Tampax, took it out, and then put it back in its plastic holder. He stroked the rabbit's foot on her key chain, made it hop around his desk. Then he tried on one of her lipsticks—a pink so hot it neared fuchsia—and tapped her on the shoulder to show her. She frowned, rolled her eyes, and turned away. "Myra!" he whispered. When I looked over at him, he pursed his lips and made small kissing noises. I looked down at my desk, smiled. "Want some?" he whispered, holding up the tube of lipstick. I shook my head. "Come on," he said, tilting his head, running his eyes slowly over my face. "It would look good on you." His blond hair was falling over one dark blue eye; his long legs in their khaki pants stretched out into the aisle. He was wearing Weejuns with no socks, and he had the sleeves of his plaid shirt rolled up midway to the elbow. He was killing me.

Diann turned around then, snatched her purse back. But he had kept the lipstick, and now he held it out to me. I shook my head again. I knew he didn't mean it.

"Care to let us in on the joke, Mr. Reardon?" the teacher asked suddenly—loudly—but then the bell rang and everyone started cheering and running out of there. Then years passed and years passed and now I am a fifty-one year-old nurse and Chip is a fifty-one-year-old man with a brain tumor. And in a few short hours, I will see him again. His eyes will be the same. His hair will not be.

DeWitt is sitting out in a lawn chair on his sagging gray wooden porch. His arms are crossed, his eyes narrowed, his foot tapping. He chides me all the way into his apartment, down the hall, and into his bedroom, the place where I change his dressing. "What's your problem, anyway?" he says. "You don't need to be no Norman Einstein to figure out how to *get* here on time. You *been* here 'bout fifteen thousand times. 'Bout thirty thousand! You ought to know by now. You say you're going to be here at twelve, you best *be* here at twelve. Maybe you mean twelve midnight, you want to come here at twelve midnight?"

"Norman Einstein?" I say, lowering my bag to the floor, digging around for supplies. I cover the syringes with the blood pressure cuff; I keep forgetting I'm not supposed to bring syringes into DeWitt's apartment.

"Allen, I mean."

"What?"

"*Allen* Einstein, okay?" He climbs onto his bed, rearranges his pillows, sucks at his top lip with his bottom one.

"Albert," I say. "His name was Albert Einstein."

"Whatever. Now you just showin' off."

"Would you please lie flat so I can do your dressing?"

"Yeah," he says. "After *you* wait for *me*. I got a life, too. I'm a bidness man, work twenty-four hours a *day*."

This is actually true—DeWitt does a fair amount of drug dealing. "I got one important call to make," he says. "And I got to call right now, take just a minute. Then you can do my dressing." He stares defiantly at me.

I sigh, stare back. It won't do any good to tell DeWitt that all three patients before him took longer than usual today. As far as DeWitt is concerned, there are no other patients. It won't do any good to tell him he's wasting my time just for spite. That's the plan, after all.

"Well?" he says, finally.

"What, DeWitt."

"I *could* use some privacy." He picks up the glossy flyer he got last week from the Mercedes dealer. He has a substantial amount of money coming from a settlement, something about what happened when he went to court over his gunshot wound. He turns pointedly away from me, starts punching in numbers.

I go out into the living room, sit in his oversized black leather chair. I notice the faint smell of his citrusy cologne. He has one chair, one sofa, one lamp, one television. No rug. No pictures on the wall. No curtains. Nothing to read. It's a terrible waiting room.

"Yeah, this Mr. Washington," I hear DeWitt say. "This Bob? Bob, my man! I'm calling to tell you I'm 'bout ready to zero in on my choice. Now, how long it take to get that silver one again? Black interior." Silence. Then, "Well, *yeah* I want that. I thought that come *with* it." The bedroom door slams shut, presumably so I won't hear. But I still can. "Say I want to add that other CD player instead," DeWitt says. "How much it be then?" He starts laughing. "No shit! Well, what *else* that car got?"

I look at my watch. Then I get up and go knock at the bedroom door.

"Hold on," I hear him say. And then, *"Yessssssss?"*

"DeWitt."

"What!"

I open the door. "Stop busting my balls. If you want your dressing changed, I need to do it now. I have another patient to see. You can talk on the phone while I work."

"Yo, Bob, you hear this? Nurse Ratched. Yeah, she mad as a wet hen. I catch you later, I got to use my wildy charms, get her back on track."

He hangs up, smiles at me. He has a beautiful smile, actually. Two big dimples. He unbuttons his shirt, exposes the dressing. I put on my gloves, start pulling gently at the tape, loosening it.

"Hey, Sugar?" he says.

I don't answer.

"Awwwwww. Cabbage blossom?"

One side of the dressing is loose. I start on the other side.

"Come on, Myra, did I bust your balls, really?"

This other side is more difficult to get off. I pull a bit harder.

"Ouch! Jesus!"

I step back, my hands raised high.

"Just kiddin'," he says, and chuckles. "Sheeeit. You like a rabbit, girl. Jump like a little white rabbit."

I go back to work.

"You a white rabbit?" he asks.

I study the incision. No redness, no swelling, no odor, no excessive drainage. Good granulation tissue.

"Let's make it easier for you," DeWitt says. "We take it one step at a time. Are you white?"

"DeWitt? Knock it off."

"Aw, you no fun today. You nervous. What you so nervous about?"

I don't answer.

"Where's your dog? Where's ol' Frank? *He* always fun."

"He had a play date."

This is true. The woman across the street, Theresa, has a collie named Ginger, who loves Frank. They play together a lot.

"A *play date?*" That keeps him going for the rest of the time it takes to do his dressing. Good thing I didn't tell him Frank will frolic in Ginger's kiddie pool, be served Frosty Paws while he watches *Airbud,* and come home with a booty bag full of rawhide treats. Sometimes when I think I'm the only lonely person in the world, I remember Theresa. But she's lucky. She's a widow.

A few minutes away from Chip's house, I pull into the parking lot of a White Hen. Hungry. Well, nervous.

I buy a package of mini–rice cakes and come out to the car to eat them, then don't eat them. I look into the mirror, freshen my lipstick, think of the questions I'll need to ask Chip about his symptoms. Any headaches? Any . . . changes in mentation? Any mouth sores from the chemo? Any diarrhea? "I used to lie on my bed after school every afternoon and imagine kissing you, Chip; have you had any loose stools?"

I take out the little bottle of mouthwash I keep in my glove compartment, rinse, spit discreetly into the parking lot. "How about pain, Chip, how are you controlling that? Want me to call you Zipper Head, like this other patient of mine who had brain surgery? He lived six months, Chip. Think you can make it that long? Can I make dinner for you? You can come to my house, I'll make anything you want—if the food is on the earth, I'll get it for you. You could take a bath afterward, I have a little jacuzzi. I can give you a massage; I'm supposed to, now."

I imagine introducing myself to his parents. I feel sorry for them already. I always feel sorriest for parents whose children are dying. It's not the natural way, of course. The parents always take me aside to say that they should be the ones to go first. As though I could do something about it. As though I could say, "Oh, *right!* Okay, then, so . . . which of you will be taking the disease instead?"

Oftentimes, the parents object to the season. "He shouldn't be dying in spring, he loves spring." "She shouldn't die before Christmas, if we could just have one more Christmas." Again, as though an adjustment could be made. Oh, their hearts are broken, that's all, and they try to find one thing they can fix. And all you can do is go through your nursing care plan, share techniques with them: "Encourage the patient to share thoughts and feelings." "Encourage use of stress mangagement skills: relaxation techniques, visualization, guided imagery, biofeedback, laughter, music, therapeutic touch." This is good advice, of course. It is appropriate. It is what you can do. But you tell the parents these things, and you imagine that as they nod and think of how they might comply, their chests are full of the loudest roaring. Just this roaring. And in your own chest? A dull weight. A wish that you could wave a wand, just once.

I wonder if I should tell the parents that I went to high school with Chip. I decide not to. It would only make them feel bad. Pointing out the similarites between us would only highlight the terrible differences.

The house is a large colonial, white with black shutters. The lawn is well kept; there is a garden that runs along the side of the house, full of flowers in bloom—blues, pinks, yellows. The riches of summer.

At almost the same time that I ring the bell, it is answered by the kind of older woman you see in magazine ads proclaiming you're only as old as you feel. She has the bone structure of the classically beautiful woman; longish gray hair held back at the sides by combs. She wears black linen pants, a white silk blouse, pearl studs. She has the distressed look I have anticipated—the start of a smile overtaken by grief.

I hold out my hand. "Hi. I'm Myra Lipinski."

"The nurse."

"Yes."

"Please come in." She stands aside, and I hear her small sigh, a mix of regret and relief. I enter a hallway, dark and cool and redolent with the scent of roses. And then I see why—on a small table is a cut glass vase full of them. A mauve color. Beautiful.

"Chip's upstairs, in his bedroom. His father is with him. But I wonder if we could just talk a little before you see him."

"Of course."

We go into the living room: yellow silk furniture; a floral Oriental rug, many paintings in heavy gold frames. Formal drapes. A fireplace, now holding a large basket of dried hydrangea.

Mrs. Reardon gestures for me to sit on the sofa. I do, with my bag at my feet. In this room, the bag looks more beat up than it is.

She clears her throat, smooths the leg of her pants. "Chip is not really responding appropriately to his diagnosis."

I nod, wait.

"As you know, it's a very aggressive form of cancer."

"Yes."

"He had the surgery, of course. But now he won't do anything else."

"You mean . . ."

"Well, I mean chemotherapy, radiation therapy . . . even *psychotherapy!*" She laughs. "Really, he won't consider *anything*. Now, I know none of this will necessarily keep him from. . . . I know it's not exactly a cure, but it can buy him time. And if he gets some time, even a few months, who knows what they could come up with!"

I've got a pretty good idea what "they" could come up with in a few months: nothing.

She leans forward, speaks softly. "I'm hoping you'll be able to talk him into treating this thing. Really going after it. Persuade him that it's the best thing. It *is* the best thing. It's the only thing."

"You know, Mrs. Reardon, it can be really hard when someone doesn't make a choice that seems obvious to us. But—"

"I mean, he acts as though this is some kind of joke! Most of the time he answers the phone saying 'Chip Reardon, cancer patient.' Last night, he answered it saying 'Check-Out Inn.'"

"Well, that's not . . . it's not unusual. People have different ways of coping. Sometimes, the first thing they need to do is—"

She stiffens. "Oh please, don't . . . I assure you, I know my son."

"I'm sure you do."

Silence. There is the rich sound of a clock ticking somewhere nearby.

"So," she says, finally.

I stand. "Yes. Why don't I go and see him?"

She leads me to the stairs, then points. "It's the first room on the right. My husband's name is Charles."

The bedroom door is closed; I knock softly. It is opened by a man who looks like an older version of Chip. "Miss Lipinski?"

"Yes."

He closes the door behind him, nods gravely, then gestures for me to move down to the end of the hall with him. "I understand you'll be coming every day."

"Yes, I will."

"I wonder if I could just ask you about something."

"Of course."

"I don't know if . . . Well, first of all, I'd like to ask you to be very straightforward with me about everything, all right?"

"All right."

"I really mean it."

"So do I."

"Good. So, I'll just say this. I was wondering if Chip . . ." Abruptly, he starts to sob, but it is nearly silent, and completely dry-eyed. He does not acknowledge this—does not apologize, does not seem at all embarrassed. He just stands there, staring straight ahead, waiting for his chest to stop heaving and his breathing to quiet. It is as though he is waiting for a loud plane to pass overhead. I know better than to try to comfort him. There are times you reach out, and there are times you must let someone hold a terrible thing by themselves.

After a few seconds, he continues. "I was . . . pretty tough on Chip, when he was growing up. Times were different, then." He looks at me, seeking agreement, I assume.

"I know what you mean," I say. "Children weren't raised the way they are now. My parents were really strict, too."

"I don't believe I was *abnormal*, but I was tough on him. And now I can't help but wonder if . . . I've been thinking that maybe his cancer—"

"Mr. Reardon?"

The expression on his face is that of a child's, caught in the act of doing something he shouldn't.

"If what you're wondering is whether anything you did caused this—"

"Oh, no, it's more that I . . . Well, yes. Yes. I guess that is what I was wondering. Not that I can do anything about it." He has been looking everywhere but at me, but now his gaze is direct. Pleading.

"No one knows what causes this cancer," I say, gently. "But I can absolutely assure you that it's not your fault."

"Okay. Thank you."

"And I think the fact that Chip has come here says something about his relationship with you."

"Well, he never married, you know. He's stuck with us."

"Still."

"Oh, I know. I know he loves us." He passes his hand over his eyes. "Jesus. This is so difficult."

"Yes," I say, softly.

"He's our only child."

"I know. I'm so sorry."

"My wife must have told you he's refusing any further treatment."

"Yes, she did."

"I just want you to know that I'm not so sure he isn't right."

I nod, slowly. "Okay."

He straightens, points to the door. "So! He's all yours! Do you need anything?"

"No, I'm fine. I'll just do an admission interview today; it'll take about an hour, at the most."

"Cup of coffee?"

"No thanks." I am at the door, ready to knock, when it opens. And there he is. And except for the baseballish line of sutures along the shaved side of his head, I would say he has not changed much at all. Some gray in his hair. Perhaps a very slight slackening at the jawline. But mostly he looks like the boy Chip dressed up as the man Chip.

He stares at me for a long moment, trying to place me, I'm sure. Then, "Oh, my God, Myra?" He laughs loudly. "You look exactly the same!" Not much of a compliment, I'm afraid. "Hey, Dad!" he says. "This is Myra Lipinski, remember? We went to high school together."

"Oh, yes," Mr. Reardon says. "Of course."

But he doesn't remember, I know.

"God, it's been so *long*," Chip says.

I smile, feel the warmth of a blush start to rise up my neck. Then I remind myself of what I'm here for: head-to-toe body system assessment, emphasis on neuro deficits. Evaluation of activities of daily living status—can he do independently all he needs to do for himself? Medication review—does he know what to take, when, and what it's all for? Home safety check: electrical hazards . . . "You're a *nurse?*" Chip asks.

I shrug. "Yeah."

"*Are* you still Myra Lipinski?"

". . . What do you mean?"

"I mean, are you married?"

"Oh! No." I laugh. "No, not . . . at all."

"Huh. Me neither. Never did do that. Still time, though, I guess. People could say, 'They never got out of the honeymoon phase.' And they'd be right! Well. Won't you come in? It's small, but it's home." He looks over at his father. "Dad?"

"I'll be downstairs," his father says quickly. "Call me if you need anything."

Chip closes the door behind us. Then he sits on the bed, grinning, looking up at me. "Let's see . . . The last time I saw you was sixth period English, right? That idiot Mr. Saunders. He read poetry with all the sensitivity of a 'goddamn toilet seat.' Remember that guy? In *The Catcher in the Rye?*"

"Holden Caulfield, talking about Ackley," I say. "Yes, I do remember that."

Chip points to an overstuffed chair close to the bed. "Sit down and tell me all about yourself while I get ready. And then let's go out and get a meal. I want some grease. My mother's driving me crazy with her health food. She's trying to turn me into a macrobiotic, for Christ's sake."

This is not exactly what the program is supposed to be. But do I mind? No. I'm going on a lunch date with Chip Reardon, cancer patient. After he interviews me. I watch him put on his sneakers and tie a blue bandana around his head that does a fairly good job of covering his incision. I'm trying not to feel too thrilled while I tell him what's happened in my life.

It's warm out, but with no humidity to speak of. Chip wants to walk somewhere to eat, and we decide on Ned's Place, one of my favorite restaurants, only a few blocks away. Chip's never been there; it's only been around for five or six years. It's tiny—five tables, five stools at the counter. It's in a white, freestanding building that looks like a child's playhouse—there's a little porch attached where I tie Frank when we come here, black shutters at the window, red geraniums in the window boxes. Inside, there are small shaded lamps on the wall over every table, as though the place is half '40s nightclub. The menu features a drawing of burned toast coming out of a smiling toaster. Once I asked Lindy, who, along with her husband, Al, owns the place, why she put a picture of burned toast on the menu. "Al likes it," she said.

Everybody who goes to Ned's loves it, including Frank—Lindy always gives him great scraps. The best time is early morning, when the regulars are lined up on the stools, hats on their heads with the bills turned emphatically frontward. Nearly all the regulars are men, ranging in age from their late teens to their late eighties. They don't bother Al, who stands quietly cooking at the grill behind the counter, but they're after Lindy all the time. Once, when she was giving it back to them pretty good, one of the guys said, "Jesus! Does anybody know when laryngitis season starts?"

There's a cop named Brenda who comes in there every morning, and she allies herself with Lindy—once, she up and handcuffed a guy who was mouthing off too much. She didn't release him until he promised to leave a ten-dollar tip. Sometimes, if the place is really busy, Brenda will run around and take orders, then go back to her own breakfast. I tried to help out once, but Lindy fired me, saying I made the customers feel bad about what they ordered. "I didn't say a *thing!*" I said. And Lindy said, "You didn't have to. Your little nursey face said it all."

When Chip and I come in, Lindy looks up from wiping down the counter. "Hey, Myra! Where you been? I've got the butt end of a ham saved for Frank."

"He didn't come with me today," I tell her. Then, pointing to Chip, I say, "I brought him, instead. This is Chip Reardon."

"How you doing," Lindy says, and Al offers a manly nod—the upraised chin variety.

"You want a table?" Lindy asks.

Always, I sit at the counter. But she can see that today I want some privacy.

"Sure," I say, and head for one in the corner.

"Not that one," Lindy says. "John Harris is coming in."

I look at my watch. "It's way too late for him." John is a big deal in our little town—has a finger in every pie. He's like the mayor without being the mayor, and he has a permanent table at Ned's.

"He's got a meeting," Lindy says. "He's probably taking out a contract on somebody."

"Yeah," one of the guys at the counter says. "He's taking it out on you, Lindy, for not *ever* keeping a goddamn *coffee* cup filled!"

Lindy looks up from the dishwasher, where she's been loading plates. "You want more coffee, Freddy?"

"I guess I do."

"Well, I guess if you ask me nice, I'll think about it."

"Aw, Jesus," Freddy says. And then, in a singsong falsetto, "Oh, please, Lindy, could you find it in your heart to give me a little more coffee, *please?*"

"That was pretty nice," she says. "Now, I'll think about it."

Freddy gets up to fill his own cup.

Chip and I sit at a table near the door. It's where Lindy sits to refill the condiments, when the place quiets down. That's usually only at three o'clock, when they close. Not that they really close. They put up the "Sorry!" sign, but then they hang around and cook for the next day, and if someone comes in and wants to eat, they feed him.

Chip scans the menu, muttering, "Great. Oh yeah, great." He looks up at me, nods. "You were right, this is exactly what I wanted." He orders a double cheeseburger, fries, and a chocolate malted. I start to order, then remember my diet.

"Just coffee," I tell Lindy.

"Aw, bullshit."

"Okay, a burger, then."

"Fries?"

"Okay. And a malt, too."

She scribbles down our orders. Then, looking more closely at Chip, she says, "Whoa. What'd you do to your *head*, fella?"

I feel myself stop breathing. Then Chip says, "Well, I had a little surgery. They took out a tumor."

"Oh, my God," Lindy says. "I'm sorry. I thought you had an accident, I had an uncle, he had a toboggan accident, and he had stitches in his head just like that."

"I wish it were that."

"I'm so sorry." I have never seen Lindy blush, but she is colored a bright red now.

She goes back to the counter, yells the order to Al while she slaps away the hand of a regular who has tried to untie her apron.

"I'm sorry," I tell Chip.

"Happens all the time," he says. "I'm used to it."

"It won't take too long for those sutures to be gone. And your hair will grow back quickly."

"Right."

There is a moment of silence, and then Chips says, "So, how come you never got married?"

"Well. Never got asked, outside of Billy Harris, who asked me to marry him in kindergarten. But that didn't count, because he proposed to all the other girls in the class, too. After that, though . . ." I smile, shrug.

"Oh, listen, I . . . It's none of my business. I'm sorry if I embarrassed you."

"It's okay," I say. *"I'm* used to *it."*

He smiles. And then his face changes and he looks away, turns his fork slowly upside down, then right side up. He leans across the table, speaks quietly. "How do you think I got this, Myra?" His voice is so plaintive, so vulnerable.

I shake my head, my throat tight.

"No clue?"

"No, not really."

He sits back. "Okay. So you're going to come every day, right?"

"For the time being."

"Uh-huh. Check my incision, and then all that other stuff: See if I'm starting to get confused, see how many times a day I barf, or have a seizure, or writhe in pain. Is that it?"

"Well—"

"'Fun, huh? And let's not forget the all important 'patient's thoughts and *feelings*'! Let's see if I can remember. 'Problem: Grieving, anticipatory. Intervention: Redirect negative thinking.'"

I swallow. "Very good."

"I know you've been told I'm 'refusing treatment.'"

I say nothing, take a drink of my water. Hearing him so matter-of-factly recite the things that can—and probably will—happen to him, has shaken me. Most people deny that such things will occur. Most people, in fact, go through a long period during which they deny their diagnosis altogether. Because it doesn't belong with them. It doesn't fit. Because they don't have time for it. They think, despite all evidence to the contrary, that there's been a terrible mistake. Later, after they come to accept their diagnosis, they often think nothing else will happen—all those terrible symptoms they heard about were just things that happened to other people; it will be different for them. Because they are Christian. Because they meditate. Because so many people love them. Because they are needed so much. Because they have learned their lesson, and now they will be good. And then: If they do have to die, it will be like this: They will by and large remain themselves. And then one day, they will turn off a ball game and say, "All right. I'm ready to go upstairs and die, now." But then comes the time when there is no more denying.

"Myra," Chip says. "I want to tell you something, and I need you to hear me. I need you to hear me. Just last year, a stockbroker I worked with got bad colon cancer. He was a good friend. I saw what he went through with aggressive treatment. I'd rather just . . . I don't want to endure all that for the promise of a few months. Well, not even the promise. The remote chance."

"I understand."

"Do you?"

"Yes, I do." I think of Mike Connelly, a patient I took care of when I was just out of nursing school and working on a medical floor. He had a rare lymphoma. The first day he came in for treatment, he told me, "You know, I served twice in Vietnam. Green Beret, real gung ho. I was never afraid of dying, not once. But I sure am now." He was sitting on the bed talking to me, and he looked so big and strong, the plastic identification band on his thick wrist so silly. He went through hell trying to save his life, using both conventional and experimental therapy. The last time he left the hospital, he looked like he'd been through a much worse war than Vietnam ever was. And he died three weeks later. Everything he'd tried had done exactly nothing.

"I'd like to stay as normal as I can for as long as I can," Chip says. "And when things start to go, I'm going to go, too."

"Well, you can't exactly program your time of death."

"Of course you can."

I look at him, start to say something, then don't. Now is not the time.

Lindy comes over to the table, sets down two chocolate malts with a flourish. Then she goes back to the counter to take care of the man who has begun bellowing about needing another spoon. "Relax, you old fart," she tells him. "Remember your blood pressure."

"It's you that *give* me that high blood pressure!"

"You wish," she says, sniffing.

Chip leans over toward me. "I really like this place."

"They have a Halloween party every year; if you want to come, you have to dress like something on the menu."

"What do you come as?"

"Me? I never go."

"Why not?"

"Well, you know. Parties."

"What about them?"

"I hate them."

"Oh. That's a good reason not to go to them."

I take a big drink of my malted. Delicious. Forty-five million calories. "When I was a little girl," I say, "I used to think people who went to parties dressed like that all the time, that they were a certain class of people. There were people like my parents, who dressed the way they did—you know, Sears—and they never went to parties. And then there were the people who went to parties and they got up every morning and put on their silks and satins and tuxes and went down to breakfast and talked about where they would be going that night."

Chip nods. "I didn't know there were bones in bodies. I thought if you made a cut through an arm, it would be all pink, solid flesh, kind of like baloney."

"I knew the deal with bones," I say. "But that's all I knew about what went on inside. I thought there were little cast-iron pots in our stomachs that held all the different kinds of food we ate. Like, there was a little pot for potatoes, a little pot for applesauce . . . One day I was eating applesauce and I got very worried, because I figured the pot must be close to full, and surely it would overrun, and that would kill me."

"What did your parents say when you told them?"

"I didn't tell them. I never told them anything I worried about."

"Why not?"

"Oh . . . They wouldn't have been much help."

One of my earliest memories is of a time I awakened from a nightmare. I went into my parents' room and stood beside their bed. "What," my father said, not opening his eyes. "I had a dream," I said. "I'm scared."

"Anna," my father said, and my mother turned over to say, "So, Myra, you said yourself, it was just a dream. Go back to sleep, now. Look at the time." I hadn't yet learned to tell time. But I did learn that night that there were things I must not ask for.

Lindy puts down our platters in front of us, and Chip stuffs a bunch of french fries into his mouth. "Paradise," he says. "Perfect." He picks up his saucer-sized burger, admires it, puts it back down on the plate to salt it. "When I was a little boy, about three or four, I guess, I was sitting outside one summer day and I all of a sudden realized that I swallowed my spit. I was just astounded at this, and I ran inside to tell my mother. She said, 'Oh yes, dear, we swallow our saliva.' I said, 'Well, what did we do *last* year?'"

I laugh, watch him take a huge bite of his burger, then cup his hand beneath it to catch the drippings. I hand him a few napkins.

"I thought nuns were a third sex," I say, and take a bite not much smaller than Chip's.

"Okay," he says. "*I* thought 'technical knockout' was when one man knocked another one out with 'technique.'"

I laugh so loudly Lindy looks over at me, one hand on her hip.

"Hey Lindy," I say. "What's something you used to believe when you were a little kid that turned out to be completely wrong?"

"Everything," she says.

"Tell me one thing."

She stands still, thinking.

Al leaves the grill and comes to the counter to tell us, "I thought if I looked into the mirror at my own eyes for too long, I'd go crazy."

Lindy turns to him. "Huh. Then you must have spent a long time looking. Anyway, she didn't ask you. She asked me." She comes over to our table, says in a low voice, "I thought men's penises were about forty inches long. I swear to God. I thought they folded up like a yardstick so they wouldn't hang out beneath the cuff of their pants."

"And?" Chip says.

Lindy looks at Chip for a long moment, then at me. "They're all like that," she says. "Pigs."

"I know it."

"I know it, too," Chip says.

"I thought you made babies by lying down and praying together," Al yells over to us. He flips a pancake up in the air, then turns to point his spatula at Lindy. "Don't you say a word, either."

A man at the counter whom I've not seen before spins around, coffee cup in hand. He's wearing a faded blue mechanic's uniform with "Buzzy" embroidered over the pocket. "I'll tell you one," he says. "When I was about six years old, I used to lie in bed at night and imagine cutting a sheet of paper in half. And then cutting that half in half. And so on and so on. And I would make myself cry, because for some reason it frustrated me, thinking that eventually some piece would get cut out of existence, that you could *do* that. I guess it scared me."

"It is scary," Chip says. And right then everything between us changes. Because we remember what's beneath his kerchief. I can feel us both doing it, together. Both of us thinking, *oh, yeah.*

A young woman I knew who had breast cancer told me that after she was diagnosed, she couldn't go to movies anymore. She used to love them, but she found that they took her out of herself, and reentry was too hard. "It's better to just stay aware of it, keep it at a slow boil," she said. "If you forget, however briefly, it's like you have to deal with the shock of being diagnosed all over again."

When that woman's hair started falling out, she saved it in a manila envelope and kept it in her night-table drawer. I think she was going to use it to have a wig made. But then she died suddenly—

much sooner than any of us thought she would, two days short of her thirtieth birthday. Her mother kept the envelope, moved it to her own night-table drawer. "I don't know why I'm saving this," she told me. "But how can I throw it out?"

We eat everything on our platters, then order dessert. Chip gets cherry pie, and I order Al's famous rice pudding—famous for its inconsistency. One time, it will be delicious; the next time, it will taste like wallpaper paste. Today, it's great.

On the way home, Chip gets tired. He doesn't say so, but I can tell. It's not in his gait; it's in his face—the sagging of certain fine muscles, the effort that shows in his eyes. I suggest we stop at a playground we're walking past, tell him I want to sit on a bench and watch the kids. There is a line for the slide—all boys. On one of the swings, a lone little girl about eight years old sits still, lost in a book. Two mothers with babies in matching buggies sit on the bench across the playground from us, earnestly talking. I remember being at this playground as a child. My mother would sit on the bench and knit, staring straight ahead; she steadfastly—though politely—refused the attempts at conversation by the other mothers. Her friends were back in Poland, she told me, those were her friends. Eventually, everyone learned to leave her alone.

After a while, I say, "How come *you* never married, Chip?"

"Oh . . ." He stretches his arm out along the bench behind me. The hairs on the back of my neck stand at attention. "Well, for one thing, I thought I had all the time in the world. And I kept thinking maybe the next one would be even *bett*er. Stupid. I had an uncle who was a real womanizer—he was my hero, in a lot of ways. When he died, he was surrounded by five women. I always thought that was the coolest thing. Now I'm not so sure. Now I wonder about him having to dissipate so much . . . energy. Who knows, maybe it's what he really wanted. But I think maybe I should have learned how to be with only one person, at some point in my life. It would help, now. But I never learned how to do that." He looks over at me, smiles. "Don't you wish we could have do-overs?"

"You only had one girlfriend in high school," I said. "For two whole years."

"Yeah, Diann. She wasn't really the only one."

"Oh. I didn't know that."

"Nobody did. She suspected, though." He leans back, sighs, then turns to look at me.

"We got back together, not long ago. She's a divorce lawyer, now, she has her own practice. Does real well."

"No kidding." Well, of course. Of course he would still have someone. In the pit of my stomach, something twists.

"Yeah, we hadn't seen each other for years, but we'd always kept in touch. She got married right after college, and then, a few years ago, she got divorced. She moved to New York, just a little ways from me, and we began seeing each other again. But we had some problems. Same old stuff—I kept seeing other women. We broke up right before I was diagnosed." He picks at a piece of paint which has loosened on the bench.

"So does she know?"

"What?"

"Diann. Does she know about you?"

"Oh, sure. She was the first thing I saw when I woke up after the surgery. But I don't see the point in . . . She called the other night, wants to come and visit me. I can just see that, her staying with my parents. They always hated her."

"Really?" *Good.* "Why?"

"I don't know. Got off on the wrong foot, maybe. It was odd."

"Why doesn't she stay in a hotel?"

"Well, she wants to be close by. Here in Ashton."

"She can stay with me." I don't know why I've said this. I don't think I mean it. I think it was just a knee-jerk response, sticking up for the underdog.

"Really?"

"Well, I do have a two-bedroom house. Although it's small, it's really very small."

"That's so nice of you, Myra."

I look at my watch. "We'd better get going. I need to let my dog out."

I stand, shoulder my bag. Chip looks up at me, one eye squinted against the sun. "But you'll come back tomorrow, right?"

"Yes, same time. And we'll really need to do some paperwork then, Chip. Or I'll get fired."

"Don't worry. I'll give you whatever you need."

Oh, those words.

He stands, stretches, and we start walking. His gait is steady, if slow. He took one pain pill, with dessert. He had minor difficulty reading the numbers on the check, which he insisted on paying. Other than that, he was fine.

A block from his house, Chip says, "I used to believe that when we slept at night, we were dead. So death was just a longer version of that rather pleasant experience. I wish I still believed that."

"Maybe it is that."

"Yeah. Maybe so. It's what can *precede* it that's the problem."

"I used to worry about going to heaven," I say. "I thought it would be boring."

He laughs. "You're an interesting woman, Myra. I'm glad you're my nurse."

"I'm glad, too." It is such a relief to hear him say this. I was afraid to ask if he minded an acquaintance serving in this most intimate of capacities.

Outside his house, we shake hands. And I can't help it, it's electric.

"Do you . . . would you like to go to a movie or something, sometime, Myra? It's boring, waiting around. Not working."

I laugh, flustered.

"I mean it, would you like to?"

"Well . . . yes. Sure."

"Maybe tomorrow?"

"Why not?"

He starts up the steps, turns back to wave at me. Then I head for my car, which is right where I parked it just before the world bloomed.

Frank is wild to go out when I get home, spinning in circles so fast I can hardly get his leash on him. I take him for a long walk through the woods by my house, watch him zigzag in and out of the trees. I throw sticks for him, and it comes to me that it is a miracle I am able to do this: use my arm, full strength. Follow the course of the stick clearly. Walk without fatigue or pain. Assume, with blind confidence, that I will be able to do this tomorrow and the day after that and the day after that. Spend an afternoon with someone who has been told their number is up, and you will will regard everything you do later that day with grateful wonder. I mean, even laundry.

Home again, I check my messages. One from Theresa, saying she was sorry, she'd had to bring Frank back earlier than usual, she had a dentist's appointment she'd forgotten about, she hoped he wasn't too wild from being cooped up.

"Are you too wild, Frank?" I ask. He barely looks up from getting a drink.

The next message is from Marvelous, calling to remind me to bring her a recipe tomorrow, one I'd told her about last time I saw her. I found it in a magazine—it's very easy, an all-in-one-pot chicken and rice and exotic spice thing that's very good. I made it and ate it every night for a week, which is what I always do when I make things that "serve six."

The third message is from Grace. She'd been crying, it sounded like. "He slept way too long today. I know he's got something bad. I must of did something. There's no fever, though, so does that mean he can't be sick? Can you call me?" A pause. "I wish you were there, you're not there, are you? . . . Okay, good-bye."

I call Grace back, and she says, "Oh, my God, I'm sorry. He's, like, *fine* now. I guess he was just sleepy. I would have called you back, but I forgot."

"It's okay."

"But are you still coming tomorrow?"

"I'll be there."

"Does it hurt him to watch TV with me? It wasn't violent, just a *Frasier* rerun."

"No, that won't hurt him."

"I didn't think so."

"You know a lot, Grace. You just need to learn to trust yourself."

"Yeah, I guess. Oh, one other thing. I gave him some beer in his bottle, but I way diluted it with water. That's okay, right?"

There is a long moment while I think of where to begin, but then Grace says, "Just kidding." And then, "Myra?"

"Very funny, Grace. I'll see you tomorrow."

I go into the kitchen, open the refrigerator, contemplate the contents. I finished the last "serves six" thing I made last night. I take the lid off a carton of strawberry yogurt, smell it, put it out on the counter. Then I pull out the three shortbread cookies I have left, take them and the yogurt over to the kitchen table, and sit down. I like to eat the yogurt using the cookie as a spoon.

After I finish, I go back to the refrigerator and look around some more. I take out some goat cheese, get sesame crackers from the cupboard, and eat crackers and cheese standing over the sink. Then I make a little salad, which I dress with a very nice vinaigrette. I eat the salad in the living room while I watch the weather report for tomorrow. Eighty-two and dry.

After my salad, I look in the refrigerator once more, eat a strawberry. Then I take the Ben and Jerry's Heath Bar ice cream out of the freezer and have a few tablespoons of that from the carton while I load the dishwasher with detergent and start it. It's not very full, but it's been four days.

And now, the evening. Spread out before me, as they say.

Every night, this hollow-stomach time comes. You'd think I'd get used to it. You'd think I'd have given up on certain things. But I see ghosts. The back of a head, coming up over a chair. His razor, left at the side of the bathroom sink. Things belonging to our children, left lying around. Those things change with the passing years: fire engines and dolls have become car keys and CD cases, gigantic sneakers. These days, the kids are only around when they're home for a visit from college. Oh, I keep up, even as someone who's lost a child says, "If he'd lived, he'd be twelve now."

I used to pay attention to stories I heard about women finding someone late in life. But so few of them were never married. The odds of being fifty-one and finding someone for the first time are formidable. Even for the women who are really good looking and have social skills.

And so.

I come into the evening like I'm coming onto a stretch of bad road. Tighten my hands on the wheel. Sit up straight. Wait for it to be over. The best time is about half an hour before I'm going to go to bed. I have an astounding array of bath products. I buy books and stack them up at the bedside, and I dip into them like a box of Whitman's every night: a poem or two, an essay, a short story, and then some of whatever novel I'm into. I don't like mysteries. I don't like thrillers. I don't like historical fiction. I like stories about our time, featuring women, where a lot of the action takes place in kitchens. I like when the women talk about childhood memories and relationships and being fat and the dreams they have at night. I like sad books, too; have ever since I was little. Growing up, "The Little Match Girl" was my favorite story. Now that I think about it, the reason I loved it is obvious: Child abused in life gets the reward el grande—a date with an angel.

Not that I have been truly *abused* in life. Unless being ignored is abused. It does hurt, being ignored. But I don't stay home and mope. I don't. I go to movies, I go shopping, I take myself out to dinner. Occasionally I see plays or concerts. Once I drove in to hear the Boston Symphony Orchestra, but I didn't like it. The way coughing was a mortal sin. The restrained applause. The age level, frankly, of the audience—I felt like a toddler there. And anyway, if you really want to listen to music, put on a CD and lie down, a pillow held tight against your chest. Weep to the beauty, if you like; it's a satisfying cry.

I suppose I should work harder at having female friends, at least. Then I could go out and do things with someone. But in spite of my great desire for intimacy, I've always been a loner. Perhaps when the longing for connection is as strong as it is in me, when the desire is for something so deep and true, one knows better than to try. One sees that this is not the place for that.

When I was seven, my mother once arranged for someone to come over and play with me—a new neighbor had a daughter my age. The little girl came over, I played with her in my room for about fifteen minutes, then told her—nicely, I thought—"Go home, now." Despite my mother's embarrassed urgings, I refused to do anything but sit on the steps and wait for the girl to leave. My mother apologized profusely to the girl's mother when she came to collect her daughter. After they left, she brought me into the living room and sat me on the sofa. "Shame on you, Myra," she said. "Shame! What's the matter with you? Didn't you like that little girl?" I remember thinking, *Why did she ask me that? Of course I liked her. There was just nothing more to do. We were all done.* But I didn't say that. I knew it was the wrong answer, and I didn't know the right one. Instead, I sat staring at my lap, counting my breaths in, waiting for her to make some noise of disgust and go back to cleaning. It took four breaths. I remember, because that was the number it usually took for her to give up on me again.

Things didn't improve much. Teachers' comments on my elementary school report cards regularly offered variations on a theme: *Myra is a pleasant child but spends too much time alone. Plays alongside, not with, other children.*

I guess what I believe is that, for some of us, things end up fitting best inside just one soul. Maybe it's genetic, maybe it's environmental, maybe it's just rationalization, who knows.

On my walks, I like to hear the sound of my sneakers against the earth; I like to linger where I want for however long I want; the things that mean the most to me are simply not translatable. In the autumn, I look up into the paint-box trees and can only sigh and feel the pleasant ache that such a glorious sight brings. What would I say to a friend? "Look. Aren't the trees pretty?"

Sometimes I feel like I'm looking down at myself, thinking, *Woman alone, living lonely life.* Those are the times my inside edges feel raw. Most times, though, I just don't think about it. I walk through the days: Saturdays, I cook for the week and pay the bills; Sundays, I do the laundry and sew. I plant new annuals every spring, new bulbs every fall. On my birthday, I buy myself a present, the price of which must exceed $150. At Halloween, I dress as a witch and Frank as a clown (Butterick #4601) to answer the door for the kids. I give out regular-size candy bars, too, not those gypy two-inchers. (I also give out a few movie-size candy bars to randomly selected trick-or-treaters, who are always so shocked they forget to say thank you.) At Christmas, I have a small tree, each ornament chosen with care, a wrapped Oinker Roll for Frank beneath it, a few new toys for him, too. If someone were to say to me at any given moment, "Quick! Are you happy?" I would answer, "Well . . . Yes. I believe I am."

I do go to bed early. Sometimes it's only eight, and in the summer, the sky's hardly dark enough for me to sleep. It's mornings I like, the promise of them, the unknowability. No dim accounting. Instead, a blank slate. A chance.

After my soak in Crabtree and Evelyn's rose-scented bubble bath, I go into my office and make a few notes on Chip. "Admission procedure deferred on first visit per patient request," I write. And then, "According to distressed parents, pt. is refusing any treatment beyond surgery. Will work with patient and family toward realistic decision-making and acceptance of patient's wishes. Will encourage as much independence for as long as possible." And then I put my pen down, stare at the page. What can it feel like for him to wake up in his parents' house? Does he think, *Here I am, then. What an end.* Does he look at his watch? Out the window? Does he run his hand over his cut head, fingering the sutures and moving his lips to count them, making sure he can still do that?

I go into my bedroom, lie down and close my eyes, then cross my arms over my chest. Body language. I suppose I am guarding my heart. I think of us at Ned's Place, eating lunch and talking so easily. Sitting there, I felt some stubborn gate creak open. I felt I could say anything. I think of Chip's arm stretched out behind me as we sat on the playground bench, my softening at the center.

It might not be hopeless. I once went to a Bernie Siegel workshop for nurses and cancer patients. One of the stories told there was about a guy who went to a hospice to die of his advanced liver cancer. Once there, however, he did very well; and finally he said he didn't want to be there any more, he wanted to go home and work in his garden. And he did. Three years later, they could find no evidence of his tumor.

That wasn't a brain tumor, though. But maybe it could happen with a brain tumor. We don't understand everything. Really, we don't understand anything.

I crawl under the covers, start to drift off, then jump at the sound of the phone ringing. I answer it and hear Chip's voice, saying my name. *Don't let this be a dream,* I think. But it is not a dream. It is Chip, asking if we could make a meal together, asking if I know how to make pie.

"Well . . . what kind?" I am squeezing the receiver, smiling so hard I have to bite my lip to keep from laughing out loud.

"Lemon meringue."

"Do you like the really sour kind?"

"Best kind."

"We could make that. I use my Aunt Lala's recipe: citric acid, that was her secret ingredient. Once I made it and ate the whole thing myself in the space of three hours."

"Okay, so this time cut it in two."

"This time . . . ?"

"I mean, how about tomorrow? Why don't we make pie for dinner at your house and then go to the movie?"

"Well . . ." *Yes. Yes.*

"Myra, I need to get out of here. I need somewhere to go that isn't so . . . hard. Why don't you 'evaluate' me at your house? Could we? Why don't we just do everything there?"

Why? Because it's unprofessional. Because it will exclude his parents, who are part of my care plan. Because it will make what's happening to me worse.

"All right," I say.

"So tell me what time to come over. And where you live."

He can't drive. Surely he's been told that. The possibility of seizures, for one thing.

"I'll come and get you when I've finished seeing patients. You're right on my way home." Of course he is not. "It'll be about five."

"Good. And Myra?"

"Yes?" He might say anything, now. All these wonderful surprises. He could say anything.

"I'm having a problem with . . . I'm constipated."

"Oh! . . . Well, see? If you'd have let me do an admission interview, we would have discovered this."

"Sorry."

"You have Colace, right? That's one of your medications?"

"Yes."

"And you're taking it, right?"

"Well . . ."

"Take some milk of magnesia tonight. Take the Colace, too, and then *keep* taking it. It's the codeine doing that, binding you up."

"All right. I'm sorry to . . . you know."

"Forget it. I'm your nurse."

"But you're more than that. You feel like a friend."

Sometimes, your spirit can rise and sink simultaneously. "Well . . . Yes. I am your friend."

"So! I'll see you in the morning."

"No, five o'clock, Chip. P.M."

"Oh. Right. I guess I wish it were morning."

Foolishly, the indicator rises.

"Myra?"

"Yes?"

"I just want to say what a relief it is that it's you who's going to be taking care of me for this . . . for all this. What a surprise and a relief."

"Well."

"I mean it. You're very . . . comfortable."

"Thanks." I guess.

I hang up the phone and look out the window at the sky, the pale blue now overtaken by the moody colors of dusk. You never know. You never know what's going to happen from one day to the next. I can vouch for that. So can Chip. So could anyone, really. Oh, it's overwhelming, sometimes, how much we really are all sharing the same, leaky boat.

I lie quietly for a while, watching the dark come, and then I get up and turn on all the lights.

I'm going to make a pie. I'll surprise him, have it all done so he won't have to wait for anything. So we'll have more time.

My visits today are going smoothly. Tiffany did a terrific job on Rose's apartment—took out all the garbage, stocked her refrigerator, did the laundry, even washed and curled Rose's hair. Ann Peters's eyes are improving, and her daughter has agreed to put in the drops on weekends.

Fitz Walters bought a new hat, a red feather at the band, and his happiness at this small thing is nothing short of inspiring. "I'll take those ladies' breath away when I show up in this," he told me, modeling it; preening. He walked across the room, a cross between Fred Astaire and Chuck Berry.

"What ladies?" I said.

He chuckled.

"Fitz?"

He waved his hand. "Go on, now."

"No, really. What ladies are you talking about? The ladies from your church, those ladies?"

"Aw," he said, "you just giving me a hard time, ain't you? Yeah, you like to give me a hard time. You know who I'm talking about! At the Pussy Cat Lounge, *those* ladies. You know."

"Yeah, I do. And you'll knock them out, Fitz, you look like a movie star in that hat."

"That's what the guy who sold it to me said! Said I look like Sidney Poitier."

"Exactly." I checked his blood pressure. A little higher than usual, but only from joy. One night, I'll ask if I can go with him to that lounge. Try to differentiate for him between the real and the silicone. Not that he can see, but maybe he'd want to know.

DeWitt was quiet, actually engrossed in some paperback novel with a torn-off cover, which he wanted to read rather than talk to me. That was fine; I was in a hurry. I did ask him what the book was about.

"You ain't old enough to know," he said.

Early in the afternoon, I pull up in front of Marvelous's three-plex, note that her dirt yard has been raked carefully and the porch swept, as usual. "I am blessed," she tells me all the time, sitting in her tiny, third-floor walk-up. The place is spotless on the inside, if falling apart—literally—on the outside. She has a gigantic velvet Elvis painting on the wall above her reading chair, red plastic flowers in a jelly glass on the kitchen table. Her bathroom has a matching pink rug, toilet seat, and tank cover. On her bedroom wall are pictures of her long-dead husband, her children and grandchildren. The floors gleam; she has window boxes filled with purple-and-white petunias. She has an old, floor-model radio and a television that doesn't much come in. She had the components for a very nice VCR stacked up on her floor one day, but gone the next. I didn't ask. I knew. Her thirty-year-old son, Rodney, whose ways of making a living are not exactly by the book.

I have never heard Marvelous rail against all she must endure: prejudice, poverty, illness. The nastiest I've seen her is one day when she was talking about the rich people for whom she used to clean. "Lord, they be complaining," she said. "Sitting there in the lap of luxury and whining from the time they step out of bed 'til they step back in it. Sometimes I want to say something to them, say, 'Here now, you know what? You missing something in your soul, be plain as day you missing something *bad*.' But they don't listen to me. They don't *see* me. They say (and here she made her voice high and affected), 'Oh, *Marvelous*, how you get that toilet to shine so!' Like they couldn't figure that out they own self. Like they that stupid. And like I should be proud my talent in life is cleaning toilets! I'll tell you why they walk around looking at my work before I go, singing my praises. They looking to see did I take something."

She has affixed her colostomy bag perfectly today, as she has the last two times; really, there is nothing for me to do for her anymore. She understands everything; she knows who to call for help if she runs into problems.

After I've checked her blood pressure, we sit together at her kitchen table drinking iced tea. I give her a copy of the recipe she requested, tell her I increased the amount of ginger called for by half. Then I say, "I have bad news, Marvelous. Bad news for me, anyway. I don't need to come and see you anymore. You're an expert now; you could teach other people."

She smiles. "I could, at that."

"I'll have to stop seeing you. As a nurse, anyway. I hope I can still come and see you as a friend."

"Well, of course you can. You *are* a friend. Since the first day, Myra. I liked you right away. You not a phony like so many."

"Oh, well."

She frowns. "You know something? You need to learn to take a compliment."

"I guess. Yes. *Thank* you."

"You need to let the light *in*."

"Well, that's . . . right."

She looks around the kitchen, sighs. "My son's coming tonight; I think I'll make this recipe you gave me. I don't know what I'm going to do with that boy. Trouble. You lucky you never had children. They bust your heart wide open."

"I don't know. I think I might have liked having children."

"Well, first you got to get a man. You found a man, yet?"

I look at her, say nothing.

Her eyes widen; she puts her drink down. Since the first day I met her, she's asked about me and men. And always, I've said there's no one. I've also said that I don't really want someone. But today is different.

"Oh, myyyyyyyyy!" she says. "Little Miss Lonelyheart finally got a fish on the line."

"It's not exactly like that."

"You got the fever, girl, steam coming out your ears. All you done was think about him, and your whole self change."

"Come on, Marvelous; it isn't that obvious."

She turns in her chair, points to a corner of the cabinet. "You see that toaster over there?"

"Yeah."

"Go look at your face in it."

I laugh.

"I mean it! You think about that man and then you go and look at your face."

I stop smiling, look down into my tea, stir it with my finger.

"What? You want to tell me about him?"

"Oh, Marvelous, it's completely wrong. He's one of my patients. He's very ill. I shouldn't be having these feelings."

"Honey, ain't no 'should' when it comes to feelings. Ain't nothing wrong with just *feeling* anything! 'Sides, you ever seen that movie, *West Side Story?*"

"Yes."

"Remember that song in there, 'bout how when love comes real strong, *ain't* no right or wrong? That's the truth, Ruth." She leans forward, looks deeply into my eyes, then pulls back, laughing, slapping her knee. "Oh, yeah. What can you do, it get you by the throat and you pinned to the floor. You got no control." And then, serious, "But it's good. It's *good.*

"Did you feel that way, Marvelous? About your husband?"

"Old Gerald?"

"Yeah."

"Oh, my sweet Jesus. Yes, indeed." She gets up, opens her refrigerator. "I got macaroni salad. I got hot dogs, too."

"Yes," I say. "Thank you." And then I wait for her to feed me more.

* * *

Late in the afternoon, I go to a gas station pay phone to check my messages. Two. One from Rose's doctor, increasing her daily dose of insulin. The other from Diann Briedenbach. I stand perfectly still, watching a well-dressed man pump gas into his car while he admires mine, and listening to Diann's voice, which has gotten quite low. "Myra! This is Diann *Briedenbach!* Long *time*, huh? How *are* you? Listen, I'm calling because Chip told me about your offer to let me stay with you when I come to visit him. That's so generous of you! I'd like to talk to you about a few things. Could you call me? Any time. Really, any time." She leaves the number, but I don't write it down. Messages can get lost. Power failures, for one thing. It's a good thing I left the house earlier than usual this morning—she called just after I left.

Chip is waiting on the steps outside when I arrive to pick him up. He's wearing a white shirt, sleeves rolled up, blue jeans, and his navy-and-white kerchief. I pull up to the curb and he comes over, leans in my side, looks around in the proprietary way men do when they check out a car. "Nice machine!"

"It is." Oh God, he's wearing cologne. What can it mean?

"I didn't notice it yesterday."

"It was here."

He walks around to his side, climbs in, slides the seat back. "Okay. Let's drive to Venezuela."

"Buckle your seat belt, first."

"What if we could drive there. Would you?"

I look at him.

"I'm feeling like that guy on TV who had six months to live, remember that show? He looked healthy as hell, and he was running around, living till he died. I mean *living* till he died. Only he never died."

"Right. I remember that show."

"Of course, that guy didn't have to eat forty pills a day and he didn't have a cracked skull and he could *remember* things."

I say nothing, shift.

"So. Are you ready to make pie?"

"The pie is done."

"Really?"

"Yes. And I have the perfect plates to eat it on. Yellow and white."

"Or we could eat it right out of the pie plate, bite for you, bite for me."

I stop at a red light, smile over at him. Then the light changes, and I pull away a little faster than I have to. Quite a bit faster.

He laughs. "Great."

And then we keep quiet, listening to the radio, each of us having our own separate fantasies, until we arrive at my house and see a red Lexus pulled up in front of it. A tall woman opens the door, climbs out.

"I wonder who that is," I say, at the same time that Chip says, "Diann!"

She starts walking over to us as I pull in the driveway. Waves gaily. She is wearing tortoiseshell sunglasses, has her hair (silver streaks now mixed in with the black) pulled up carelessly and clipped to the top of her head. Her silk pants and top are the cool turquoise of swimming pool water; over them, she wears a white linen blazer, sleeves pushed up. She has a wide silver bracelet on one arm, an expensive-looking watch on the other. Silver hoop earrings. Espadrilles. Nice woven purse. She comes over to me as I finish climbing out of the car, pulls off her sunglasses, and smiles. There are her blue eyes. Those eyes. There are her straight, white teeth. She's lost nothing. She extends her hand, and I take it. "Myra *Lipinski*," she says, though she is not looking at me any more. "Nice car!" she says, but she is not looking at it, either.

From inside my house come the outraged barks of Frank, who, for two days in a row, now, has been left home. Well, he'll come with me tomorrow. Tomorrow, everything will be back to normal.

I pull my nurse's bag up higher on my shoulder. "We were just going to have some pie," I say. "I . . . made a pie. Come in." I go first, alone. They follow, together. I have never been so ashamed of my back.

Ethel Schwartz boiled three bones for Frank. Two of them she wrapped in Hanukkah paper and froze so that they would "last" until we got home; the third, she has just given him now. He goes to the corner of the kitchen where he is allowed, collapses happily, then looks up to me as if to say, "Go ahead; I'm fine."

"I wonder if I could just have a private moment with you before we do the pills," Ethel says, holding onto my arm tightly, speaking in a low and tremulous voice between her clenched teeth. She often clenches her teeth when she speaks; otherwise, her dentures make small, clicking sounds. I've told her those dentures don't fit, that she should have them adjusted. She always waves her hand and says, "My teeth should be my biggest problem."

She does this every week, asks for a "private moment" with me. Then her husband, Murray, has a "private moment" with me. Then we all sit at the dining room table, and while they silently fume and avoid looking at each other, I dole out the fifty or sixty pills they'll each need to take that week. I line them up in Medi-Minders, the divided plastic cases that keep their pharmaceutical lives, at least, in order. His case is blue. Hers is pink and decorated with decoupaged pictures of flowers she clipped from seed catalogs, seed pearls, pink mini-rhinestones, and bits of ribbon.

53

She yells down the hall toward Murray's bedroom that I'm here, then takes me into her bedroom. She keeps her heavy drapes closed, and it's always dark in there, claustrophobic. She turns on her night-table lamp and sits on the bed, and I take my usual position in the Queen Anne chair she keeps in the corner. I pile four lacy pillows onto my lap so that I can lean back.

Ethel crosses her legs and wearily examines her fingernails, painted a dark rose color each week by the traveling manicurist. Then she sighs and says, "I'm telling you, Mary, I don't know if I can take it anymore; he's driving me bananas."

"It's Myra."

"What?"

"My name is Myra."

"Oh. You're right. *Myra*. But anyway, I mean it, Myra, it's gone too far. Listen to this: Yesterday, he took the drapes in the living room—and I'm sure I don't have to tell you those are very expensive drapes, I had them custom-made—anyway, he takes those drapes and he yanks them apart and he *duct tapes* them to the wall. As God is my witness, he *tapes* them to the wall! I said, 'Murray, what the hell are you doing?' You know how he answers me? You know what he says?"

She stares at me; blinks once, twice.

"What did he say?" I ask, finally. She likes when I enter into the conversation this way. It makes her feel that I'm on her side.

"He said nothing. Can you believe it? Not one word. He tapes my *drapes* open and then he sits down in his recliner and picks up that damn *Golf Digest* and says *nothing!*"

"Hmmm." My back hurts a little. I change my position.

"I said to him, 'Murray, what are you, crazy? What are you *doing*? If you want the drapes open, then *open* them. What is it with the tape? You just *open* the drapes.' And you know what he says to me?"

"Nothing?"

"Oh, no. Not nothing. Absolutely not. I wish you could have *heard* what he said, I only wish you could. He starts in with me about how I'll just shut them again. He starts yelling about 'Too much darkness! Too many curtains all over the house!' Now I ask you, what are curtains for? What are curtains *for*? You *close* them for your *privacy*! And then he starts screaming at the top of his lungs, he says we got too many *things*. All over the house, too many things. Too many scatter rugs, too many knick-knacks—and you know and I know that *that* is what makes a house a *home*—but he is yelling and carrying on that he feels like a prisoner in a junk store, that he can't *move*. I swear to you, Mary, every person in the building must have heard him. Think of how it felt for me to face my neighbors the next time I saw them—my dignity in shreds, you can just imagine.

"And that's not all. Next he starts in on my doll collection, which I can tell you means a lot more to me than he does. It is not in his way, there is no way he can say it is in his way, you know how I have my darlings all together in that locked case in the dining room—but he is yelling about *that*, about what kind of person am I, a grown woman who has sixty-five *dolls*. Well, I had an answer for him there. I said, 'Listen, you know Demi Moore, that actress you're so crazy for?'—like she'd bother to look at him if he was handing her a million-dollar bill. But anyway, I said to him, I said, 'Demi happens to be a *very* serious doll collector! She is *crazy* for the Gene Marshall doll, which I was one of the very first to get!'" She settles back on her rump, hikes up a slipping bra strap. "So then what do you think he says?"

I sneak a look at my watch.

"All right," she says. "Okay. I can take a hint. I know you're too busy to listen to me."

Now I feel bad. She's just an old lady who used to have dreams, whose life has disappointed her. I know she picks out one of her baby dolls to rock every night, Murray told me once when he was complaining about her.

"No, Ethel," I say. "I was just thinking it must be frustrating for you when—"

"The *point* is, Marsha—and I'll be brief, here—the point is, he's losing his marbles. Okay? Plain and simple. He is cracking up. All of a sudden, everything I do is wrong: his sandwich is cut straight across rather than on the diagnoal; I buy the wrong detergent—like he should know from detergent!—I park too close to the curb, I park too far from the curb. He wants I should stop wearing the perfume I have always worn, it is my signature scent which, by the way, he is the one who first *gave* it to me!" She takes in a breath, studies me. "*Ma Griffe*, I don't know if you know it, do you?"

I shake my head no.

"Well, it is a very clean and *classic* scent, but now he says the smell bothers him. Meanwhile, he puts on his cheap cologne a bottle at a time. He who wears his underwear for days in a row, I kid you not, I have to pry it off him! I'm telling you, I'm very sorry to say this, but I think he needs to be placed."

I have no idea what to say. I'm too tired; I got very little sleep. I lay in bed reviewing the stupid things I did last night. Examined myself from all angles, like an EKG looks at a heart, only less sympathetically.

"This is what I'm asking you: Will you just have a close look at him today? Just see if you notice anything you could maybe tell your supervisor? This is all I'm asking."

"Sure," I say. "I'll look at him."

"You want some rugelah before we start? It's fresh; I just this morning defrosted it."

"No thanks. I ate a lot of pie last night." Six pieces, actually.

"Up to you," she says, slightly offended as she always is when I reject her offers of food. She opens the bedroom door to yell to Murray that I'd like a moment with him, turns back to look at me significantly. Which is exactly the way Murray looks at me when I come into his bedroom.

"She's driving me batty," he says quietly, closing the door behind him.

When Frank and I walk into the house at four-thirty, I hear the sound of the shower running. No one has ever used that shower but me, and it feels odd, somehow, to hear it working for someone else.

I sit on the sofa, hear the water being turned off, then the sound of the bathroom door opening. It's kind of nice to come home and hear the evidence of another human being, but mildly irritating, too, as when someone you like calls just as you're ready to sit down to a really good meal. I mean, do I *want* to hear the shower just now? Do I want to have to talk to someone else? Not really. I want to do my notes from today's visits, and then call DeWitt's doctor to let him know I'll need to see him for at least another week or two. I can *do* that, of course; it's just that I feel a sense of inhibition about it.

As I sit having a debate with myself over free movement in my own house, I hear Diann coming downstairs. And then she is standing in front of me wearing a long, white summer dress, barefoot, her hair wet, her face free of any make-up. She looks like an ad in a magazine. Frank leaps up and runs to her, sits on her feet.

"*Frank*," I say.

"Oh no, he's fine." She scratches him behind his disloyal ears. "You're so full of love," she tells him. "Aren't you?"

"A bit overeager."

"It's nice!" She squats down, hugs him, then comes to sit on the sofa beside me. Frank follows, lies beside her. *Who buys the damn Snausages around here?* I'm thinking.

"God," Diann says. "I'm so glad it's you! I thought you weren't going to be home until later. I was in the shower and I heard someone come in, so I beat it right out of there." She smiles. "You know how you never want to be in the shower when the murderer comes."

"Better to be in the kitchen, making lasagna," I say.

"Pardon?"

"A joke. Not a good one."

"Oh."

"I meant, you know, like it would make a *difference* where you were, if it were a murderer."

"Oh! I see. That's funny."

"Well. No, it's not."

A moment, now. Each of us tight with the other.

And then she says, "I really want to thank you again for letting me stay here."

"That's okay. It's fine."

"I never got the chance to tell you last night; you left so fast."

Frank finally tears himself away from Diann and comes to lie down heavily beside me. I have an urge to smack him, but pet him instead. "Well, you know, I really had to get some things done. And I thought it might be nice for you and Chip to have some time alone."

She nods. "It was."

The phone rings, and with some relief I go to answer it.

"Hey," Chip says.

"Oh, hi. Hold on; she's right here."

"Wait a minute, Myra! I'm calling to talk to you! Why did you leave last night?"

I say nothing.

"I know she's probably right there, but was it because of Diann?"

"Oh, no. No."

"Well, I wish you hadn't left."

"Okay." I don't know what else to say. I suppose I wish I hadn't left either—it only made things worse. But I felt so foolish. We were all sitting at the table, eating pie, when Diann asked why I became a nurse. I meant to say something pithy and intelligent, and ended up going on forever, talking like a person starved for company. Talking like what I am.

I told them that the summer I turned fifteen, my mother was hospitalized for a hysterectomy. She developed a nasty infection, and so her stay there was prolonged. In the room next to her was a sixteen-year-old boy, dying of some kind of terrible disease. I used to see his legs when I went past his partially open door. They were thin and so white, lying on sheepskin, uncovered. They were always in the same position, always very still. I learned about his age and diagnosis from one of my mother's nurses. "It's very sad," she said, "especially since it looked for a while like he was going to make it."

"Where's his family?" I asked, and she said, oh, there was always one of them with him. At least one, sometimes two. Always somebody there.

"Well, why don't they talk to him?" I said. "I never hear them!" My mother, embarrassed, said that was enough, now; no more questions. The nurse said it was all right, it was natural for someone to be curious. But she didn't answer the question.

Once, walking past the boy's room, I pushed the door open wider so I could see all the way in. There was a visitor sitting by the bed, but whoever it was didn't notice me; the chair had its high back to the door. The boy was awake, and when the light from the hall came into his room, he turned toward me. He was bald, and his thin face was full of a terrible longing. I swallowed, raised my hand in a silent greeting. He stared; then, slowly, raised his hand back. The visitor turned, saw me, and came over to shut the door. She was an old woman, his grandmother, I assumed. She held knitting in her hands, a pale blue sweater she was making. I wondered if it were for him. I thought, *It's terrible if it is—he'll never get to wear it.* And then I thought, *It's terrible if it's not—it means they're showing him they've given up.*

I wrote a letter to him. It said, "My name is Myra and I'm fifteen. I'm here every day visiting my mother, who is right next door to you. If you want, I could visit you, too. I could bring a deck of cards and a transistor radio. Maybe you could come outside in a wheelchair."

My mother was upset when I told her about the letter. "Why are you doing this?" she said. "You, Miss Antisocial!" And I couldn't tell her, because if she could ask such a question, she could never understand the answer. He was my age! He lived in a small room, attended by medical personnel and family members who almost never spoke. He did not get phone calls, he did not put records on a turntable, he did not read books or swim or stay up late watching monster movies. He did not smell cut grass or walk barefoot down a warm sidewalk. He did not slowly peel back the wrapper from a Snickers bar and sniff before he bit; he did not go to ball games or swimming. Day after day, he lay in a room with the shades pulled, silence hanging in the air like fog. How could you see that and not want to do something?

When I got no answer to my letter, I sent another. Which he never got to read, because he died. When I heard that, I locked myself in a hospital bathroom and wept. And vowed that I would never be helpless in such a situation again. I would make it so that I could walk into any sick person's room and offer comfort, especially when that comfort was so sorely needed, so sure to be taken.

I went on and on, talking about how I decided after high school to go to nursing school, how I loved every minute of it. I said I found learning about the body to be an exercise in sustained astonishment. How could I not? The eye, the way it translates an image! The vigilance of the brain; the elegance of the skeleton; the dark mystery of hormones; the specificity of muscle tissue types! I described reading about the awesome workload of the heart; the complicated balancing of the respiratory system; the dependence of nerves on the myelin sheath; the swift passage of red blood cells coursing through the sixty thousand miles of the circulatory system.

Even as a student, I was the one they called to start IVs when no one else could. I got NG tubes down fastest: I, not even twenty, my hair in a ponytail, my life experience nil, threaded a tube down an innocent nostril while some formerly dignified patient, now robbed of individuality, sat upright in a patterned cotton gown, hands clenched, eyes watering, trusting me. And forgiving me.

I surprised myself by being so good at these technical things. The suffering, I knew I'd understand. Knew I'd want to relieve, and would be able to relieve. The technical part, I came to see, I was able to do because of the catalytic effect of love.

I had been staring at the wall as I spoke, lost in a reverie. It was as though I were speaking to myself, creating with my words some sort of movie of my life. Confirming it, validating it. I said I thought my job saved me from a thousand hells, that I couldn't imagine ever finding anything I liked better. That what it gave me was too much to be measured; too much, finally, to be told.

And then, suddenly, I snapped out of it. The lights came up. I looked over at Chip, then Diann. They were silent, just watching me. I said something about needing to run some errands, and fled.

I went to a bookstore and drank coffee and read magazines until the place closed. Then I went for a drive. Then I went to the grocery store that stays open all night and bought Ajax and a couple of oranges and sunflower seeds for the bird feeder.

When I came home the house was dark and quiet—Chip gone, I assumed, and Diann asleep. I let Frank out for his final pee, and then went to the refrigerator for the pie. I brought it into bed with me and finished it. Then I lay awake until some time after four. I thought of how you open a too full cupboard and everything comes falling out. I thought of how in my job, my hands regularly touched things others wouldn't dream of touching. I thought of how people hated hospitals and did not like to be reminded of what went on there. I thought of a time when I was twelve and ate dinner at someone's house, and when I was finished eating, she said, "Wow, you were *hungry*," and her mother shushed her, and I was suddenly so ashamed. I thought of Chip and Diann staring at me, the calm blueness of those stares, their utter apartness from me and those like me.

I press the phone closer to my ear, hear Chip saying, "Listen, you know how Diann was going to come and get me to bring me over there? My parents wanted to know if you'd come here today. Just for today. They said they have a few questions about the medications."

"Sure." Out of the corner of my eye, I see Diann's legs. They are crossed. Evenly tanned. Doesn't she know she shouldn't lie in the sun like that? Although maybe it's that cream, there's a cream that will tan you, with no side effects that they know of. Yet.

"Then I thought maybe we could go out," Chip says. "Diann and I and you, too." I start to excuse myself, but he says quickly, "Please don't say no, Myra."

I look at my watch, out the window.

"Myra?"

"All right."

I hang up, tell Diann, "Chip's parents need to talk to me. So I'll go over there to see them, and then I'll bring Chip back here. He thought maybe we could all go out somewhere."

"Oh. All right." She shrugs. "Isn't it odd, the way there's this sort of . . . party atmosphere?"

"Yeah."

"His attitude is so hard to understand. Don't you think? I mean, why isn't he grieving?"

"He is." I pick up my nurse's bag, sling it over my shoulder. "I'll be back in about an hour."

"Okay." She stands, yanks at the waistline of her dress. "I wish you didn't make such good pie. After you left, I ate that *whole piece*."

"Oh, well."

"No, I really shouldn't have. I'm glad you tossed the leftovers; I probably would have had more for breakfast. And lunch. I've gained five or six pounds the last couple weeks; I look like a beached whale."

"No, you don't."

"God, Myra, you're so lucky never to have *worried* about any of this stuff! I always thought it would be so much easier, so much *better*, to be like you!"

I stand with my hand on the door, open my mouth to say something, then shut it. I feel a small rush of anger moving from my stomach up into my throat.

"Oh, you . . . Please don't think I . . . What I *meant* is, you always seemed so much *wiser* than those of us who were running around desperately trying every new fad, you know? You were—"

"I'll see you later, Diann." I start to leave, but she comes over and stands between me and the door.

"Myra, I know how it sounded, what I just said. But I didn't mean it that way."

"It's okay." I reach around her to open the door.

She steps out of the way, her hands clasped before her, speaks quietly. "I hate when this happens. I hate when you say something wrong, and suddenly you're in this hole you can't get out of. And everything you say to try to convince someone of the truth just makes you sound like more of a liar. Will you please just consider that I *really* didn't mean what you think?"

"What makes you think you know what I thought, Diann?"

She sighs. "Look. I know you won't believe me, but I mean this: I always admired you. I always did. That's all I meant to say."

I step outside.

"I wish you weren't leaving. I hope we'll get a chance to talk, later."

I take a few steps down the sidewalk, hear her call my name. I turn around, say nothing.

"I . . . Can I still stay here?"

"Nothing has *changed*, Diann. I said you could stay here. You can stay here."

"Okay. Thanks."

"You're welcome."

"Why don't I make us all some dinner?" she calls after me. "Pasta? A salad?"

"Fine."

She closes the door, and the words I put to the rhythm of my steps are, *Why don't you just leave, huh? Why don't you just leave?*

When I start the engine, I look at myself in the mirror. I don't know why I'm so mad at her. She may be a lawyer, capable of star-spangled lying, but I do believe her. And damn it, I'm starting to like her.

Chip's parents are waiting for me at the front door. They lead me into the living room and we sit down—all of us, I notice, close to the edge of our seats. I lean back, meaning to communicate something I don't really feel: relaxation. Confidence.

"Chip's upstairs, getting ready," his mother says.

I nod.

"I understand he'll be seeing you at . . . your place?"

"Well, he—"

"Oh, we have no objection. It's just that occasionally we'd like to talk to you as well. There are certain things that may come up. Things we may need you to do."

"Of course. You're welcome to call me, any time. I believe I gave you my number."

"Yes." Mrs. Reardon smoothes back the hair at one side of her head, checks her watch. Recrosses her legs and neatens the crease line in her pants. Then she looks over at her husband, pointedly raises her eyebrows.

"I can't," he says quietly.

She sighs.

"I can't!" He turns toward me. "Myra, my wife wants me to tell you that we both believe Chip should aggressively pursue other options; that he is no longer capable of making decisions for himself, and we should intervene on his behalf. There's a clinic in Switzerland we heard about. But as I told you before, I'm just not sure—"

"As you told her *when?*" Mrs. Reardon asks. "When did you two talk about this?"

"It was just in passing," I say. "It wasn't really a conversation."

"Ah," she says. "Well, I'm just his mother. Why should I be included?"

A long moment passes. Finally, I say, "You know, all of this takes time to work out. There are so many—"

"We have no time!"

"Elaine," Mr. Reardon says.

"No! We have no time! That's the truth! We're going to sit around here talking about his 'feelings' and his 'options' and his 'right to participate in the decision tree,' and while we're talking and talking and talking about what to do, he's going to die! Doesn't anyone but me understand what's really happening here?"

Mr. Reardon crosses the room, sits on the arm of his wife's chair, takes her hand. "Maybe we're not quite ready to do this now," he tells me.

Mrs. Reardon stands, looks at me. "You don't even know him." She leaves the room.

I clear my throat, reach for my nurse's bag.

"I'm sorry," Mr. Reardon says. "We've been . . . We haven't even had any sleep, lately."

"I understand."

"Really, we just would appreciate knowing how he's doing from your point of view. On some sort of regular basis."

"I'd be happy to tell you that. And . . . Well, you know there will come a time when he can't come to my house any more. When he'll only be here."

"Right. That will not be a good time."

"No."

"I talked to his doctor the other day. If he gets no further treatment, that time will come pretty soon."

"It's hard to say when."

"Around six weeks, tops, is what he predicted, before—"

"It's a guess."

"Rather an educated one, though, wouldn't you say? I hired a pretty damn good oncologist."

"I know you did. But it's still a guess."

Out of the corner of my eye, I see Chip coming into the room. His father stands, and the expression on his face changes to one of forced cheer. "Well! Out for the evening!"

Chip is wearing a blue blazer over his jeans, and a blue-and-white striped shirt. His blue kerchief over his head.

"Thought we'd go out to dinner," Chip says. And then, "Hi, Myra."

"Actually, Diann's cooking," I tell him.

"Really?"

"Yes."

"She never cooks."

"She is now."

"What time will you be home?" Mr. Reardon asks.

Chip turns toward him. "What time will I be *home?*" He starts to laugh. "Dad. Jesus. What could happen?"

In the car, we ride in silence until we hit the freeway. The more speed I pick up, the more Chip seems to relax. He turns on the radio, then says loudly over the music, "You can see why I need to get out of there."

"Oh, they're just . . . They want to save you, Chip."

"I know that." He stares out the window. Then, more quietly, "I know." He turns toward me. "How about you?"

"Do I want to save you?"

"Yes."

"I wish I could."

"I wish you could, too."

A car honks loudly, narrowly misses us. My fault; I strayed out of my lane. "Or you could kill us both," Chip says. "We could go together."

"'NURSE AND PATIENT GREASED ON LINDBERG STREET,'" I say.

"'PATIENT'S PARENTS ENRAGED,'" Chip says. "'NOT WHAT *I* HAD PLANNED,' SAYS MOTHER.'"

I look at him, smile. He shrugs. "I don't worry so much about her."

"I know. It's your dad who's the vulnerable one."

"You understand everything, Myra."

"Well."

"No. You do."

The Stones come on the radio, singing about how you can't always get what you want. First, we are silent. Then we sing along.

When we pull into the driveway I cut the engine and open my door, start to get out. Chip grabs my arm. "Listen. Before we go in, I want to tell you something. When you said all those things last night, I was . . . I didn't say anything right afterward because I thought it was just so beautiful, Myra. Really. I was sitting there, trying to take it all in. All those amazing facts about bodies. And then you were gone."

I look away, embarrassed.

"Next time you tell me something like that, something about yourself, I hope you'll stay. I wouldn't mind getting to know you a lot better."

"I can smell the garlic from here," I say. As though it followed.

Diann and I are in our pajamas, loading the dishwasher. "He gets a few words wrong now and then," Diann says. "Did you notice when he said, 'How much time is it?'"

I smile. "Yes."

"But other than that, he seems so normal. Just a guy with a bad haircut wearing a kerchief. And popping pills every now and then."

"I know."

"When will it . . . get worse?"

"I don't know."

She takes the sponge, starts wiping down the counter. "I'm not sure I can do that part, you know. I've never . . . Well, I'm just not sure I'll be able to stay for that. I don't know if he wants me to, anyway."

I busy myself wiping wine glasses that are too delicate for the dishwasher. I bought them years ago. This is the first time I've used three at once.

"Do you think he wants me to stay for . . . everything?"

"I think you'll know when the time comes, Diann."

She rinses out the sponge, leans back against the sink, her arms crossed. "You know something? This is the first time I've ever been with him that I didn't feel competition all around me, all the time. It was never easy with him, not in high school and not when we got back together all those years later. You'd go out to a restaurant with him, and the waitress would be all over him. Or the waiter. Everywhere you went, people just . . . And even if he didn't pay any attention to them, it was still so irritating.

"More than that, though, there was this kind of aloofness in him. Even when we were alone, I felt continually frustrated trying to reach him, to get to *that place*. There was never any sense of sureness. Of certainty. Even if he told me over and over that he loved me and seemed to really mean it, you could feel this holding back. He never really gave himself away—not to me, and not to anyone else, either, as far as I know. The irony is that now, when I think he might finally let himself be fully loved, I don't think I can do it." She contemplates the floor, then looks up at me, naked faced. "Myra, tell me. When he dies, what will it be like?"

"It will just be him," I say. "Leaving. I don't know how else to describe it, really. Unless something dramatic happens, something really fast, you'll just sort of see him disappear. There'll be less and less of him, until he's gone." If I add that witnessing such a thing can be deeply rewarding, that often times a dying patient becomes a radiant instructor, someone wonderful to be next to, she'll probably stay. If I tell her it's unbearably hard, which it also is, she'll probably not stay.

I look at her, meaning to say that attending someone's death is really very difficult; not many people can do it. That it's best to admit it, if you can't; there's no blame in that. That it may not even be worth it to do it, because oftentimes the memories you're left with are so grim. Better to remember him as he was. Better to say good-bye now and go home before the going gets tough. Leave him to the care of his family and professionals like me. Leave him to me. But when I open my mouth, what comes out is, "I think you should try to stay with him for as long as you can. I'll be here. I can help you."

"But if he lasts for weeks and weeks . . ."

"Your work?"

"Oh, no. That's not a problem. I can work pretty well from anywhere. No, I mean it's a long time to be *here*. I can't ask you to put me up that long. I'd need to get a hotel room."

"No, you wouldn't."

Later, lying in bed, I wonder who has entered my body and made it say these things I don't mean. I turn onto my left side. Then onto my right. I sit up, rub the back of my neck. Turn on the bedside light and pick up a book. Put the book down and turn out the light.

Finally, quietly, I cry for a while. And then I take in a deep breath, oxygenate the three hundred thousand air sacs in my lungs. Does he know that? One of the three bones in the middle ear is no bigger than a grain of rice, how about that? I've got so much I could tell him. I look down at Frank, asleep at the side of my bed. Then I look out the window at the black sky, at the stars separated by unimaginable distances. When he took my arm today, I liked that, I liked so much when he took my arm. I make this thought into a shape, and sleep with it.

Woman, you 'bout as crabby as a politician fresh out of lies,"
DeWitt says. "You *mean!* What's your problem, you got Monday
morning blues?"

I say nothing, finish taping his dressing. I need to stop by the office
before I go home, pick up some more tape, more 4 x 4's too. Saline.

"I didn't do nothin', I know that. It ain't *me!* He looks at me from
under his heavy lids. "You ain't got a thing to complain about today; I
been Sean Connelly."

"I'll see you tomorrow, DeWitt."

He takes my wrist, gently. "What's the matter now, really? Is is
something I can help you with?"

His brown eyes are so rich and honest, so open. I mean to say no,
thank you; but instead I burst into tears. Frank comes running over,
sniffing nervously first at me, then at DeWitt.

"Whoa, call off your bodyguard," DeWitt says, moving away.

"Like he'd hurt you," I say. I reach for my nurse's bag, open up a 4
x 4, blow my nose into it.

DeWitt pats the bed. "Sit down. Tell ole DeWitt all about it." Seeing
the pat, Frank jumps up on the bed and curls himself into a neat ball.

Frank's not supposed to get on the bed. Frank's not even supposed
to even be here. One of these days I'm going to get into real trouble
for all the rules I break.

I stand looking at DeWitt for a while, and then, the hell with it, I sit down, too. It feels so good to be the one taken care of for a change, such a relief. I have a notion to kick off my shoes, lie in the crook of DeWitt's arm, and ask him to sing me a lullaby, to read me a story that is simple and has a happy ending. Instead, I sit shyly looking down until DeWitt takes one of my hands between his own, and then I start crying again.

"You pillowed, honey?"

I stop crying.

"What?!" he says. "It's not such a dumb question. I seen plenty of womens act like you and the problem is? . . . P-R-E-G-N-U-T!"

"I'm not pregnant."

"You sure? I got some of them tests in the bathroom. *Accu* . . . Accuknocked-up, something, I don't know what they call it. But you can take one. Go ahead, check yourself out."

"You have pregnancy tests in your bathroom?"

"Sure do."

"Why?"

"Why you think? I thought you's a nurse."

I don't know what to say. You never really know anyone.

"You in love, right?"

I look up sharply.

"Bingo. Give that man a cigar."

I sigh, stare at the wall.

"He don't love you back, is that what you think?"

I nod.

"Maybe he don't know you love him."

"It wouldn't matter."

"You got to try. Hell, girl, you got to *try!*"

"Oh, DeWitt, you say that like . . ."

"Like what?"

Like I would have a chance. Like I am an attractive woman who can decide to go after something she wants with some sense of confidence. "He's one of my patients, DeWitt. And he's a dying man."

He nods slowly, blinks. Then he says, "We *all* dyin', baby."

"Yes, but some of us have longer than others."

"You got an agreement with somebody important? You got some guarantee you won't step out in the street and get run over by a city bus? Happened yesterday. Downtown Detroit. Some guy tear-assing across the street, going back to the office after his workout. Carrying his gym clothes, thinking 'bout how his body in such great shape. Now what is he? A memory."

"Oh, I know. I know what you're saying. Well, anyway. Thank you." I stand, pick up my bag. Frank hops off the bed and heads for the front door. He's ready for the next patient. Grace, who believes that there's something wrong with her baby's scrotum.

"Why don't you bring this chump over, let me size him up?"

"Bring him here?"

"Yeah. I want to meet him. What's his name, anyway?"

"Chip Reardon."

"You're shitting me."

"No."

"His name is *Chip?*"

"Yes."

"What the hell kind of name is that?"

"I don't know. A white name."

He grins. "You said it, not me. But anyway, bring him on by. Tomorrow. I'll help him find a new name for himself. Give that boy some dignity."

"Maybe I will."

Only yesterday, Chip asked if he could come to work with me some time. Said he'd wait outside during the visits, that he'd just like to see where I go.

On the way down the steps outside DeWitt's apartment, I ask Frank, "Do you want to bring Chip here tomorrow?"

He looks up at me, wags his tail.

"Should I ask him?"

He barks, happily. "You're a good boy," I tell him. "Smart."

* * *

"Look," Grace says. "See how it's all swollen?"

She points to her baby's scrotum, which is completely normal. Nonetheless, I look carefully before I tell her that.

"Are you sure?" she says.

"Yes. Tell me what concerns you. Have you noticed a change?"

She looks away, blushes. She's wearing a gray T-shirt over her tiny jeans, no more than a size four, I'd guess—you'd never know she recently had a baby. She wears no shoes. Purple toenail polish, most of it chipped off. Plenty of makeup, including a glittery eye shadow. Her blond hair is twisted up and held in place with a long, silver barrette. She's a pretty girl. And smarter than she knows. I wish she'd look up from her life and reach for something.

"I haven't seen no change because I haven't exactly been checking out the equipment. I don't want to give him a complex or something."

"Well, he's fine. Completely normal. How's he doing otherwise? Eating okay? Sleeping more?"

She looks at him, runs her finger along his cheek. "He's okay." She shrugs. "He's not that interesting, really."

"Is that what you really think, Grace?"

She smiles.

"Is it?"

"He ain't interesting that you can, like, talk about him to someone else. You can't say, oh he said this and he said that."

"No, he doesn't talk yet. But he does do some interesting things, doesn't he?"

She picks him up, sits on her bed, lays him out gently along the length of her lap. "I seen him the other day just . . . watching. He's going to be way smarter than me." She slides her fingers into his tiny hands. "Watch this." She pulls up and her baby hangs on grimly. "Strong."

"That's a reflex," I say. "That will disappear."

She looks up at me, stricken.

"Oh, the ability will come back. But he'll be doing it because he wants to."

"Well, that will be even better." She looks past me, out the window. "What's it like outside?" Her longing is so subtle. In some ways, she's very grown up. Certainly she has displayed admirable equanimity in coming to terms with all she's had to give up. She was a cheerleader; she still wears the little silver megaphone around her neck. Posters of rock stars are on her wall, tickets to concerts she attended. Bottles of cheap perfume and tubes of lipstick are lined up on her dresser, along with plastic cases of blusher and eye shadow, held together by rubber bands. Stuffed animals are on her bed, yellowing paperbacks beside it. She reads every night. Mostly romances, but she will try other things. I brought her an Anne Tyler once, and Grace said the characters were strange, but she liked it.

"It's nice out," I tell her. "Not as hot as yesterday. Why don't you take Kurt out? Put him in his stroller and take him for a walk?"

"Well, he bends over like a rag doll in that thing."

"He's fine."

"Don't his organs get smashed if he sits like that?"

"No, he's all right in it."

"Okay. Maybe I will take him." She goes to the mirror, lets down her hair and starts brushing it.

I put my stethoscope back in my bag, think about the notes I'll need to make. *Mother's involution complete. Confidence still lacking.*

"How long did it take you to be a nurse?" Grace asks, suddenly.

"Four years."

"Oh."

"But you can go for two years, too. You'd get a different kind of degree, but you'd still be an R.N."

"I don't want to be a nurse," she says. "I was just curious. Being a nurse is—I mean, I'm sorry, not to be rude—but it is *gross*. Somebody give *me* a bedpan . . ." She shudders.

"Nursing's not for everyone, that's true. What about you, what do you want to be?"

"Happy."

"Well," I say, putting my bag on my shoulder. "That's a good thing to aspire to. That's the best thing." We smile at each other. When

Grace smiles, you see her as one step away from a flat-chested little girl, reaching for her mother's hand.

In my maternity textbook photos, the new mothers were always very attractive. They would be sitting up in their neatly made hospital beds with a wide ribbon in their hair, smiling down at the infant held close to their nonleaking breasts. Off to the side there would be evidence of The Father: half of a masculine torso, perhaps. A successful-looking masculine torso wearing a suit.

In practice, there were some mothers who resembled those photographs, if not in looks then in spirit. But most of the mothers I saw were different than that. Such as the bitter unmarried woman I once cared for, a sharp-boned thinness to her, her eyeliner perpetually smeared, the spike heels she wore in with her maternity jeans tossed into her clothes locker, a distance between her baby and her even when she held him close. There were also a fair number of older women who had other children at home—sometimes many children—who kept their cups from their meal trays and filled them all day long with coffee from the visitors' lounge. Who turned their babies over to the nurses so they could go out and have a smoke, talk to other mothers about the goddamn laundry piling up at home that *he* wasn't *about* to do. Whose nightgowns were old and stained and whose bouquets were those that someone else left behind.

None of those women thrilled to the sight of a heartbeat in their baby's fontanel; none held tiny feet in their hands and felt moved to simultaneous laughter and tears. None bathed newborn bodies with a sense of great wonder and fear.

If there is something I mean to do for Grace, it is to let her know all that is before her in that baby, to help her see the rightness in being profoundly grateful for something even when it is so hard. I see the connection starting to form: There is a line between her boy and her that makes her feel something when he feels something; there is a start of primal ferociousness growing beneath her breastbone, taking its rightful place there.

A re you sure everyone knows I'm coming?" Chip asks. His voice is light, insubstantial. One heel taps rapidly, though sound-lessly, against the car floor.

"They know," I say. I don't know why he's so nervous. I wish I'd brought Frank, who makes everybody relax. But he really needed to go to the groomer's. Diann will pick him up. It's kind of nice having a roommate. Yesterday she bought groceries, and she brought home an English cucumber, which I'd never tried. Very good—hardly any seeds.

"Maybe I shouldn't actually go in with you, though," Chip says. "Maybe I should just wait outside."

"You don't have to come in. But you're welcome to."

"But do they know about the way I look? " His hand goes to his wound. Checking. Still there.

"Here's what I told them. I said you were a friend of mine from out of town who is recovering from some surgery, and that you wanted to come to work with me. They're all fine with your coming in. Even Ann Peters, which really surprised me. She wants us to have tea with her, in fact."

He nods. Then, abruptly, he asks, "Would you mind turning the radio off?"

"Not at all." I take a quick look at him. "Does your head hurt?"

"No worse than usual."

"Do you need to take something?"

"I did."

I pull into the parking lot of a White Hen, turn off the engine. "You okay? You still want to do this?"

"Yes. I do. I'm just . . . I was trying . . . Oh, goddamn it. What's today?"

"Tuesday."

"Tuesday." He says the word as though he's tasting it. "Okay. And it's . . . June?"

"It's August," I say, gently. And feel my stomach lurch.

"August . . ."

"Seventh."

"Okay." He takes a huge breath in, smiles. "God. It's embarrassing."

"Yes."

"And . . . I'm not sure I know anymore when I don't know." He sighs, turns to look out the window for a long moment. Then, turning back to me, "Who can be with me, Myra? Not Diann. Not Diann, she can't do it. This is so lonely, I'm in here so *alone*. That's the thing that hurts the most. Somebody draws this small circle, you step inside. Somebody stops the bus and tells you you have to get off and you're not nearly where you wanted to go, but you have to get off. And nobody will look at you the whole way down the aisle. If only they would *look*."

I take his hand and do that hardest of things; sit still and say nothing. He lets me hold this small part of himself while he quietly weeps, and we sit there watching people come out of the store with bags full of things for their ordinary lives. And I would bet everything I own that Chip and I are feeling the same thing: a longing as wide as the world. On my wrist, a watch ticks. Second by second goes by. This is how the days pass. In this small, measured way. You can see it. The second hand moves relentlessly around the clock face. Forward. Forward. Forward. More than once in my life I have wanted to just stop everything.

* * *

DeWitt has cleaned his apartment; there's the scent of Pine Sol everywhere. He offers his big chair to Chip, then sits beside me on the sofa. "So. Where you from?"

"New York City," Chip says. "But I was raised around here."

"You like living there?" He scratches his chest lazily. He is in his stocking feet, and one little toe shows through one of the holes.

"I'm not sure anyone does, really."

"So how come you stay?"

A long moment passes, and then Chip laughs. "You know what? I don't have a good answer for that." He's so nervous; his hands are clenched, his back ramrod straight.

"Well, his work," I tell DeWitt. "It was a good place to be for what he does."

"What line of work you in?" DeWitt asks.

"I'm a stockbroker."

DeWitt leans back, stretches his arm along the top of the sofa. "Yeah, I'm a bidnessman myself. I know sometime you got to do what you don't want to do. That's so, later on, you *can* do what you want to do."

"I guess that's the way it works." Chip looks around the living room. "How about you? Have you lived here long?"

"Twenty-seven years," DeWitt says. And then, abruptly, "What do you say we take a tour through my candy store? You *tense,* man. You got to re*lax.* That's the first thing. I got something for everything, and I got something for you."

"DeWitt," I say.

"Just a little something, on the house."

"DeWitt!"

"It's all right, Myra," Chip says.

"No, it isn't!"

"Now, now, now." DeWitt goes over to his hall closet, where he pulls down a large cardboard box. "This just something between us boys. 'Less you want some, too."

79

"No, I do not."

"Not like you never seen me under the influence before."

"I'm well aware of that, DeWitt."

"Aw, put your feathers down. I ain't gonna hurt your little friend, here. I know more than most doctors do 'bout drugs, that's the God's honest truth. I'll just help him relax. Give him just a little something to make him feel *good*. He got a right to feel good! Give me a little something too, then we both feel good. And then we gon' find him a new name."

"All right," I say. "That's it. We're leaving."

"I wouldn't mind a new name," Chip says.

I stand, pick up my bag. "Come on, let's go."

I head for the door. No one follows me. I stand in the hall, call Chip's name, hear nothing but the low sound of the men's voices. I wait for what seems like hours but probably is less than five minutes. Then I come back to the living room.

"I am responsible for you, Chip," I say quietly.

He smiles. "Oh, Myra. No, you're not." He tosses something in his mouth, swallows it.

"What was that?" I ask DeWitt. "What did he just take?"

"Two and a half milligrams of Valium."

"That's all?"

"That make you a little less nervous yourself? That make you relax?"

I say nothing.

"That's all he took."

Chip leans his head against the back of the chair, his eyes closed. I could kill DeWitt.

Chip sits up suddenly, opens his eyes wide. "We're ordering out for Chinese. Shrimp with lobster sauce. You want some?"

There's no way I'm taking Chip home. All I need is for his parents to see him like this: lids at half mast, a foolish grin on his face, his balance equivalent to that of a baby who's just begun walking.

"I'm taking you to my house," I tell Chip. "Until you . . . For a while. What did you really take?"

"Valium. Val-e-yum."

"I don't think so."

"Awwww. Don't you trust DeWitt?"

I shift, say nothing.

"You should trust him," Chip says. "He's a honest man."

"He's a drug dealer!"

"Yes. As I said. He's honest. People need drugs; he just acknowledges that simple truth. It's hard here. People need drugs."

"People need a spiritual bank account," I say. "Not drugs."

"Oh, come on, Myra. Haven't you ever taken rec drugs?"

I say nothing.

"*Never?*"

"I did, once."

"What did you take? Pepto-Bismol?"

"No. For your information, I took acid."

"*Whoa!* Really?"

"Yes."

"When was that?"

"In college. A bunch of us did it. It was my first year, our dorm floor went on a little outing—to "bond," you know. And my roommate and I and about six or seven others, we took acid." I look at him, shrug.

"So what happened?"

"Oh, it was . . . Well, it was on a sugar cube. This brown stain in the middle of a pure white sugar cube. It looked to me like sin on a soul. And I put it in my mouth and I waited for it to dissolve, and as soon as it was gone I got this terrible, panicky feeling. It was like realizing you'd just stepped into quicksand. I sat down in a field—we were out in this beautiful park—and I just waited. And after a while, I started to feel this sense of such . . . wisdom."

Chip laughs. "Right. *'We are all one.'*"

"Yes. Yes. And my roommate lay down next to me and she said—in this terrifically calm voice—she said, 'I think I'm going to die now.' She really thought she was going to die, but she was so *calm* about it."

I realize, suddenly, that I'm talking about dying to a dying man. But Chip appears unfazed. It seems that for the time being, he has put thoughts of his own death out of his mind. As we do.

"So she's lying there," I continue, "saying this stuff, and at first I thought, oh God, maybe I ought to do something. But I didn't. I just sat there. And then *I* got really calm, too. I remember thinking, well, that's okay that she's dying. That's all right. It's the Mighty Journey. It's good. It's natural. I started looking into the centers of all the wild-flowers, and I saw this pattern that seemed to me to be echoed every-where, within and without, you know, and I started saying '*It's all right here.*' Over and over, '*It's all right here.*'" I laugh, look over at him. "I don't know. In some ways, I guess I still think that."

"Sounds to me like you had a pretty good time. I'm surprised you didn't take it again."

"Oh, it didn't stay a good time. There came a point when I had to pee. But I wasn't really *sure.* I mean, I had the sensation, but it was . . . separate. It was as though I were holding the feeling for some-one else."

"I know exactly what you mean." We are at a stoplight, and I look over at Chip. His eyes are closed. He's smiling.

The light changes, and I shift gently, not wanting to disturb him. "I got up and headed for the bathroom—it was one of those park bathrooms, log cabin type, forest green trim, very cozy—and I went in there and I saw myself in the mirror. And there were all these pul-sating red *blobs* on my face. But I didn't get upset. I was fascinated; I just kept looking.

"But then the sink started to melt off the wall. And I remember I all of a sudden felt this terrible sense of regret. I thought, I'll never see the world right again. I went into the stall to pee—it seemed to take about an hour and a half; it seemed that was all there *was* in the world—and then I came back outside and I couldn't find anyone. For a long time. And then . . . I don't remember this part, but I guess someone found me. At any rate, I got back to the dorm. And that night, I lay in my bed thinking, oh please, let me just be done now, let me come down. I couldn't get comfortable—no matter how I arranged myself. I was just too *aware* of everything. Finally, I lay flat on my back and held a pillow to my chest and stared at the ceiling, thinking, all I have to do is wait. I just have to let time pass and everything I think I've lost will come back to me. And my roomate—who had not died, of course—was weeping. Just crying and crying. And when I asked if she was okay, if she needed something, she said, "No. It's good. It's good."

I shake my head, look over at him. "Wow. I haven't thought of that for a long time."

He nods. Barely.

"Chip? Are you all right?"

"It's good, Myra."

"But are you—"

"I'm all right! Really!" He sits up, looks out the window. "Hey, we're by Carroll Lake, aren't we?"

"Oh. . . . ten minutes or so. Why?"

"I'd like to go there."

"It'll be dark soon."

"Right. So let's hurry."

The sun is starting to set when we arrive, flattening against the edge of the horizon. No one else is there. We sit on the sand, near the life-guard's chair. There is a wild wind blowing—the tree branches look as though they're wrestling with each other.

Chip picks up a handful of sand, lets it sift through his fingers. "I'm fucked, aren't I?"

I say nothing.

"Aren't I?"

"It's bad, what you have."

"Have you ever heard of anyone with this recovering?"

"No. But I haven't heard of everyone. Do you know what I mean? Sometimes I think there must be people walking around with terrible diagnoses who never go to the doctor. And who knows how long they live?"

"I'm fucked."

I say nothing, draw a line in the sand, make it into a cross, then, quickly, an asterisk.

"Hey, Myra, are there really sixty thousand miles in the circulatory system?"

"Yup."

He sighs. "I don't know so much. I won't have a chance to learn about so *much*. That's one of the things that's just driving me crazy. That and . . . Well, okay, I'm not going to bounce any grandchildren on my knee, but I've got some time left. And what should I do with it? I think I should do what I really love. But, you know, I'm not sure what I love. Honest to God, Myra. I feel like I've lived my life in a beekeeper's suit.

"I do know, though, that I love being surprised by things like that amazing number. By being shown what's right before me that I never knew. I mean, did you ever take a look at all the shelves in . . . in that room in the library? Where you look things up? Did you ever see all those books? Tomes dedicated to the life of the alligator!"

"I guess I haven't. I've used a reference room, but I've never *browsed* there."

Chip stands, brushes the sand off himself. "Okay. Let's go. I want to show you." He's wide awake now.

"You really want to?"

"Yeah."

"The library closes at nine."

"What time is it?"

I squint at my watch. "Eight twenty-three."

"Well. It's no problem for you to get somewhere fast, is it?"

I throw my keys up in the air, catch them.

The library is almost empty when we arrive. There is no one, not even a librarian, in the reference room. From the children's room, though, we hear the sound of laughter. "Bedtime story hour," I tell Chip, as we stroll past the low bookcases.

"What's that?"

"Oh, the kids come in their pajamas and hear a story."

"Cute."

"Yeah, it is. I go, sometimes."

"Do you?"

"Yeah."

"Why?"

"Well . . ." I'm embarrassed now. "I like to watch them."

"Ever talk to them?"

"*Talk* to them? . . . No."

"Why not?"

"I don't know. I like to just watch them."

"I have to say, I never much liked it when my parents read to me," Chip says. "It was never just for pleasure—I always had to *learn* something. I'd hear a story and then I'd have to take a little quiz. Were your parents like that?"

I smile. "No. No, I had to take the test before the story—I'd have to have been good enough that day to be read to that night." A memory comes to me of sitting next to my father as he read a book to me, *Parakeet Pete*, it was called, wondering what about the story made him so angry. I listened carefully to the words, inspected the pictures closely, thinking, *What? What is it?* But it wasn't the book. It was the way he saw life, his dark take on everything, the bleakness of his soul. I don't think I ever once saw him smile. And my mother? She read to me like she swept the kitchen floor: It had to be done, it wasn't the *worst* job she had to do; it was, at least, over quickly. It's funny; it took such a long time for me to understand that my parents never wanted children. I was in my twenties before I realized that nothing I might have done—or not done—would have made any difference. My grades didn't matter, my interests, my aspirations. Once my mother put a picture of herself as a beautiful fifteen-year-old next to my sophomore year school photo and sighed. But if I too had been beautiful, I don't think that would have mattered, either. I don't think so.

Chip goes over to a table, sits down, looks around the room. "It smells good in here."

"Yes. Books."

"And it feels good, too. There's a kind of residue. People have been here. Thinking."

"Yes." I feel the same weighty richness in the air. A rough equivalent to the sound the pendulm of a large grandfather clock makes, swinging. Or to the sight of someone's head bowed over a book, a wash of late afternoon sunlight illuminating the pages. If we were in bed, holding hands, lights out, I could tell him these things.

"Myra, show me those blood vessels, will you? I want to see them. I'm going to just sit down."

I look at him.

"Just a little tired. Really."

I find the section on anatomy, pull down a book called *The Illustrated Guide to the Human Body*. I bring it to the table, find a page with a map of the circulatory system. Chip stares and stares at it. Then he lays his head down on the page. "You know, I used to believe, when I was a little boy, that if I lay my head down on a page and concentrated, everything on that page would transfer into my head."

"Whereas I thought the technique was to put your head next to a smart person's, and if they wanted to, they could transfer things from their ear into yours."

"Come here," he says. "We'll try it."

I laugh.

"Come on."

I put my head down next to his, align our ears. "Ahhh," he says. "I *feel* it."

He's not the only one.

Over the loudspeaker comes the low voice of the librarian telling patrons to bring to the desk the materials they want to check out; it's closing time. Chip looks at me. "Guess that's that."

"We can come back again."

"Oh well, what for?" He stands, tucks in his shirt, rearranges the kerchief on his head. Everything has shifted.

We walk down the steps to the first floor, see a couple probably somewhere in their eighties walking arm in arm out the door. Their heads incline toward each other: old love. I imagine their house, their bed, the dust on the windowsills that neither one of them can see anymore, the bowl of oranges on their kitchen table, photographs albums stored on the high shelves of their closets.

And now, just ahead of us, a mother with two young children dressed in look-alike pajamas. She is carrying an armload of children's books, telling her two girls that if they don't start moving faster, they won't have time for another story before bed. Then, lunging suddenly toward her younger, a toddler who is moving away from her toward an open display of birds nests, the mother drops her books. Some land at her feet, others a good distance away, near us. Chip picks up a few, hands them to her. She smiles and distractedly thanks him, but when she looks up and sees his kerchief, her face fills with pity. And fear. She will not reprimand her children about anything for the rest of the night, I know. She might hug them so tightly before they go to sleep that they will pull away in happy confusion.

Chip stands taller, raises his chin. I want to take his arm, but instead just move closer to him.

We say nothing on the way to the car. Then, as we pull away from the library, I say gently, "So, I'll just take you home, now, all right?"

A moment. The deejay on the radio exuberantly announces the weather for tomorrow. Hot and humid. "If you don't mind," Chip says, "I'd like to come home with you."

My heart lifts.

"See Diann."

"Oh, uh-huh."

"She can take me home later."

"Right. That's fine."

As for me, I will find something to read while I listen to the busy silence of the two of them behind the closed door in the room down the hall from me. I know they'll have sex. Diann asked me last night if it could hurt him. And I said no. I saw his chest slick with sweat, his face full of the sweet pain of pleasure. No, I said, it wouldn't hurt him—a little increased intracranial pressure with orgasm, big deal. Take it slow, I said. Make sure everything's all right with what you're doing before you . . . go on.

I am his nurse. I am his nurse. My job is to monitor signs and symptoms, supervise medications, to educate and support. My job is also to help him enjoy what is left for him, no matter who it's with, no matter what form it takes, so long as it's legal. Then, thinking of DeWitt, I amend this to: so long as it doesn't hurt anyone else.

I feel a tear slip down my cheek. Quickly—and with great, misplaced anger—I wipe it away.

I am lying in bed reading *Rosie's All-Butter, Fresh Cream, Sugar-Packed Baking Book,* the recipe for chocolate orgasms. Close as I'm going to get.

I am also trying very hard to hear everything that's going on down the hall from me—without shame, it's my house. Not that I've had to try *so* hard. You can see why Diann was a cheerleader. At one point, she actually roused Frank from sleep—he looked around blankly before he put his head back down on his paws, sighing. "Want up?" I asked him, patting the bed beside me. He wagged his tail, refused.

Now there is the low sound of Chip and Diann talking. Maybe they're reviewing the good time they just had, doing the usual postcoital filling in of scorecards. The postcoital experience for me is always similar to how you feel after a massive cheat on your diet: You shove food in your mouth, barely chewing; then, afterward, you don't know where to look. Shame lies curled in your belly; you want to grab hold of your need and shake it.

I hear Chip laugh softly, then Diann. Oh, how did this happen? How is it that I am lying in my bed in the place that is supposed to be my refuge, listening to a man I so much care for make love to another woman? On my sheets! That I spent a long time selecting—and from Bloomingdale's, not even Bed and Bath!

I get up, pull on a pair of jeans and a T-shirt, go down into the kitchen and open the refrigerator. Frank comes into the room with his Frisbee in his mouth. "Wrong," I tell him, looking to see if I have all the ingredients to make orgasms. A little bit short on nuts—the irony does not escape me—but enough to make do. I turn on the oven, take out the mixing bowl. And turn the radio on.

As I'm finishing my third orgasm, I see Chip and Diann coming down the stairs. He's fully dressed; she's in a beautiful blue silk robe.

I turn my attention back to the *American Journal of Nursing*. An article on renal failure.

"What smells so good?" Chip asks.

I point to the kitchen. "Treats, have some." There's no way I'm going to call these what they are.

He goes into the kitchen, and Diann sits at the table with me. "I'm sorry," she says quietly.

"For what?"

"For . . . well, I think I might have been a little . . . loud."

"I was down here," I say, ambiguously. And then I look up to see Chip, who has come out with a plate full of orgasms. He sets them on the table, takes one. Diann looks longingly, but takes nothing.

"Diann," he says, pointing to the plate, his mouth full.

She shakes her head. "I'm not really hungry." She pokes at the edge of one of the smaller squares, takes her hand away, then picks it up. "What the hell." She breaks it in half, eats one half; then, quickly, the other. "I remember the first time I made brownies," she says. "I was so proud. I took them out of the oven, left them on the stove top, and went to my bedroom to do homework while they cooled. When I came back, they were all gone—my brothers and sisters had eaten every one. That was one of the many times I wished I were an only child."

"Be glad you weren't," I say.

"Oh, but wasn't it . . . didn't you get so much *attention?*" Diann asks.

"No," I say. People who had brothers and sisters hate it when you tell them this. They want you to prove them right, support their fantasy that you spent much of your time seated between two adoring parents who took turns stroking your hair and praising you. They don't want to hear about silent dinners, awkward vacations, the long hours when your parents went out and you sat in the living room waiting for them to come home.

I go into the kitchen to get a carton of milk and some glasses, set them on the table. "Here's how great it was being an only child," I say. "I used to cut children out of magazines to be my brothers and sisters. I taped them up on my bedroom wall. My mother would yell about tape on the walls and take them down. Then I'd cut out some more."

"I pretended a frog was my brother," Chip says. "His name was Sherman. I kept him in a cardboard box in a corner of my room with a screen over it. When I did my homework, I put him on the desk and held him down to keep him from hopping off."

"You never told me about him," Diann says, laughing.

"Oh, sure," Chip says. "When you have brothers and sisters, your fantasy is to be an only child. When you're an only child, your fantasy is to have brothers and sisters."

"I guess I didn't really want to be an only child," Diann says. "I liked playing with my sisters, and I *loved* my little brother. Although I was often terrible to him. Last time I saw him, he reminded me of the time I—"

Chip stands suddenly, then heads for the downstairs bathroom. We hear the sounds of him vomiting. Diann looks at me, wide-eyed. "It's all right," I say. "I'll take care of it." I go to stand outside the door, hear the toilet flush, the tap water run. When he opens the door, I say quietly, "You okay?"

He laughs, embarrassed. "I just . . . it all of a sudden came on! I mean, I didn't even feel sick!" I nod, not wanting him to ask me if this is because of the cancer. "Guess I ate too many brownies," he says, and I can tell from the way he is not quite looking at me that he knows it's not that.

* * *

The next morning, I call Dr. Samuelson to let him know about Chip's vomiting. He increases the dose of steroids. I make the change in the chart, then call Chip's parents to let them know. His mother answers the phone. When I tell her there'll be a change in medication, she asks why. When I explain, she says, "That's it. He's doing too much. He needs to stay here. I just can't have him wearing himself out this way."

I say nothing.

"Miss Lipinski?"

"Yes, I'm here."

"You all seem to think this is some kind of game."

"No, I—"

"Perhaps you're unaware of the fact that we have signed papers, all of us, so that Chip's father and I can make decisions for him should it become necessary. I think that time is here. I'm going to have to ask that Chip stay with us all the time now. And I think, too, that maybe he should have another nurse."

"Mrs. Reardon—"

She hangs up.

Fifteen minutes later, the phone rings. Mr. Reardon. Asking me to continue seeing Chip. Asking me to let him continue coming to my house.

"Maybe it would be best if we were all to get together," I say. "I think we need to talk about this."

"Well, my wife has agreed to let Chip do what he wants."

I tap my pencil eraser on my desk, stare at my calendar. Then I say, "May I speak with her?"

When she comes to the phone, before I can say anything, she says, simply, "Take him, I don't care."

"I'd like to come and see you, Mrs. Reardon."

"I don't want to see you. I said, take him. That's what you want. You don't need to see me. I'm not the patient."

"May I please come and talk with you?"

Silence.

"How about tomorrow afternoon?"

A long pause. And then, "At what time?"

"Four o'clock?"

"Yes," she says, sighing. "All right."

I hang up the phone, stare out the window, imagine her doing the same, her well-manicured fingers to the hollow of her neck, her blue gaze steady. I do understand, I want to tell her. I do.

A little after eleven that night, I am working in my office when I hear a noise. I look up and see Diann, dressed in shorts and Chip's T-shirt. "Can I come in?"

"Sure." I close Grace's chart. "Is he all right?"

"Yeah. Sleeping."

"You can't, though, huh?"

"Well, I'm used to staying up a lot later. But he gets so tired. You know."

"Right."

"So," she says, sitting down in the armchair across from me. "Big meeting tomorrow!"

"Yes. I really need to get some things straight with his mother."

"Good luck. You know, his Dad's a real peach, but that mother . . ."

"Chip told me you two had never gotten along."

"That's putting it mildly. From the first time I met her, she was always very cool toward me. And then I slept with Chip for the first time in her house."

"You did?"

"Yeah, it was toward the end of our senior year. I'd decided to go ahead and *do it,* even thought I always thought it was tacky to do it in high school. But my rationalizaton was that this was close enough to graduation. And I was so in love with him, even then. I really thought we'd stay together forever, get married, have the two kids, the four bedrooms . . . Anyway, Chip's parents were out of town, they'd gone to New Orleans. And we made love in his bedroom, on these very tasteful boy sheets, I remember they had a thin, navy blue stripe. His mother had decorated his room like something right out of a magazine, but there wasn't much *Chip* there.

"There was some blood, of course. We washed the sheets, and I remember being so impressed that Chip knew how to use a washing machine—I didn't until after my first year of college. But we washed the sheets, bleached them, even, and I was sure no one would ever be able to tell a thing. Then I ran into her and her husband a few days after that and I swear she knew everything. Her husband was very friendly, as usual, but she didn't crack a smile, didn't say a word. She just stared at me, like, *I know exactly what happened between you and my son, you whore.*"

"Huh. I wonder if Chip told her or something."

"Oh, God, no. He would never have done that. He's had a hard time with his mother all his life; he's never confided in her about anything. You can't get close to someone like that. She's interested in one perspective: her own. And I'm not sure she would ever have approved of anyone for Chip."

"Well, it'll be an interesting meeting."

Diane picks up a seashell I keep on the windowsill and looks at it, turning it over and over. "I'm sure she's beside herself that *I'm* around again."

"She hasn't really mentioned you. Her big issue is that she wants Chip to pursue much more aggressive treatment. She feels he's not taking his illness seriously."

"Oh, he's taking it seriously. But his way of doing that is to—"

"I know." *I'm the one who told you.*

She puts the shell down, stands. "Well. I guess you're busy."

"I do have to get some work done."

"I'm sorry for interrupting."

"It's all right."

"Would you mind if I watched televison? I'll keep the volume low."

"Go right ahead." I open Grace's chart, pull my chair up closer to my desk.

Diann leaves the room, and I make a few more notes, then close the chart again. I don't really have to work. I can do this tomorrow.

She's out there watching television in some stranger's house, wondering if all the plants have died in her apartment where she too lives alone. She came here to try to take care of the man she has always loved, and she's failing.

I go into the living room, sit on the sofa beside her.

"Oh! Hi!" She wipes quickly under her eyes; she's been crying. Then she laughs, embarrassed.

"Mind if I watch with you?"

"Not at all. Of course, I'm not really watching."

"Should I turn it off?"

"No. I just like the sound of voices, talking about something else."

"Right."

"Myra, I have to . . . You know why I got up? I need to do some wash." She starts crying again. "He pissed the bed."

"Oh, Diann."

"I came into your study to tell you, but then I just couldn't. I don't know why."

"Well, this is going to start happening, Diann. Once in a while at first; then more and more frequently. How was he about it?"

"He was . . . mixed up, mostly. He'd been sound asleep. I felt it right away, and I jumped up and started yanking the sheets off—I saved the mattress, by the way. And he . . . Well, I told him I'd done it." She stares at me, starts laughing through her tears. "And he believed me. Told me I shouldn't drink so much water before I go to bed. I put on another set of sheets and he went right back to sleep."

"But weren't his pajamas all wet?"

"Well, he . . . wasn't wearing any."

"Oh. I see."

She looks away, then back at me. "Myra, I just want to say . . . I mean, I know you care. For him. And I'm sorry that . . . Well, I'm just sorry."

"It's all right." I look at the television. Judy Garland. *A Star is Born.* "This is good. Maybe we should watch this."

Diann squints at the screen, leans forward. "Oh, I love this movie. *The Man Who Got Away.*"

"Right."

We smile at each other, sharing the unfortunate irony. And then I lean back in my chair, sigh deeply. "Oh, God. God." I stand, stretch. "I'm going to put the sheets in. And then, do you want some popcorn?"

"I'll do the wash. That part I can do. And then I'm going to get my glasses and then I would *love* some popcorn."

Rose is in the hospital. This is not unusual; she seems to require a brief stay there every few months in order to keep her diabetes under control. So I've changed my usual schedule and have come to see Grace first. She's distracted—avoiding eye contact, fidgeting, not really answering the routine questions I ask about her and her baby. At first, I think the change in schedule has thrown her off. But it's more than that. After I put her chart in my bag, I sit on her bed and say quietly, "What's up, Grace?"

She lays Kurt in his daybed, gently pulls his tiny T-shirt down to cover his belly. Then she sits on the bed beside me. "I been talking to my mom about giving him up."

I try not to let my surprise show. "Oh?"

"Yeah. I bet he could get adopted by somebody who'd take real good care of him."

"I supppose that's true."

"It's the best thing for him. I don't have much prospects."

"Well, Grace, you're only fifteen. A lot can happen."

"Do *you* think I should keep him?"

I look at Kurt, his clear eyes, his pink cheeks, his reddish whorls of hair. Grace has been wonderful with him. But it's difficult to suggest that raising a child is the best thing for a fifteen-year-old to do.

97

Finally, I say, "I guess I'm a little surprised that this has come up. I thought you'd decided definitely to keep him."

"I had. But me and my mom were talking the other day, and she . . ." Grace pushes her face into her hands and starts to cry. "You don't know. I'm trying so hard."

"Oh, Grace, I do know, I do know how hard you're trying. And you're doing a great job."

"I just love him so much. And I don't want to wreck him." She reaches around me for the Kleenex box on her night table, wipes at her nose. "I know that somebody else could give him so many more things, too."

"More material things, perhaps."

"What do you mean?"

"More clothes, more toys . . ."

"Yeah. Schools." She reaches toward him, starts to stroke the top of his head, then stops. "And . . . Well, this is it. I mean, it's at the now-or-never stage. At this point, he's still young enough . . ." She looks at me. Swallows.

"It's your decision, Grace."

"Yeah. But this is what I was wondering. I know it might be unfair for me to keep him, okay? But now that I've had him, how can I go back to *not* having him? I know this kid at my school, she had a baby girl when she was fourteen, and she gave her up. But she didn't want to. And she's allowed to see her and everything, but all it does is tear her up. See, what I think is, you *can't* really give a baby away that grew inside you. It doesn't work. He's just always there anyway. Part of you. You might as well have him in your house if he's taking up so much room in your insides."

I smile, touch her hand.

"Anyways. My mom says I have to decide by tomorrow."

"So . . . you'll let me know?"

She walks over to her window, looks down onto the street. "Sure. I'll call you. 'Cause if I let him go, you won't need to come see me every week."

The truth is, I'm only authorized for two more visits, anyway. She must have forgotten that. But there's no need to bring it up now.

I pick up my bag. "I'll respect whatever decision you make, Grace. But I just want you to know that you've done everything right, and you don't have a thing in the world to be ashamed of. "

She won't look at me, but she nods.

On my way out, I see Grace's mother, Millie, sitting in the sun parlor reading a magazine and smoking a cigarette. She's a cashier at Stop and Shop; it must be her day off. I wave, and she nods curtly. She doesn't like me, has never seen the need for me "coming around." She pushes herself out of her chair, comes over to the door to stand beside me. "She tell you what we talked about?"

"Yes."

"I don't know what sense it makes for her to keep him."

"It's a hard decision."

"Yeah. One that she has no business making." Millie takes in a drag, exhales only slightly away from my face. One arm is crossed over her stomach, the other holds the cigarette up high. I see that she has lost one of her acrylic nails. She's wearing a pair of black shorts, a white shirt knotted at her waist, blue plastic bedroom slippers. Her hair, red this week, is up in a high ponytail. "She can barely decide what she wants for dinner, for Christ's sake."

"I don't know, I think Grace has grown up a whole lot in the last few weeks."

"You have kids?" Millie asks.

"No, I don't."

"Yeah, I didn't think so." She looks me up and down. "You even married?"

"I'm not."

Another drag off the cigarette, a slow nod. "Well. Thanks for what you did for her and the kid, anyway."

"It was a pleasure to see her. And Kurt." *Not you,* we both hear.

She opens the door, raises her eyebrows expectantly. For one moment, I think about going into Grace's room and asking if she and

Kurt would like to move in with me. But I don't. I walk out to my car, thinking, *As soon as I get home, I'll call social services. Millie has her weapons, and I have mine.*

But then I start the engine, and my anger fades. I know why Millie's doing what she is. All around me, it seems, mothers are trying to save their children.

On the way to DeWitt's, I get paged. Diann. When I find a pay phone and call her back, she says, "Oh, thanks for calling. I need to ask you something. Hold on for just a minute?"

I hear her call Chip's name, say something to him about needing to talk to someone from work. Then, "Okay. I'm in your office. Is that all right?"

"It's fine." *Don't touch anything.*

"I called because Chip and I were just sitting outside having coffee. And he dropped his cup. I mean, it just fell out of his hand. I know it doesn't sound like anything, but there was something so *weird* about it. You know?"

Yes. I know. The brain, being taken over by cancer cells, fails here, fails there. First, you mean to say "blueberry" and you say "cranberry." Then you wet the bed. Then you start to write something and you can't spell anymore, nor is your handwriting quite your own. "It's . . . to be expected, Diann."

"Oh. Uh-huh. So there's nothing they can do for it? It's nothing you should call the doctor about?"

"No. I'll let him know next time I give him a progress report. But it's not anything surprising. He also might . . . Well, just to let you know. He may start stumbling a little. Or falling."

I hear her start to cry, then stop abruptly. "Jesus."

"I know."

"It's so scary. It's so *evil.*"

"I know."

"Well. I'm sorry, I got scared; but I guess there was no need to call."

"There was a need. You had a question about something that concerned you. You can call me anytime."

"Okay. Okay. Thank you. Oh, one more thing. We're going to a movie this afternoon. And then, will you come with us to dinner? Chip wanted some Mexican, we were going to go to Tippi's."

"No, thanks, I—"

"He told me he was going to ask you to come along. And I think it would mean a lot to him, Myra. I don't want you to tell him no. Please don't tell him no."

"All right. I'll come."

I hang up, close my eyes for a moment, then get back to work.

"I'm stoked out," DeWitt says. "Illin' big time."

He does indeed look sick—bags under his eyes, a terrible weariness to him. I check his pulse and his blood pressure, put a thermometer in his mouth. When I take it out, I tell him it's normal.

"Damn. I like to have a fever when I'm sick. Where's Frank?"

"Not with me today. Is your incision hurting?"

"Naw. Where is he?"

"He's with someone who's visiting me for a little while. Let's do your dressing, I want to take a look under there and make sure you're not getting an infection."

"It ain't that. Most likely be that *bait* I had for dinner last night. I invite this new lady out, she say she want *sushi*. I say, baby, what you want with that Jap crap. She say, oh, Dewitt. And I know I ain't gon' get laid without I eat some shit like that. So I do, and then what happens? I spend half the night in the Porcelain Room, both ends open for *bidness*."

"Well," I say, loosening his dressing. "At least you had some pleasure before the pain."

"Sheeit," he says. "That's the worst part. I had to take her *home* after, she live with her mama, which, believe me, if I'd been apprised of *that*, wouldn't never have *been* no date. And I *paid* for that dinner! Paid for us both and left a good tip, besides!"

"Sometimes you win, sometimes you lose." I throw away his old dressing, inspect his wound. Healing slowly, but healing.

"Oh, no. I *always* win, baby."

I look at him.

" 'Cept this time."

I do his new dressing, silent, lost in my own thoughts. When I'm finished, DeWitt says, "Bring your dog tomorrow. He a more scintillating conversationalist than you. You getting boring as shit."

"Call me if you get worse," I say.

"Call *me* if you get better!"

I sigh, lean against the door frame.

"What?"

"Just . . . Give me a break, DeWitt. You know?"

"Aw, toughen up. Don't you know you my friend?"

I stop at a McDonald's for a quick lunch. At a table nearby is a young mother with her son, about four years old. "My head hurts," he tells her. She ignores him. "Mom," he says, "My *head* hurts."

"I know, sweetie," she says, staring off into middle space.

I take the last bite of my fish sandwich, finish my Coke. Then, "Miss?" I say.

The woman looks over.

"Excuse me, but I couldn't help overhearing what your son said. And I just wanted to tell you that I'm a nurse, and it's very unusual for a child so young to have a headache."

She stares at me. "He just bumped it. In the car just now, when he was getting out."

"Oh. I see. Well, I'm sorry."

"It's all right."

I get back in the car and sit still for a while, trying to remind myself that not everyone is dying. And thinking that, some time, I ought to try hanging up my cape.

* * *

On the way to Fitz's, I get stuck in heavy traffic. One of the bad things about doing the work I do. But I can't imagine doing anything else.

I turn on the radio, tune it to the classical station. Did they dream the music they wrote, those composers? Did they rise up in the morning full of something that made them feel tight at the center, then write out the notes and feel the slow release? And when they played it for the people they loved, did those people really hear it? I wonder sometimes about the nature of relationships, if anything that was once perfect in them is ever sustained. Every time I go to a restaurant alone, I feel a little sorry for myself until I see so many couples staring past each other, seemingly so *without*. Why enter into anything, when you end up scraping the bottom so soon? And yet the alternative makes for such sad echoes off the canyon walls of self, I know that.

I think of my parents, esctatic looking in their wedding pictures. Years later, neither of them wore their rings; they were tossed in a dresser drawer. Once, when I was around twelve years old, my mother found me sitting on her bed and playing with those wide gold bands. "What are you doing?" she asked. "Nothing," I said. She held out her hand, I put the rings in them, and she put them back in the dresser, saying, "Leave them there." *Why?* I remember thinking.

I wish I hadn't agreed to go to the restaurant tonight. Enchiladas suisas for the fifth wheel, please. What an odd trio we will be. What will the waiter think? *Pretty good looking guy, if he'd lose the kerchief. Beautiful woman. And . . . must be a friend.*

"I got something to tell you," Fitz says.

I look up from my bag, where I've been digging around for my stethoscope. "What's that?"

He's been cheating on his diet, I suppose. He's neglected to take his medication.

"I'm getting married."

I sit back on my heels. "Really!"

"Sure enough."

"Who's the woman?"

"Well, she called Misty Dream, down at the club. But her real name Miss Angela Brooks."

"Well, Fitz. Congratulations!"

He nods, smiling widely. "Yes, indeed. Thank you."

"Will you be doing this soon?"

"Tonight."

"Tonight!"

"Yeah, after the last show. We found a minister stays up late."

"And . . . will she be living here with you?"

"Naw. I'm moving to her place. You can come and see me there, she got a real nice brownstone in the South End. Those girls make good money! I'll be the house husband, take care of her. That's all she needs, someone just to take care of her, a man to come home to that's different from the rest. And that's me, I'm different! But I can cook for her, I know how to cook, once I get shown where everything is. I'll clean too, I'm very clean!"

"I know you are, Fitz. You keep your place looking great."

"That's the same thing *she* said. I had her over last Sunday afternoon, made her a chicken dinner. She was so surprised how I keep things. How I made her such a nice plate of eats. You know what she did when I put that plate in front of her? She started crying like a baby. Say she misses so much back in Alabama. Say she started out so different, when she were a little girl. We had a long talk, and then, I don't know, just seemed right, I popped the question. Sure did. On bended knee! I loved her a long time, she got a voice like velvet, but I have to say I surprised my own self saying those words, 'Will you marry me.' I been a bachelor for a long time! And you know what? She said yes quick as lightning. Just as grateful as can be. All it is, she need love the same as everybody else. A place to come home and be natural. You see someone such a big star like that, you think they got everything they need. But then you give them some chicken and biscuits and the truth comes out." He chuckles. "Yeah, the truth comes out."

I unroll the blood pressure cuff, put the stethoscope around my neck. "Well. I'm really happy for you. Now let's see if all this good news has helped out your blood pressure."

I check it, take the stethoscope out of my ears, smile, and say, "Guess what."

"You don't have to tell me," he says. "I already know."

Ann Peters is dressed in a white linen pantsuit when I arrive, a matinee-length pearl necklace, matching studs. After our visit, she's going into Boston for lunch at the Four Seasons.

I use the guest bathroom to wash my hands before I administer her eyedrops. Whenever I go into that bathroom, I always want to linger, just to admire everything. The high arch of the gold faucet, the leaded glass of the window. The curtains are like nothing I've ever seen, some sort of translucent fabric, a pale gold in color. They are so full of presence they might as well speak. The marble floor is richly veined; the soap at the side of the sink always unmarred and delicately scented; the towels so plush.

Mrs. Peters uses a floral handkerchief to wipe her eyes delicately after the drops have gone in. We are sitting in the breakfast room: French decor in the traditional colors of blue and yellow, murals of the countryside on the walls.

"Have you ever eaten at the Four Seasons?" Mrs. Peters asks.

"No."

"Really? *Never?*"

"It's not exactly my kind of place."

"Oh, but it's wonderful. Really, you must try it some time. I'll tell you what, I'm very good friends with the hotel manager. I'll arrange for you and a friend to have dinner there, on the house. In fact, let me give you a weekend."

"Well, that's very nice of you. But I really can't accept."

She straightens, sits back in her chair. "I would like you to notice something, here."

"Yes?"

"I'm not asking you. I'm telling you. You've been so kind to me. I've so much appreciated everything you've done."

I laugh. "But that's—"

"Myra." She puts her hand over mine, looks directly into my eyes. "Please don't make me explain how much your company has meant to me. Your care. I'm afraid it would be rather embarrassing for me."

Before this moment, if you'd asked me if I mattered to this patient, I would have laughed and said no. But now I think of the times I've spoken to one or the other of her children, neither of whom has time for her. I think of the photographs I've seen in heavy metal frames in her house: no one sitting too close to one another; no one smiling from the inside out. I realize now that perhaps I am the one she's most comfortable with, and it breaks my heart.

"This is much too generous, Mrs. Peters. But . . . all right. I'll take you up on it."

"I'm so glad. You'll get a call from the concierge later today. I'll arrange everything for you. You'll just need to let him know the dates you want to come."

"I will. Thank you."

"I'm thrilled to do it for you, Myra." She looks at her watch. "And now, I think my driver must be waiting."

I walk out with her, pull the heavy front door shut. And then I watch as she is driven away. Her head seems so small, framed in the rear window of a car driven by a stranger who is focused mainly on getting a big tip.

At four o'clock, Chip, his parents, and I are seated in his living room. For what seems like a long while, there is only the sound of the grandfather clock ticking, the occasional bird call coming from outside. Finally, Chip says, "So! Are we done yet?"

Mrs. Reardon looks at me. "I'm not sure what the point of this is, Myra. I told you I've agreed to let Chip do as he sees fit."

"Yes, I know that. But I thought it might be helpful for all of us to . . . Well, just to make sure each of us feels as though we understand—"

"There's nothing difficult to understand," Mrs. Reardon says. "It's simple. What Chip wants is to make no effort whatsoever to help himself."

"Ma," Chip says. "*Jesus!*"

"Don't give her a hard time," Mr. Reardon says.

"I'm not!" Chips stands; then, abruptly, sits back down. He turns toward his mother, shakes his head. "What do you want, Ma? You know what the prognosis is. You know I'm not going to be cured."

"I don't know that," she says. "And neither do you. I read in the library just the other day about a man in Italy who had exactly the same thing you do. When he was diagnosed, they had very little hope—his sister had died from a brain tumor just two years earlier. But he had surgery and then radiation, and he lived. They checked on him fifteen years later and he was *fine*—married, working full time. And the father of two daughters!"

"Myra," Chip says. "Help me out, here."

"There are exceptional cases, that's true," I say. "But the chances for cure are really very—"

"You don't know!" she says. "No one does."

I lean forward, speak directly to her. "I think what needs to be decided here today is how we can best support Chip in the decision he has made."

"*He* has made? I'm not so sure about that."

"What are you talking about?" Chip asks.

She says nothing.

"I *came* here knowing what I wanted to do. What are you suggesting? I decided my*self* what I want to do, which is *nothing*, Ma, can't you get that through your head, what will get that through your head? I know everything! Don't you think I researched the hell out of this before I decided I didn't want to go through the treatment? Don't you think I'd want to live if I could?"

"You don't listen to anyone else's ideas," she says. "There are things going on in other places that—"

"I researched *everything*," Chip says. *"Ma!"*

"You never used to be a quitter," she says.

"I never used to have a brain tumor. I'm going to die. I know that. I want to finish what's left of my life in the way I want. It doesn't make *sense* to me to do what you want. And I know it doesn't make sense to you what *I* want to do. But what else is new? That's the way it's always been between us."

"Chip," Mr. Reardon begins, but his wife interrupts him.

"Say it," she says, her chin high.

"Say what?" Chip's voice is so quiet it's barely audible. He's staring down at his hands shoved between his knees.

"Oh, I think you know what."

He looks up. "Ma. I love you."

She inhales sharply, and I see her mouth start to tremble.

"I love you and despite everything I have always loved you and I thank you for what you've given me and are trying to give me now. But you have to let go. It's time. Give me some peace, Ma. Please."

I stare at my bag, at the mantel over the fireplace. Finally, I hear Mrs. Reardon say, "What exactly do you want me to do, then, Chip? Tell me. And I . . . I will help you."

Here is the great privilege of being in this profession. What you see people do! How you come to understand what they are capable of, how huge their hearts are. And cracked open, how wise.

Chip packs a small bag to bring to my house. A way of formalizing what he's already been doing. For a long time, on the way back, we say nothing. And then he says, "So."

I smile. "So."

"Here we are."

"Yes."

I make a right turn, stop suddenly for a child who rides his bike out in the street directly ahead of me. Chip rolls down the window, starts to say something to the boy, then doesn't. I feel it, too. *What will be, will be.*

A few blocks from home, Chip says, "You know, it was driving me crazy, her pushing me to get more treatment. But now that she's going to stop, I kind of miss it. It makes me kind of scared. Everything's realer."

"I know."

"It's almost like anger at her was keeping fear at bay."

"Yes."

He clears his throat, taps his fingers rapidly on his knee. "So. You ready?"

I look over at him. Nod.

At home, Diann has begun a marinara sauce. She's making spaghetti and meatballs. I pour myself a glass of chianti, then leave Chip in the kitchen washing lettuce while I go into my office to check messages. Four. The first is from Grace, who says she is keeping her baby, and could I make a visit tomorrow instead of Monday because he stares so much at the light coming through the window and is that normal and do they make sunglasses for babies. Next, Marvelous, telling me she agrees with her doctor that she's all right without me, but she *would* like me to come to lunch any time. She has tomatoes from her daughter's garden coming out her ears. We can have BLTs, she says, and you can bring the B.

The next message is from a soft-spoken concierge at the Four Seasons, wondering when I would like a room, and telling me with what I can only describe as restrained glee how very happy he will be to accommodate any date, *any* date at *all*. The last message is from Chip's doctor, who says that he understands there's been a change in plans, and am I sure this is the wisest course. For me, he means, he's thinking of me. Call him tomorrow and let's talk about this. I stand for a long moment before my desk, swirling the wine that's left in my glass. Then I go ahead and drink it.

I awaken to a crack of thunder that shakes the house. Rain is wild on the roof, against the windows. Frank, who is terrified of thunder, is nowhere to be seen. I get up, kneel at the side of the bed, and raise the dust ruffle. He's squeezed under there, shaking. "It's all right," I tell him. He stares at me, wags his tail apologetically. "Come here," I say, patting the floor, but it's no use, he won't come out.

I shut my windows, then remember that most of those downstairs are open as well. I come out into the hall, turn the light on, and see Chip on his way up the stairs. For a moment, I feel embarrassed about my sleepware—my gray T-shirt and many-times-washed striped bottoms. But Chip is in his T-shirt and boxers—I'd call us even. "Are you going down to shut the windows?" he asks.

"Yes."

"I just did."

"Oh. Thank you. Did any water come in? Anything I need to wipe up?"

"A little. I got that, too."

"Well, *thank* you."

"You're welcome."

We stand there for a minute, listening to the rain, and then Chip says, "Myra, would you check my bood pressure or something?"

"I—*now*, you mean?"

"Yeah. I feel weird. Kind of dizzy. And just . . . weird."

"Sure, let me go and get my cuff. Maybe you should lie down. I'll be back up in a second."

"Would you mind if I went into your room? Diann's asleep."

I turn around. "She's sleeping? Through this?"

He shrugs.

"Sure, go ahead, go to my room."

I go into my office, grab my nurse's bag. I stand there for a minute, thinking. It could be nothing. It's probably nothing. Then I sigh, sit down in my desk chair. Nothing. Right.

I go back upstairs, pass the closed door of the guest room, then go back to open it and peek inside. Diann does indeed appear to be sound asleep. I can see her clearly in the light from the hall; she's on her side, facing me. "Diann," I whisper. I want her to be awake, in case I need her. "Diann!" She doesn't move. I close the door, head back to my room.

Chip is stretched out on the bed, Frank beside him. I laugh out loud. "How did you do *that?*"

"What?"

"How'd you get him up there?"

Chip looks at Frank, who looks back at him. "I don't know. He just came out and jumped up on the bed. Is that okay?"

"Yes, it's fine, but he has *never* come out from under the bed when it's thundering. He gets really scared."

Chip scratches Frank's butt, and Frank raises his head appreciatively. "He seems fine now."

I sit on the bed, take out my blood pressure cuff and wrap it around Chip's arm. Has he lost more weight in this last week? Why have I not noticed this? I position my stethoscope over his brachial artery, inflate the cuff. His pressure is normal, and I tell him that. Then I listen to his heart. After I've gotten a count, I look up into his face.

"It's fine," I say. "Eighty and regular. That's just fine."

He looks at me, something in his face.

"What," I say.

"I don't know, you . . ."

I wait.

"I just . . . like you. You have pretty eyes."

I frown, start rolling up the cuff.

"You do," he says. "A lot of green in there. I never noticed before."

"Yes, well."

"Your eyes change colors, I think."

I can feel discomfort rising in me like a wave. It makes me oddly irritable. "I wouldn't know, maybe they do." I put my supplies back in my bag, rest my hands in my lap. It's strange, taking someone's blood pressure when I'm dressed in my pajamas. It's like those dreams where you find yourself naked on a crowded street.

"So," I say, apropos of nothing. I suppose I mean it to be the verbal equivalent of putting a robe on, an effort to formalize somewhat a too casual situation.

He lies still. The rain drums, lightens for a moment, then drums on, harder. Finally, "Myra?" he says. "Would you mind if I stayed here for a while?"

"Of course not, it's all worked out, you *are* staying here." *Oh God, I think, he doesn't remember, he's getting confused.*

"No," he says. "*Here.*" He pats the bed, and Frank moves closer to him.

"Oh!" Who knows why people ask for the things they do. Who knows why certain things suddenly bring you comfort. "Sure. I'll go down to the sofa." Chip has never had the pleasure of sleeping with a dog; I'll give that to him.

"No," he says. "I meant I wanted to stay here with *you.*"

I swallow, say nothing.

"Just for a while."

I nod. "Okay."

"Is this your side?"

"Well . . . Yes."

"Okay, I'll move over."

He climbs over Frank to the other side of the bed, punches the pillow and lies down. "There's no night stand over here," he says, looking around. "No light."

"I haven't exactly needed one."

"You always sleep on the same side?"

"Yes, don't you?"

"Yeah, I guess I do." He looks over at me, smiles.

I smile back, then climb awkwardly back into bed. I am overly conscious of every part of myself. My legs and arms feel as stiff as if they were cast. I lean up against the headboard, smooth the sheets over me. My heart is knocking in my chest. Frank, panting happily, makes the bed shake, and for some reason, this embarrasses me.

There is a long moment of silence, and then Chip says, "Why don't you lie down?"

"Well, I . . . thought you wanted to talk a little, maybe."

"You can talk when you're lying down."

I start laughing. "You know what? You know what just came into my head? 'That wouldn't be professional.'"

"Right," he says, smiling. Lightning flashes, and we both look out the window. A loud crack of thunder follows, and Frank jumps off the bed and crawls under it again.

"God," Chip says. "Quite a storm!"

"I know."

"Did they forecast this?"

"I don't think so."

He looks over at me. "Nobody knows anything."

"Well."

"I don't think they do."

"They're right a lot of the time."

"They're wrong a lot, too."

"Yeah. They are."

"You know," Chip says. "I first went to the doctor a couple of months ago. I was having terrible headaches. The guy told me it was my sinuses and gave me something for pain. It didn't help, so I went back. He gave me stronger medication. It still didn't help, so I went to another guy. I told him what was going on, and he said, oh hell, it's not your sinuses, it's *stress*. He put me on antidepressants. Then I went a third doctor, who actually might have gone to med school."

"It's hard sometimes," I say.

"What is?"

"It's not always easy to make a diagnosis right away. Most of the time, it *isn't* . . . that."

"Shouldn't they make sure, though?"

"Well, they usually do. Eventually."

"Yeah, when it's too late."

I say nothing.

After a moment, he says, "I know."

"What?"

"In this case, it wouldn't have made any difference, right?"

"Probably not."

"Yeah . . . What time is it?"

I look at the bedside clock. "Three forty-three."

He takes in a deep breath, closes his eyes. Then opens them. "I'm sorry, Myra. I'm keeping you up."

"It's all right. The thunder would be, anyway."

"Are you tired?"

"No."

"Me neither."

He reaches over, takes my hand. I stop breathing. "I just want to do this," he says.

"Okay."

"The rain. It makes you kind of . . ."

"Yes."

After a while, he says, "It's awful to know how you'll die."

"I know."

"Do you ever wonder about that, about how you'll die?"

"Sure."

"And what do you think?"

"Oh, on a good day, I think, 'Massive MI. Cerebral hemorrage. Airplane crash.' You know, instant death."

"And on a bad day?"

"It depends," I say. "There's so much to choose from."

"Do you ever think you'll die from a brain tumor?"

"Honestly? I never have thought that."

"I never thought I would, either. Myra?"

"Yes?"

He is silent so long I think maybe he's fallen asleep. But then he says, "Do you think if you got a diagnosis like mine, you'd consider suicide?"

Now it is my time to be silent. The truth is, I've considered suicide plenty of times, but for very different reasons. Sitting alone at my kitchen table, I've looked out the window and thought, in the most dispassionate of ways, "Well, soon I'll have had enough." It's because I know what I'm headed for. More beauty, yes, the world is rich with beauty. But more of everything else, too. Unrelenting loneliness, of course. But also this: Sometimes, reading the paper, I have to put it down. Sometimes when the news comes on the radio, I have to turn it off. This ongoing parade of tragedy. And even if the world were right, there is the wisdom of biology. The old must make way for the new. Why should I insist on hanging around after a certain age? To begin fearing the small descent down my stairs? To fret over the cost of a can of beets?

In school, we had to spend a week working in a nursing home. One afternoon, I sat in a room where old people in wheelchairs gathered to sing. I looked at their faces, and some were joyous, but most were not. And I remember thinking, *Not for me.* For one thing, I would not have the relief of family visiting; I would be one of those for whom the staff made birthday cards out of construction paper. Apart from that, I have always thought that there can be very good reasons to leave life by your own hand. Without bitterness. We come, and we go. As we should. The earth turns on its creaky old axis and gives what it can and takes back what it must. Why not awaken each morning thinking, *It's a good day to die,* and then go about living, if such is our choice. Or fate.

I want to answer Chip's question honestly, to say that suicide does not seem like a horrible option at all, under certain circumstances.

But I am his nurse as well as his friend. I don't want to influence a decision that must be his own. And so I say, simply, "I might."

"I'm strongly considering it," Chip says. "I think you should know that."

"Yes."

"Not quite yet," he says.

"No."

The rain goes on and on. I think of flowers in their beds, drowning, birds huddled miserably in their nests. Chip leans over to kiss my cheek once, twice. I lie still as stone.

Then, "I guess I should go back to bed," he says.

"Okay."

"Thank you, Myra."

"I . . . You're welcome."

He stands, then grabs for the headboard. Instinctively, I grab for him. "It's when I stand, sometimes. That's when it happens. I get dizzy."

"Does it go away after you're up for a second?"

"Yeah."

"It could be your medications. It could be orthostatic hypotension—your pressure drops when you stand up."

"Why don't I stop taking them?"

"If you do, you'll . . . have some problems."

He nods. "Yeah. I know." He sighs heavily. "It's been so long since I was me."

He comes around to my side of the bed, stands there. Then he sits down, and I start to sit up.

"Don't," he says.

I lie back down, breathe out slowly.

"Yes," he says. "That's right. Now close your eyes, would you?"

I close them, hear him turn my bedside light out.

"Good night, Myra." His voice is so soft.

"Good night."

He hesitates, and I think that perhaps he's going to kiss my forehead. But he doesn't.

And yet he does.

In the morning, I come downstairs early, go into the kitchen to start coffee, and find Chip sitting at the tiny breakfast table. "Hey," I say. "Good morning." I am embarrassed. Bad enough that he saw me last night in my pajamas. Now there's my mussed up hair, my ancient bathrobe, my morning breath, and my slippers. They are Bill and Hillary Clinton, a gift from one of my patients a few Christmases ago.

"Good morning." He shoves a piece of paper in his pocket. He's wearing a light blue T-shirt with his jeans, and his long legs are stretched out before him, his bare feet crossed at the ankle. There are deep circles under his eyes.

"You're up early," I say.

"Yeah, I never went back to sleep. Did you?"

"I did." I reach up into the cupboard. "Want some French roast?"

"That would be great. I was going to make some for all of us, but I couldn't . . . I didn't know how to use your coffeemaker."

"Yeah, they're all different," I say, though my coffeemaker, the rough equivalent of those provided to hotel guests, couldn't be easier to use. I measure out the coffee, pour in the water, flick the switch. Then I join him at the table.

"Who are you seeing today?" he asks.

"Let's see. Friday. First Rose, then . . . Well, actually *everybody*."

"Mind if I come along?"

"Of course not."

"I can take Frank for little walks while you go in and see people."

"Why don't we just leave him here with Diann? He loves her."

Chip leans back in his chair, puts his hands behind his head. His new growth is crew-cut length; if he'd even out his hairdo, he could stop wearing the kerchief. But he seems attached to it.

"You know what, Myra? You look pretty good in the morning."

"Oh, God." I go over to check the coffeepot, to see if it's ready to give up a cup. Half a cup.

"I like your robe."

I stare down at my battered red plaid. "Well. Thank you."

"And your slippers, too . . . Who is that?"

"The Clintons."

"Great."

I reach up into the cupboard, take down two cups, hear the shower turn on upstairs, and take down a third. With a kind of edgy pleasure. *Family*, I'm thinking.

And now I hear Frank's tags jingling as he comes down the steps. He comes into the kitchen and greets us, snorting and smiling. He puts his head in Chip's lap and stands there, lazily wagging his tail. Chip pets him and I watch those long, slow strokes.

After I've returned some phone calls, Chip and I head out. The sky is clear, a deep blue. Hard to think it's the same sky that poured down so much water last night. "Your doctor wanted to know how you were doing," I say, as we drive down Main Street. "I said fine, considering. Is that the right answer?"

"That's the right answer."

His doctor also wanted to know if I was really all right doing this, of course, having Chip stay with me. And I told him that I understood how unusual it was, but I was fine. How about another nurse seeing him, and you just being . . . his friend, the doctor asked. No, I said. It's fine.

Chip suddenly sits up straighter, points out the window. "See that florist?"

"Yes."

"Stop there, will you?"

I start to tell him I don't have time, but he says, "I'll be really fast," and so I pull into a parking place. "Wait right there," he says. After a few minutes, he emerges with a small bouquet of roses. A vibrant yellow. "Roses for Rose," he says.

I imagine those flowers by her bedside, offering glorious relief to all that surrounds them. I see her reaching out to touch each half-open blossom. "That's nice of you, Chip."

He turns up the air conditioner. "Do you mind? It's hot as hell out there already."

"I know it."

"It's *summer*."

"Sure is."

It's not idle conversation. He's asking me. Diann told me that last time she drove him, he asked if a stoplight were a semaphore. "I told him yes," she said. "Should I have done that?" I said it probably didn't matter. "But what would you have said?" she asked. And I told her I would have told him it was a stoplight. She sighed, looked away from me. "I can't do this," she said. I told her she was doing fine, and I noticed how beautiful the shape of her face was from that angle. Heartlike.

"Oh, *flowers*," Rose says, after Chip presents them to her with a flourish. "Where did you find these?" She's still in her nightgown and robe; we must have awakened her.

"Just a shop on the way," Chip tells her. "Do you like them?"

"Yes. They need a vase. Flowers have to have water, or they'll die."

"Do you have one, Rose?" I ask.

"I don't know."

"Well, I'll tell you what, we'll just use a jar. How's that?"

"Not so good." She frowns, shuffles over to her kitchenette. She

121

pulls a tall glass out of the cupboard, hands it to me. "Here. This is better. You cut the stems, I don't like to use scissors. It's bad for a diabetic to get cut."

"Where are your scissors?"

"I don't know."

I sigh, take a quick look at Chip, who shrugs, then smiles at me.

"Okay, how about a knife?"

"Oh, sure, I have that." She opens a drawer, takes out a large butcher knife. "This was my mother's. I remember she always used it to chop nuts for Russian tea cakes, we had them every Christmas. Russian tea cakes." She leans closer, squints at it. "Well, I wouldn't eat anything cut with *that*."

"It'll be fine for this." I take the knife from her, cut the stems, and arrange the flowers in the glass. Then I hand Rose her bouquet.

"Ohhhhh!" She holds the roses up to her nose, inhales deeply. She smiles shyly at Chip. "See, I didn't know I was getting *flowers*."

"Well," he says. "You did."

"You're a very nice young man."

"And you're a very nice lady."

Rose straightens, adjusts the collar on her robe. "Where do you live?"

"Well, actually, I'm living with Myra, at the moment."

Rose gasps, spins around, and wags her finger in my face. "You didn't tell me you got married, you rascal!"

"We're not married." I dry the knife I've washed, put it back in the drawer.

"You're not?" Her face clouds. Then she says, "Well, that's all right. Don't worry. That's how they do nowadays. Lots of people do it." She sets her flowers down on her kitchen table. "Now. How about some tea for the lovebirds?"

I look at my watch. Ten minutes behind schedule. "I'm afraid we can't, Rose," I say, at the same time that Chip says, "We'd love some."

"*Chip!*"

"Oh, it's a fight," Rose says. "Don't fight."

"*Myra*," Chip says.

"Rose, " I say, "you need to get your insulin now. I have to give it to you right now so you can be ready for Tiffany. Then you need to get dressed, okay? She'll be here soon."

"Oh, she left."

"Who did?"

"Tiffany."

"She's not supposed to *be* here, yet. I want to give you your shot so you can get ready for her, remember?"

Rose starts to cry. "But she's *gone*, Tiffany's *gone*, I got a *new* one now!"

"Oh!" I say. "Oh, I'm sorry, Rose, I didn't know. I'm sorry. Who's the new one, what's her name?"

"I don't know. But not 'Tiffany.'" She pulls a filthy handkerchief out of her robe pocket, blows her nose.

I check my watch again, go over to the refrigerator and take out Rose's insulin. It's close to being used up; I'll need to call her pharmacy. I take my pen out, make an X on my wrist to remind me to do this later. No time now.

"Okay, Rose, go over to your bed, please, and let me give you your shot."

She stands still, her head down.

"Rose?"

"I have to tell you something first,"

"Yes?" I draw up the required number of units, cap the needle, grab an alcohol swab.

"Can you come here?"

I walk over to her with some impatience. "What is it, Rose?"

She looks quickly at Chip, then back at me. "He'll have to leave," she whispers.

I start to say something to Chip, but he's heard. "I'll wait outside," he says. "It was nice to see you again, Rose."

"Yes. It was nice to see me." As he walks out the door, she yells,"I wish you all the happiness!" She shuffles over to her bed, flops down, and hikes up her nightgown so that I can inject her thigh. She squeezes her eyes shut, as usual. Says, "*That* time I didn't even feel it!"

as usual. Then she leans forward to tell me, "He shouldn't wear that kerchief on his head."

"No?" I swab off the injection site, pull Rose's nightgown back down, break apart and discard the needle in the cardboard box designed for used syringes that she keeps under her bed. It's almost full; I'll need to get her another one.

"No. That's for *girls.*"

"I'll see you Monday, Rose."

"Is that tomorrow?"

"No. Tomorrow's Saturday."

"Oh. Isn't that funny." She gets up, accompanies me to the door. "Happy honeymoon! All the best to you both!"

In the car, we ride in silence for a while. Then I say, "Chip, I like it when you come with me. But you need to let me run my own show."

"I'm sorry."

"I don't want you to feel bad, but I have to tell you that."

"It's all right. I just thought, you know, it would have been nice to spend a little time with her."

"Well, yes, it would have been, but I can't do that when I have all the rest of these patients to see. Today is just a tight day."

"I understand."

I stop at a light, listen to the quiet. Then, "I'm sorry," I say.

"It's all *right.* I'm the one who should be apologizing to *you.* Jesus, Myra, why do you *always* . . . ?"

"What?" I say.

"Nothing."

I look over at him. "*What?*"

"Green," he says, gesturing with his chin at the stoplight.

I turn right, put on some speed so that I can get to Ann Peters's and Fitz's sooner. I don't feel like hearing the usual lecture from DeWitt on how most people learned to tell time in grade school.

"Is this our first fight?" Chip asks.

"Oh, I'm just . . . tense. I'm late."

"It happens all the time," Chip says. "People fight on their honey-moon."

By the time we get to DeWitt's, I've more than made up for lost time. We're actually ten minutes early. He ought to love that. I knock on the door, and hear him bellow through it, *"What?"*

"It's Myra," I say.

He yanks open the door, walks away from it without having seen me. "Some people wear a watch and actually *look* at it," he mutters, walking down the hall. "If I wanted you to come this early, I'd've *told* you that. I'm not ready, I'm on the phone. Conference call. You going to have to wait, and I don't want to hear nothing about it. I got a bid-ness to run."

He turns around and, for the first time, sees Chip.

"Oh," he says. "I didn't know you was here."

"Hey, DeWitt."

"'Be right there, my man."

Let's see. I'll give Frank to Diann, and DeWitt to Chip. Wish them all the happiness.

After I do DeWitt's dressing—remarkable progress, the wound is nearly healed—I get into the car without Chip. I'm going to finish my work day alone. Chip is staying at DeWitt's—they're going to watch a movie together. I had plenty of misgivings about leaving Chip there, I did everything but pick him up and carry him out, but they both insisted it was fine, and in the end, I had to simply leave without him. DeWitt said he had roast beef sandwiches, they'd eat some lunch and enjoy some "fine art" entertainment. Chip wasn't particularly interested in seeing the Schwartzes again, and I need to spend a fair amount of time at the agency's office, picking up supplies and doing paperwork—it would actually be better not to have Chip there. I told them I'd be back in a few hours.

"Make sure you not late, neither!" DeWitt said, walking me out, and when I started to say something back to him, he said, "Aw, relax. I don't want you in this neighborhood after a certain time of the day, is all. Be a little funky for you. And anyway, your boy be tired by then."

I pull away from the curb, look up at DeWitt's window. I hope none of his clients come over. But so what if they do. Nobody will hurt anybody—all of that happens outside DeWitt's place. It's actually more dangerous bringing Chip in and out of DeWitt's than letting him stay there for a while. And if Chip were to meet a client, it would at least be interesting for him, a better movie than the one they're planning on watching.

I was once at DeWitt's when a customer came to do a deal with him. It was because I'd been late, that's why our paths crossed, and DeWitt was none too pleased about it. "She just leaving," he told the man. "She ain't even 'posed to be here in the first place and she *know* that. She be out of our way in a second."

"Oh, that's no problem at all," the man said. He was well-dressed, a light-skinned black man wearing diamond studs, rings on every finger, and several gold necklaces. He sat in the living room with me as I finished making notes on DeWitts's chart and made polite chitchat. He mentioned the beautiful weather, asked if I had any children, told me he had a couple. Or maybe three, he wasn't quite sure. As soon as I shut the door, they got down to business. I know, because I stood there listening, wondering if I should do anything about it. Wisely, I didn't. I remembered all the places there are in the world, and my place in it.

When I arrive at the Schwartzes, Ethel answers the door in tears. "What's wrong?" I ask.

"It's Murray. He's in the hospital."

"Oh, Ethel. When? What happened?"

"Just this morning. We were having breakfast, and he stood up and said his chest hurt so bad and then he just fell down. And I called the ambulance and by the time they got here, he was . . . he couldn't . . . Oh God, Mary, I can't live without him. You don't know. He's in the CCU. I just came home to get some things packed, and then I'm going back there. I won't leave him until he comes home. I know what I used to say about him, but I love him, he's my husband, I'm married fifty-five years to him. I don't know life without him. You must think—"

"Ethel. I know how much you love him. Finish packing. I'll drive you back to the hospital."

"Oh, thank you. Thank you." She wipes at her nose with the back of her hand.

"It's all right."

"I'm almost finished, I just need to find a robe that . . . I never saw such a slob. I tell him, I say, Murray, did it ever occur to you—" She stops, turns to me. Opens her mouth and then closes it. And then, very quietly, "Oh, my God."

"I'll go and take care of your medications," I tell Ethel. "You'll need to take them with you. You go ahead and finish packing. I can get you there in less than fifteen minutes."

In the kitchen, I put away the milk that's out on the counter. Note the list for groceries on the refrigerator that both of them have contributed to, though Ethel's blue ink has crossed out Murray's black "salami." I put the breakfast dishes in the dishwasher. Dole out pills for a week. In Murray's bedroom, Ethel packs his bag. I believe she feels her love for him like a second skin, and that although her hands pack clothes, her mind is back in the hospital room with him, straightening his bedcovers, adjusting the blinds, holding a spoonful of trembling Jell-O up to him, saying, *Here, Murray, take it, open up, darling. Stay.*

Chip is stoned out of his mind. I lead him down the hall, tell him to wait at the door, and then go back to stand before DeWitt, who's lying back in his recliner. Probably because he cannot get out of his recliner.

"What did he take?" I ask.

"Mary wanna."

"I can't believe you did this, DeWitt."

He looks up at me, red-eyed. "Did what? Made him feel a little better? Let him have some fun?"

"You—"

"I didn't do *nothing* wrong. And that's the truth. You go home and think about it, little girl. World is way different than you think. You ask my friend, there; you ask Chip. He got a load lifted, that's what happened to him. His head stop hurting and he didn't throw up. That's some kind of tragedy. You uptight, woman, and you need to get unwound. Maybe you need to get laid, I don't know what your deal is. But for now you get out my house, I ain't gonna stand for some bitch yelling at me 'bout nothing."

I stand there for a moment. Then I say, "I won't be back here, DeWitt. I'll arrange for another nurse to come and see you."

"Aw, now, you—"

"That's all I have to say."

I start down the hall, and he calls after me, "Get on back here, now. Just relax, all right?"

I take Chip's arm, open the door.

"Myra!" DeWitt calls.

I slam the door shut.

Late Monday afternoon, I am on my way to my last visit. Chip is with Diann; they were going to go into Boston to visit the Museum of Fine Arts. I warned Diann that Chip might get tired; she should pace things. She said she knew that, Chip had already told her. She'd planned on them walking around for a bit, then having lunch at the café. I pictured them sitting there, a plate of cheese and fruit before them. I've been to the museum many times, but never with a date. It must be fun.

Margaret Thornton is a ninety-year-old woman I'm seeing just once, as a favor for her regular nurse. She needs a vital-signs check, evaluation of the ankle edema she's started to develop, and administration of some antibiotic drops for an ear infection.

Margaret lives in a retirement hotel where each resident has a bedroom, a bathroom, a small kitchen, and a sitting room. "How do you like living here?" I ask, after I've finished our visit and am packing up my bag.

"Oh," she says, looking around as though she too is seeing it for the first time. "Your own home is always better. But after a while, I just couldn't keep up with it. The stairs, you know. It's all right here, but for God's sake, how often can you play bingo? Yesterday, I applied for a job in a bookstore."

I laugh. "Really?"

"Really. I volunteer at the library twenty-five hours a week. But I need some cash—I haven't bought an article of clothing in years. And besides, I just . . . Well, to tell you the truth, the people here are just plain hard to be with sometimes."

"I can imagine." I zip my bag, head for the door.

Margaret walks along with me, continues talking. "For meals, I sit at the same table with the same people every day. There's one woman, Catherine, she's ninety-three, and I can go and have a cup of coffee with her—you know. But there's another woman with Alzheimer's and I've seen it progress so fast over the last year. I . . . well, I feed her, now. I mean, I literally feed her. It's so sad, I go and get something to cover her up, and then I just sit there with the spoon . . . I know the staff would feed her, but they're not very careful. I think she deserves more than that."

I know exactly what she's saying. The baby bird tenderness you feel for someone when you feed them. The regret. The way you attempt to give them back some dignity: small bites, so the mashed potatoes don't fall out, a precise dabbing at the corner of their mouths after the slow, slow sip of coffee.

"Another woman at my table," Margaret says, "is named Evelyn, and she comes from a wad of dough. She's always talking about her family members, what degree this one has, and that one. And saying that she taught the ballet. Well, maybe she did." Margaret leans in closer to me. "But I taught with Martha Graham." She stands back, nods. "Yes, I did. One of the women who works at this hotel, she knows that and she told Evelyn that I taught with Martha Graham and that I have a bit of education myself. So now Evelyn won't talk to me or anyone else at the table; she eats her meals without saying a word." She shrugs. "What can you do with someone like that?"

I smile. "I don't know." I can see Evelyn, head held high, staring pointedly away.

"The other woman at the table is always talking about people stealing from her. Betty's her name. Every day, it's another story of what 'they' took from her. Today at lunch she said someone had taken her girdle. Now, who in the hell would want to steal a dirty old girdle?"

And now, I can't help it, I start laughing. "Well, I know," Margaret says. "Exactly." She laughs herself. "I'll tell you. As soon as you give up your car, you're done for. Oh, you have some friends that say they'll take you out, but they get tired of it, and they fall off. Your world gets very narrow."

I look at my watch, then say, "Listen, I've got to get going now. But how would you like to see a movie with me tonight?" I've never done this. I feel so nervous, like an adolescent boy asking for his first date.

Margaret stares at me. "What's your name again?"

"Myra. Lipinski."

"Well, Myra, I would love to go to a movie. And I don't care what we see. It can be trash—I'll just be so happy to be sitting in a theater and smelling that popcorn."

"I'll pick you up at six," I say. "We'll have dinner first."

As I open the door to leave, she says, "Oh, wait just one second!" She goes into her kitchen and returns with a paper bag full of cookies. Gingersnaps, I can smell them.

"Thank you, but I don't want to take your cookies," I tell her.

"Please," she says. "I bake every day, I just love to bake. And I can hardly ever find someone to *take* anything. Their diets, you know, or this, or that. There's nothing worse than having all this stuff you want to give away and then not being able to find anyone to take it. You finish these and I'll give you more, any kind you like."

"Well," I say. "Thank you."

"Thank *you*."

When I come home from the movie, it's late, 1:00 A.M. Margaret and I snuck into a second feature, and after that we went to an all-night diner for pie and ice cream. When I open the front door quietly, Frank pushes his head in the crack, and I pet him, whispering, "Yes, I see you, good boy." Then, coming into the room, I see Diann sitting on the sofa, a magazine in her lap.

"Hi," she says.

"Hi." I close the door, scratch behind Frank's ears. "Is Chip sleeping?"

"He's not here," Diann says. "He went home. Said he was going to spend a night with his parents."

"Really?"

She shrugs, returns to her magazine.

I head for the kitchen. "I'm getting something to drink. Do you want anything?"

"No thanks. I got us a bunch of different drinks today, though—they're on the bottom shelf of the refrigerator."

I come into the living room with a bottle of cranberry juice, sink down into a chair.

"How was the movie?" Diann asks.

"Movies," I say. "We went to two. That Margaret, she's delightful. Best date I've ever had."

"Do you date much?" Diann asks.

I look at her. "Are you serious?"

"Well . . . Yes."

"I date about three times a year. They're desperation dates. You know. The last time I had a date that wasn't like that was . . . God, it was in high school. The night of the senior prom, I went to the mall for something to do and ran into Danny Roth, you remember him?"

"Wasn't he a preacher's kid?"

"Yeah." I take a long drink, put the bottle on the floor. "He was walking around killing time, he didn't have a date, either. We decided to go to the drive-in. It was actually kind of fun—we talked for a long time about whether there was life after death, I remember that. He thought no."

"Really? A preacher's kid?"

"Yeah. And I remember I said I thought there was, and that you got to pick what you would look like in heaven, too. He said that might be enough to make him believe in it."

"I can't believe you went to a drive-in and talked about things like that. Didn't you make out?"

"Actually, yes. A little. It was my first French kiss."

"I'm not sure I remember him," Diann says. "What did he look like?"

"Oh, he was short. Good hair, bad teeth. Well, he was ugly as hell. But it was the night of the senior prom, it was the end of high school, everybody was leaving, you had to go and do *something*. He wrote me once, from college—did you know he went to Harvard?"

"Really?" Diann picks up her hair, makes a ponytail high on her head, drops it. "Wait. Did he have green eyes and really big black glasses?"

"No, that was Sam Goodman. I'll show you what Danny looked like." I go into my office, come back out with my yearbook from senior year.

"Oh, *God*," Diann groans. "I haven't seen that for so long! I don't even know where mine is. Can I see?"

I sit beside her, flip through the pictures until we come to Danny Roth. Diann leans in closer, inspects him. "Oh. Yes. Danny Roth."

"Right." I look at him again, and even after all this time, he seems so deeply familiar to me. One date.

"He *did* have nice hair," Diann says.

"Yeah. I wonder if he has any left."

She turns to the very front of the book, and I feel a sudden urge to put my hand over the page, to hide the lack of autographs. I think I know what Diann's yearbook looks like—no room for any more messages, all the space filled by people congratulating her on being herself and congratulating themselves on being her friend, and telling her to "never change." As though it were a choice. As though one of our greatest lessons isn't that change is the only constant. The seasons tell us, everything in organic life tells us, that there is no holding on; still, we try to do just that. Sometimes, though, we learn the kind of wisdom that celebrates the open hand. Then we know that letting go of everything is the only way to keep the things that matter most.

"Where are you in here?" Diann asks.

"Class picture and French club," I say. I feel a blush start, then stop.

She nods.

"*You're* everywhere," I say.

"No I'm not." She closes the book, and I take it from her, look up her name in the index. "Look at this. Six lines just to list the page numbers!"

I open the album to one of the pages listed. There's Diann in her strapless white formal for homecoming, Chip at her side. We both stare, and then Diann runs her finger down Chip's cheek.

"My God," she says. "He was so beautiful."

"You were too," I say quietly. "You were *always* so beautiful!"

"It was makeup."

"Right."

"Well, *some* of it was makeup. And clothes." She closes the yearbook, looks at me. "You never did wear much makeup, did you?"

"Not much point."

"That's not true. A little makeup can do some very good things."

"For people like you."

"For anyone!"

"Well." I pick up the yearbook again, flip through the pages. "Look at Sandy Weller. She got knocked up. I wonder if she's still married to the guy. He was way older than she was."

"Would you let me make you up?" Diann asks.

I look at her. Only kindness there. And a mild curiosity.

What the hell. "I might have to get drunk, first," I tell her.

"I might have to, too."

It is with a mix of apprehension and joy that I head for the cupboard that holds the booze. I've got gin. I've got vermouth. I've got us covered.

"Now," Diann says, putting down her empty martini glass with exaggerated care. "I am ready."

I eat the last of my five olives. "Me, too."

"Let's go in the bathroom," Diann says. Then, standing, "Where is it?"

We head for the upstairs bathroom, laughing. Inside me is a small figure holding her hand over her mouth. Frank follows us, lies outside the bathroom door.

Diann takes down the floral cosmetics holder she has hanging on the back of the bathroom door. "Wash your face," she tells me, digging through her supplies. She hands me a stretchy headband. "And put this on."

I put the handband on, splash off my face, sit down on the closed seat of the toilet. "Hey, Diann."

"Hmm?" She's got a couple of pencils clenched between her teeth, and her eyebrows are furrowed as she sorts through various bottles and tubes.

"Diann."

She looks up. "What?"

"Do you think we need a permit for this?"

She smiles, returns to her foraging.

"Do you know how much this would have meant to me in high school?"

She turns to me, hand on her hip. "Ha! Do you know how hard a time you would have given me if I'd asked to do your makeup in high school?"

"I would not have!"

"Yes, you would."

I consider this. She's right. I would have been too afraid. I'm still too afraid; I'm just drunk now.

Diann comes over to me, serious-faced, a woman with a mission. She lines up a handful of products up on the counter. Gold tops on frosted bottles, long black tubes, plastic cases in various sizes. Another kind of pharmacy. She picks up a bottle, shakes it. "Close your eyes," she tells me, and I sit still while she puts dots of foundation on my face.

"I would like to be really beautiful for one day," I say quietly. And then have the odd feeling that I haven't really said it.

Silence. She's working, concentrating on me, and I like it. She's gentle, she rubs upward on my cheeks in a way I can just barely feel.

When she pencils in my eyebrows, I say, "I'll bet it's great to be so beautiful. I'll bet you get everything you want."

"It's not so great," she says. "It's a prison."

I open my eyes, look at her.

"It is."

It's an awfully nice prison, I want to say, but don't.

"Look down," Diann says, and carefully applies mascara. "I'll tell you something, Myra. It makes you retarded, being pretty. You learn to rely on something that doesn't last. That isn't real. You hit the age where we are now, and you start to panic, because you've built your house on sand." She does something with eye shadow, puts some coral-colored lipstick on me. "I don't date much either, now. And I have the experience of walking in a room and having not one head turn. I know it never meant anything, when that happened. But it meant something. And being without it makes me . . . scared."

"People still look at you," I say. "You still look great."

"No," she says. "Believe me. I think one of the reasons I wanted to get back with Chip is that he still saw me that old way. Selfish, huh? Stupid."

"I don't know," I say. "I don't know what brings people together, really. I'm retarded myself."

Diann laughs. "Met in the middle after all these years, huh?" She uses a huge brush to apply blush to my cheeks. "Okay. Done. Take a look."

I start to get up, then sit back down. "Is it funny? It is, isn't it?"

"Not at all."

I stand up, look in the mirror. Swallow. Nod. And pick up a washrag.

"Don't!" Diann says. "You look nice! You're just not used to it!"

"I look like . . . I don't look good. I'm sorry. But I look stupid." I turn on the tap water.

Diann reaches over, turns it off. "You *stop* that, Myra! You leave that makeup on and you come and sit with me for a while. Then come back and look again. It looks *great*."

"I don't want to," I say, but she takes me by the hand and leads me downstairs into the living room.

"I feel like a clown," I say.

"You look just fine."

"I feel ridiculous."

"Feel ridiculous, then. Now *sit*," she says, and points to the couch. Frank, standing beside me, sits.

Diann laughs. "Can I take your dog with me when I leave?"

"No," I say. And then, "What do you mean 'when you leave'? Are you leaving?"

She says nothing.

"Diann?"

"You know, I have loved him forever. I really have. But I've been here for over three weeks and I just don't think I can do this anymore. Anyway, he doesn't want me to."

"What makes you think that?"

"He told me. He feels more comfortable with you, Myra."

"Well, it's because I can—"

"It's because he likes you. Likes *you*. Funny, isn't it, that even at the end, there's still this fucking competition."

In the morning, I come downstairs and see Diann at the kitchen table, drinking coffee. She is dressed in the same outfit she arrived in, and her suitcase is beside her.

I pour myself a mug of coffee, sit at the table with her. "You're going?"

She nods. "Yeah."

"Well, I'm sorry you are. I've enjoyed having you here. I never thought I would."

She smiles. "I know."

"Was I that obvious?"

"Even in high school, you were never easy to be friends with, Myra."

I sit back in my chair, open-mouthed. "I was *dying* to have friends in high school!"

"Well, who would ever have known? You seemed so self-contained. So . . . superior."

"*Superior!*"

"You did! You didn't seem to need *anything*."

"Oh, my God."

She looks down into her coffee cup, pushes her hair behind her ears. "In some ways, you still seem that way."

"Well, it's not true. I need a *lot*." I realize, saying this, that it's the first time I've said it out loud to anyone. It feels horrible, scalding. And yet it feels good.

Frank comes into the room, puts his head in my lap. "I know," I tell him.

"I'll take him out," Diann says.

"It's all right. I'll do it."

"No, I'd like to. I'll take him for a walk and then I'll head out." She stands, hesitates. Then she says, "I want to tell you, Myra, that I've really enjoyed being here. Even though the circumstances . . ."

"Yes."

"And I hope you'll stay in touch. I hope you'll come and see me."

"Oh, uh-huh." Here it is, my automatic pulling back. It's as though I can feel myself flattening until the shadow passes. I can feel it and so can Diann, apparently, because she puts her hand over mine and stares directly into my eyes to say, "I *mean* it."

"Okay."

"Take good care of Chip. Call and let me know how he's doing. And tell him to call me, too."

"I will."

We stare at each other for a long moment, and then she says, "I couldn't have done it, even if he'd wanted me to. It takes something that I just don't have."

"It's all right."

"How do you have it, Myra? I mean, when people are dying, how can you stand it?"

How to explain this? How to tell her that to look into a dying person's eyes can show you a view beyond that does not frighten, but comforts. The heart settles in the Hand.

"It's . . . I'm not afraid of dying people," I tell her. "I think there's a richness to that time of life. In fact, sometimes I envy people who are dying a good death. Not that I want to die, just that I want to be that aware. And to have the opportunity to say things that will be *heard*, finally, in a way they never would have been otherwise. Do you understand what I mean?"

She nods, but I can tell from her face that I've lost her. You usually do, saying these things. At least when you're talking to people who haven't attended someone's death. Not long ago I visited a gay man called William, who'd been a very good friend to Angelo, an AIDS patient I was seeing. When Angelo died, William was with him. "I'm so sorry," I told William the next day, and he thanked me. Then he said, "It was glorious, at the end." He looked at me and on his face was a mix of enlightenment and confusion. "It's been like that every time," he said. "You know?" And I said yes, I did.

It's Thursday, the two-week anniversary of Chip and me living together. This is how I think of it, though I never would admit that to anyone. We've developed a comfortable routine. Once in a while he comes with me to visit patients, but more often I drop him and Frank off at our little downtown on my way to work. He reads the paper in the mornings at the Time Out coffee shop, though increasingly he is having trouble focusing. He has lunch at Ned's, and then sits out in the common for the afternoon, or goes to the reference room at the library and looks at random books, magazines, and newspapers. When I come home, we cook dinner together or go out to eat, and he tells me things he's learned. Such as: The mourning cloak butterfly survives the winter almost completely exposed, belly up against the bark of a tree. A ninety-nine-year-old woman named Giovanna still bakes pizzelle every morning—despite macular degeneration and severe arthritis, she hangs her cane over a kitchen chair, puts an apron on over her sweatsuit, and goes to work. In Upper Volta, crocodiles are venerated because it is believed that they are spirits of the departed, protecting their former village.

I sit there when he tells me these things, taking it all in, wondering at his ability to remember, wondering, actually if he *is* remembering it, or if he is making some of it up. It doesn't matter. The stories are wonderful pieces of information that say so much more than they say. As a child, I would lean over my microscope for long periods of time, then rest my chin on my hands, smiling. This is that, again.

Chip goes to bed early, around eight-thirty or nine; he's getting more tired than he used to. Before he falls asleep, I sit at the side of the bed and talk to him. Or I read to him—short stories or poetry. He falls asleep to the sound of my voice. It makes for a tenderness in me that I've never experienced: He becomes the son I never had mixed with the lover I always wanted. He has not mentioned Diann, other than to once wonder aloud whether he'll ever see her again. She calls me every day for a report, but, truthfully, we talk more about ourselves than him. She's terribly busy; being away so long took its toll on her firm. She thinks it will be Christmas before she's back to normal. She used to try talking to Chip every time she called, but it became frustrating for both of them. "I mean, what am I supposed to *say?*" Diann asked me. And Chip said, "I really don't know what she wants to hear."

This will be my last visit to Grace. I spaced out the time between the last two, to get her used to not having me. When I arrive, I find her wearing a pantsuit, one that's a little big for her, but flattering nonetheless, a powder blue color that brings out her eyes. She's going to interview for a part-time job as a receptionist, then look at a group home. She's also planning on getting her GED in night school. "This was my mom's," she tells me, when I compliment her on her outfit. "But she's too fat for it, now. It really pisses her off. She gave it to me, and that pissed her off, too."

I bend over the bassinet to look at Kurt. He smiles at me, and my heart breaks in the happy way. He smiles with his whole body, as babies do: hands clenched and waving, feet kicking. I give him a brief exam, but there's really no reason to. Mother and baby are absolutely fine. "Any problems?" I ask.

"No, he's good. They told me he could come with me to the interview. I guess he'll be okay doing that."

"I'm sure he will. How are you getting there?

"Bus."

"I'll tell you what, " I say. "I'll drive you there."

"Oh, you don't have to do that. The bus goes right there."

"I'd like to take you."

The company where Grace is interviewing is in an industrial park, a small, nondescript concrete building painted a light green. Some sort of tool-and-die firm. I pull up in front of the place and Grace checks her watch. "Right on time," she says. And then, turning to me, "Do I look all right?"

"You look beautiful. And very professional."

Before she goes in, we stand together at the curb. "I just want to say thank you for everything," Grace says. "I wanted to get you a card, but all the ones I looked at sucked. They didn't say what I wanted."

"I know what you mean. And I want you to know what a pleasure it's been to see you and your son. You've come a long way, Grace, and I'm so proud of you. As you must be of yourself."

"Well, I still have a lot of questions, and I guess some of them are pretty dumb. But I'm not the only one who has questions. And there's lots of places I can go for answers, lots of people who are ready to help me. My mom, she can't do it. I guess it's because she's had a pretty hard life and she just . . ." She shrugs. "Whatever. But I'm ready to do the stuff I have to. I think I'm the best one to take care of Kurt, and I think he'll be all right. Actually, I know he will be. I can feel it, I'm his mom." She hoists him up on her shoulder, gently kisses his head, then looks at me. "Okay, so . . . 'Bye, Myra." She starts up the walk.

"Grace?"

She turns back, squints in the sun. "Yeah?"

"You can still call me, any time you want."

"Okay. Thank you."

"Good luck."

She nods. Then she puts down the car seat, waves Kurt's little hand at me. "Say 'bye,'" she says. And then, shyly. "He says to say he loves you."

"Well, you tell him that I love him, too." We stand there, both of us smiling, and then she turns around again and disappears into the building.

"Treat her right, " I say, to nobody. To everyone.

Murray Schwartz came home from the hospital yesterday, and the doctor asked me to visit today to make sure the new regime for medication is being followed correctly. Murray is sleeping when I arrive, and Ethel brings me into the kitchen to show me how she's divided all the pills in the Medi-minder. She's made a couple of minor errors, and I help her correct them. "Do you understand everything now?" I ask, and she shrugs.

"Anything you want me to go over?"

"Yeah. You could go over how to put up with a man who's draining the lifeblood out of me." She puts the flame on under the teapot. "He's got demands that could put a woman half my age in her grave."

"Would you like me to see if I could get a home health aide in to help you?"

"Oh, no. No. I couldn't ask you to do that."

"I'd be happy to."

She turns around to look at me. Blinks. "I'm his wife. Who else should do for him? If I get sick like that, God forbid, it will be his turn to take care of me—not that he would do such a good job as I am, oh no, not by a long shot, let me tell you. This is marriage, Marilyn. Don't let anyone tell you otherwise. For about ten minutes, you get the romance. Then you get the rest. Ah, so what. You know?

What are you gonna do?" She gets two cups down from the cupboard. "Tea?"

"No thanks."

From the bedroom down the hall, we hear Murray calling.

"Oy," she says. "You see? A hundred times a day. Two hundred. *Coming!*" she yells.

"I'll go, Ethel, and I'll tell him you're coming."

"Ask him does he want his toasted bagel now, would you, darling?"

I enter Murray's darkened bedroom, see him slowly sitting up. "I need to take a shit, Ethel."

"It's Myra."

"Aw, Jesus. I'm sorry. Raise the blind, will you? She keeps it like a crypt in here. I never saw anyone so opposed to sunshine."

"Do you need some help getting to the bathroom?"

"She can do it."

"I can, too."

"I'll wait for her. Not that I don't appreciate it, Myra, thank you anyway, thank you very much."

"She wanted to know if you'd like your bagel now."

He waves his arm in a gesture of futile dismissal. "If I say yes, she'll complain because she has to make it. If I say no, she'll complain because I'm not eating. So what should I say? I'll say yes, and eat half."

I sit on the bed, take his hand, and smile at him. "So. Murray. You're happy to be home, huh?"

He smiles back at me. "What are you gonna do?"

Later in the afternoon, I stop in at the agency to pick up supplies. Sandy, our receptionist, has a spectacular bouquet of flowers on her desk. It's all white: roses, Casablanca lilies, lisianthus, freesia, orchids, phlox, sweet peas, delphinium. "Wow!" I say. "Who sent you *that?*"

"It's not for *me.*" She pushes the vase toward me.

I laugh. "Are you kidding?"

"Take a look at the envelope. It says, 'Miss Myra Lipinski, R.N.'"

At first I just stand there, taking in the extraordinary beauty of the flowers, allowing myself to luxuriate in speculation. Of course I imagine first that it's Chip. But it couldn't be. Could it? Then I think, No, it's Mrs. Peters. She's the only one who could afford this. But maybe, somehow, it's Grace, could it be Grace? Diann?

I open the card and read, *I surrender.* No signature.

"Who sent them?" Sandy asks.

"I don't know," I look at the envelope again. Yup, they're for me. I show the card to Sandy.

"Jeez." She leans back in her chair. "That's cool. Mystery man."

The phone rings, and she turns to answer it. "*Enjoy* them," she whispers, and then, in her work voice, "Good afternoon, Protemp."

I gather my supplies, wondering all the while about who would send me such a thing. And then it comes to me. I go over to a desk, pick up the phone, and call DeWitt. When he answers, I say, "Did you send me flowers?"

He chuckles, low and long.

"Is this supposed to be an apology?"

Silence. Then, "Well, I guess if *this* bouquet ain't enough, I could spend *two* hundred dollars, maybe that get the hair on your neck back down. People talk about 'Don't get the black woman mad.' But they ain't met you!"

"This is a very beautiful bouquet, DeWitt, but it is not an apology. I can't be bought off this way."

"Read the card, ain't there some card come with it?"

"I read the card. It says, *I surrender.*"

"Aw, woman, what you want? Want me to beg and gobble?"

"I want you to accept responsibility for your behavior, DeWitt."

"Whoa!"

"And I want you to apologize."

"Well, fuck."

"As for now, I have to go."

"Aw, wait a minute. Just *wait* a minute!"

I stand still, say nothing.

"You still there?"

"Yes, I am."

"So you want me to say this all my fault."

"I want you to apologize."

"Well, if I 'pologize, I am *definitely* not saying it's all my fault. 'Cause it ain't. If I 'pologize, it just some words I got to say to get you back here, take care this dressing like it should be took care of. You sent some nurse here don't know how to find her way out of a closet if you put the door knob in her hand. Plus she sneezed, right in my open gut."

"She *sneezed* in your wound, DeWitt?" I doubt it.

"I swear to God. On my mother's grave, I swear to God and cross my heart and hope to die."

"Well, I'm sure we can find you another nurse if you don't get along with Jill."

"Yeah, *Kill*, that's what I call her. But I don't want another nurse. I *told* you, I want you to come back!"

"Well. It appears that we've reached an impasse."

"What you mean?"

"A place where we can go no further."

"Oh. I thought you meant one of them things in canyons, like in the cowboy movies."

"I'm going to hang up now, DeWitt."

"All right, I'm sorry, okay? I'm *sorry*. I'm sorry I hurt your tender little feelings that shouldn't have been hurt and *wouldn't* have been hurt if you's a *normal* person."

I sigh.

"Okay?"

"Fine."

"So . . . what time you coming?"

"It's too late for me to come today. But I'll be back at the usual time tomorrow."

"All right. You bringing Chip?"

"No, I am not." I wave back at Sandy, who's waving at me to tell me there's a phone call. "I'll see you tomorrow, DeWitt."

"Hold on, one more thing. Did they send all white flowers?"

"Yes, they did."

"Yeah, that be my idea. Fit in with the surrender theme."

"Right."

"You *got* that, right?"

"Yes, I did."

"Yeah, that's 'cause you smart, not like your friend, Kill."

"I'll see you tomorrow, DeWitt."

I pick up the other line and take an order from Mrs. Peters's doctor for a change in eyedrops, starting tomorrow. Then I call Chip, to tell him I'll be home soon and to ask if he needs anything, something I always do. No answer. I look at my watch. He should be back by now. I try the number again. No answer.

I walk quickly out the door, hear Sandy calling after me, "Hey, Myra! Your *flowers!*"

* * *

At home, I call Chip's name, then Frank's. Nothing. I go into all the rooms of the house. Empty. He might be with his parents. Oftentimes they come and get him for a while. I sit at my desk, start to reach for the phone, and it rings.

"Myra Lipinski?"

I feel a sense of dread wash over me. "Yes?"

"This is Dr. Libson, at Memorial Hospital. We're calling at the request of Chip Reardon."

"He's there?"

"Yes, he's fine, he's in the emergency room—"

"What happened?"

"Well, he took a little tumble, and we had to put a couple of sutures in his chin. They're just finishing with the dressing now."

Tears come into my eyes, and I wipe them away angrily. When is enough *enough?*

"We think it might have been a seizure, although he swears it was the dog that pulled him off balance—is it your dog he has with him?"

"Yes. Frank. Where's *he?*"

"Actually, he's in the room with Mr. Reardon. He wouldn't let us treat him without the dog being there. Of course, as I'm sure you know—"

"I'm on my way."

I arrive at our tiny community hospital in under fifteen minutes, park in a doctor's reserved spot, the hell with it. Chip is in the waiting room. "Are you okay?" I ask.

"Yeah. Somebody just took Frank out. They'll be right back, and then we can get the hell out of here."

"We can wait by the door." I offer my arm to Chip.

"I'm fine." He stands, starts walking out. He won't look at me.

Outside, I see an orderly coming toward us, with Frank. He hands the leash to me. "Great dog."

"Thank you."

"What's his name?"

"Frank."

"Great dog."

"Thanks."

Chip says nothing all the way home, until I pull into the driveway. Then he says, "Let's eat out tonight. Agostino's, okay?"

"All right. I'll just put Frank inside."

In the house, I dump some food in Frank's dish, turn on the Discovery channel for him, say "Be good!" and slam the door behind me. Then I climb back in the car.

"Why don't we walk?" Chip says. "It's only a few blocks."

"It's further than that." I start the engine. Chip is silent the whole way there. I can wait for a while. But then I'm going to ask him. There's no way Frank made him fall.

We both order eggplant parmesan. After it arrives, I say, "So. What happened?"

"Frank just jerked the leash all of a sudden and I fell."

I say nothing, take a bite of pasta. Then another.

"All right, I don't know what happened. But it wasn't a seizure, I do know that. I just fell, that's all." He stops eating, leans back in the booth. "Oh, all right, Myra."

I stop chewing, look over at him.

"When I had to sign my name at the hospital, I could barely do it. Things are just going to keep . . ." He shakes his head. "You know, right after I was diagnosed, I read a lot about brain tumors like mine. And one of the things I read was about this guy—big fellow—whose family took him on a car trip to some relative's house for Thanksgiving. When they arrived, they couldn't get him out of the backseat. The guy just all of sudden couldn't figure out how to *do* it. You know how long he sat there like that?"

"How long?"

"*Five hours.*" He stares at me, his face full of sadness, and then, suddenly, he starts laughing. "Jesus! Five *hours!*"

I can't help it; I start laughing, too.

"Do you think they brought his dinner out to him?" Chip asks.

"I hope so. And a urinal, too."

"Aw, he could have just used his empty wine glass."

I laugh harder. "It isn't funny."

Chip, who has not stopped laughing either, says, "I know."

Later that night, he is lying in his bed before sleep and I am sitting beside him. "You know what I learned today?" he says. "Before my field trip to the ER?"

"What?"

"Buttercups grow on the Arctic tundra."

"Huh."

"And: butterflies taste with their feet."

"Do they?"

He yawns. "Yup."

"Maybe people can, too."

Chip frowns. "I know *I've* never tried."

"Me neither."

"Maybe we should put some peanut butter between our toes, right now. No time like the present. Well, in my case, there's no time *but* the present."

I smile, say nothing. But then I say, "You know, Chip, I have a lot of vacation time due me. I thought maybe I'd take a few days. Would you like to go somewhere with me? We could . . . I have a free weekend at the Four Seasons in Boston. Mrs. Peters gave it to me. Would you like to go there?"

"Sure, they're nice hotels."

"You've stayed there?"

"Oh, yeah. Not in Boston, though." He closes his eyes, breathes out slowly. Then, "Oh. I meant to tell you. The drain doesn't wiggle."

"Pardon?"

"The drain doesn't turn. On the . . . thing. The puller."

"The drain? In the bathtub? What do you mean?"

He opens his eyes. "Never mind. I'm just tired."

"Okay. You go to sleep. I'll see you in the morning." I stand, and he takes my hand. "Stay," he says. "Just a little bit longer." He closes his eyes, then opens them to say, "That's a song. Right?"

I nod. And then I watch him fall asleep. In my chest is the steady tick of my love for him. In the space of a few weeks, I have so quickly gotten used to this, our life together, pretend man and wife. That's what it is, at least for me. I don't want to be without it. It would be like going back into a cave. I think, *you* stay. *Or let me come with you.* The thought comes unbidden, but naturally. It seems so natural.

These tomatoes are wonderful," I tell Marvelous. We are finally having lunch together, and we are both on our second bacon, lettuce, and tomato sandwich.

"Yeah, my sister knows how to grow them like nobody else. The goddess of tomatoes, that's what she is. She talks to them every day, and she plays music for them all night long."

"Really!"

Marvelous nods, wipes mayonnaise from the side of her mouth. "It's the truth. She puts a transistor radio right out in the middle of the garden every night, plays music for them. Classical. One year a neighbor complained, she called the cops, can you imagine? Never mind people shooting each other's faces off, call the cops on the woman playing music to her tomatoes. My sister said she'd stop doing it, but she didn't. She just turned it way down and the plants still heard—in fact, that was her best year so far. So now she always plays it that way, real soft."

I take the last bite of sandwich. "Delicious. Thank you."

"How 'bout another one?"

"Oh, no, Marvelous. I'm stuffed. But I'll sit here with you if you want another one."

"I'm full, too." She leans back, pats her belly, smiles her wonderful smile.

"You look great, Marvelous. You must be feeling well."

"I am, I'm feeling *good*, honey. But not you."

Reflexively, my hand goes to my chest. "Me?"

"Ain't nobody in this kitchen but you and me. And I ain't talking to myself. Least, not at the moment."

"I'm fine."

"Nope, something after you. Don't have to be psychic to see that. Although I do have a little psychic blood in me, did I ever tell you that? My great-great-grandmother was a fortune-teller in New Orleans. Everything she wore, every day, was *red*. Anyway, I can tell there's something weighing on your mind, Myra."

"It's just . . . I've been taking care of someone—"

"That patient you in love with."

"Yes. Chip. And I think he wants . . ."

She says nothing, waits. Her white kitchen curtain lifts, falls. Outside a woodpecker knocks against a tree. I have always loved that sound, the wild industriousness of it. Finally, I look at Marvelous. "Let me ask you something. Do you think it's wrong for someone to commit suicide? When, after very careful thought, they really believe it's the right decision?"

"This be *Chip* you talking about, right?"

"Well . . . *yes*. I mean, what do you mean?"

"What you think I mean?"

"I don't know."

"Oh, I think you do."

"I'm not thinking of suicide *myself*. I'm not thinking that."

Marvelous sits quietly, looking at me. Finally she says, "What you think I been seeing, all the times you come here? You think I never paid attention to who you really are? You think I don't know anything 'bout how you feel? I see you sitting in my kitchen, and I see *behind* you, too, girl. But to answer your question, well, who knows the answer to a question like that? Answer is in every person's heart, and all our hearts is different."

"Yes."

" 'Course, all our hearts is the same, too, isn't it the mixed-up truth? But I got to tell you . . ." She comes over next to me, pulls me against her. She is so warm, and her clothes smell so good. Ironed. "I *don't* think it's right for you. Don't you think about doing that, now."

"Okay." I don't know what else to say.

"When my Gerald died, I wanted to go right along with him. I used to lie in bed at night and pray for death, I begged Jesus to take me home. But I'm so glad now I didn't die. It took a long time, but I'm so *glad* I didn't. You hold on, baby. You'll see."

"Well. It's nice to see you, but I'm very sorry to hear you haven't used my gift," Mrs. Peters says, after she lets me in.

"Oh, but I'm going to," I tell her. "I'm starting a vacation today, right after work, and I'm going there. With a friend."

She claps her hands together. "Good! And you have a *wonderful* time and I hope you'll take advantage of *everything* that's offered you. Please do that, it would mean so much to me."

"I will."

"I really mean it, Myra."

"I really do, too." We stand smiling at each other, finishing our conversation in this most primitive and advanced of ways, and then I head for the eyedrops.

At home, Chip tells me he has packed for both of us and brought Frank over to Theresa's.

"Good," I say. "So we're ready."

"I just need to get the suitcase—it's on the bed."

"I'm going up anyway," I say. "I'll get it."

Inside the suitcase, I see a pair of pants for Chip, pajamas for both of us. My bathrobe. And that is all. I gather his pills, add our toothbrushes and his razor, changes of clothes. Next, I quietly call Theresa to make sure Frank really is all set. I sit on the edge of the bed for a while, thinking. And then I go downstairs.

* * *

At Chip's request, we drive around Boston for a while, up and down the streets of Back Bay, then through the different sections of downtown. We go to the North End for dinner, to a restaurant where there are only five tables, and eat *zuppe di mare*. Afterward, we eat cannoli at Mike's bakery. We sit at the window so that we can watch the summer traffic along Hanover Street, the slow-moving cars, the smiling couples and noisy families who walk along the sidewalk. People point to the salamis and cheeses, the fine leather shoes, the hand-painted plates. Just as it is growing dark, we head over to the Four Seasons.

"Ah, Ms. Lipinski," the clerk says, when I check in. "So nice to see you, welcome to the Four Seasons. We have something here for you." He turns and reaches behind him for a small but exquisite bouquet. "From Mrs. Peters, who hopes you will very much enjoy your stay here." Attached to the flowers is an envelope holding tickets to the symphony Sunday night. I look up at the clerk, embarrassed, but he has busied himself punching computer keys. "And I see that we have a lovely upgrade available for you, one of our junior executive suites?"

"Oh, I can't take that," I say. "I—"

"We'll take it," Chip says.

"Certainly, Mr. Lipiniski."

I look at Chip and he smiles, then puts his arm around me. "Okay?" he asks, and I say yes.

The elevator that we take up to the top floor is beautiful, the hallway too; and when we open the door to the room, I take a few steps in and then stand still. Past the bathroom, with its fine wallpaper and richly-veined marble, is a living room with a huge window overlooking the public garden. Heavy silk curtains with colors of robin's egg blue and gold, with thin red stripes. Tie-backs with tassels that must weigh ten pounds apiece. A table and two Chippendale-style chairs are arranged before the window, and a floral brocade sofa is against the wall, gold-framed prints above it. Off to the side there's an antique cabinet with a Chinese vase–style lamp turned on to a low glow, a bottle of wine, and two glasses on top of it.

I open the French doors and go into the bedroom, where there is another large window from which you can see the gold dome of the state house. There is a bench before the window, an armoir with a televison inside. And a king-sized bed.

"Oh," I say.

Chip comes in to stand behind me. "What?"

I point to the bed.

"What about it?"

"I forgot to ask for two beds. I'll call down." I pick up the phone, and Chip takes it from my hand, puts it back in the cradle. "We'll work it out," he says. And then he takes me by the shoulders, turns me around, and kisses me full on the mouth. I don't move until he steps back from me. Then, when he says, "Okay?" I put my arms around him and kiss him back.

We lie down on the bed and I begin to shiver. "Are you cold?" he asks, and I tell him no, no, I'm not cold. I close my eyes, and then do nothing but let myself feel his hands move slowly up and down my body. His hands, my body. Behind my lids I see not the man with the scars and the failing memory, but the boy with the world at his feet: running off the football field, his helmet in his hand; dressed in his suit and tie at the homecoming dance; laughing at his table in the cafeteria; jiggling his pencil at his desk, his long legs stretched out into the aisle. I see Chip Reardon coming down the hall of our high school, grinning, his books at his side, his letter jacket sleeves pushed up. He is that boy again, that one. And I am that same odd-shaped girl, leaning against my locker, waiting for him to see me. His blond hair glints in the light that comes from the windows, his blue eyes scan the crowds. And then he finds me, and he stops looking. I am the one, and he takes my hand, and we walk on together. They all look up and say nothing; I am the one, now.

And then I stop seeing the boy and I see the man with the scar. And the woman with the scar. And I stop shivering. I open my eyes and help him undress, and then he helps me.

I put my fingers to his lips, to the curled cartilege of his ears. I touch the place where they cut his head, move deliberately along that line, as if to finally heal it. I trace the high arch of his cheek-bone, the underside of his jaw, his shoulders and chest, his stomach. I reach down and feel his erect self and then take my hand away so that he can move over onto me. And then I open up and let him in.

Once, at the library, I watched two children, a boy and a girl, building a popsicle stick fortress. They did it very slowly, carefully. When it was finished, the boy stood back and said, "No," and began disassembling it. "What are you doing?" the girl asked, and the boy said, "I got another idea." He took apart the fortress using the same deliberate care with which he built it. And then he made a road, each narrow stick laid perfectly beside the next. It twisted and turned, but the path was clear, and something about it made you want to go on it.

I am in the bathtub when I hear Chip call, "Myra, did you read the letter on the desk?"

"No. What does it say?"

A moment, and then I hear him start to open the bathroom door. "Don't come in!" I say.

"Why not?"

I look down at myself, consider my nakedness. Which he just spent a good forty-five minutes considering.

"Never mind," I say.

He comes in and leans against the edge of the sink. "Want me to read it to you?"

"Yes."

He opens the envelope, pulls out a piece of hotel stationery. "Well. We are to have dinner at Aujourd'Hui tomorrow night."

"Oh, no. This is too much, Chip. Really. I have to tell her no, at some point."

"It's not from Mrs. Peters."

"Who's it from, then?"

"Me."

I sit still for a moment, then laugh.

"I mean, I can still *charge* things."

"Well, thank you."

"You're welcome." He sits on the edge of the tub.

"Want to come in?"

"No. I think I'll maybe just lie down for a while now, okay?"

I start to get out of the tub, but he tells me, "Stay. I'll be right outside. Just going to take a pain pill, though, so if I'm asleep when you come out, don't be offended."

"I won't."

He closes the door, and I lean back in the tub and close my eyes. And I had been thinking we'd just keep going, check out of the hotel in a couple of days and take a trip somewhere else.

When I finish bathing and come into the bedroom, he's still awake. "Look what *we* get," I say, and model one of the soft white terry-cloth robes that was hanging in the bathroom.

"It looks great."

"Well."

"It looks *great*."

I look at him. "Thank you."

"That's better."

I go over to the bed, lie down beside him. "Does your head still hurt?"

"Not bad." He looks over at me, kisses my forehead. "Myra? I've been lying here just . . . thinking. I lived my whole life unable to make a vital connection. Not because I couldn't; because I wouldn't. And you know what? It's the same for you."

"Well, I haven't exactly—"

"Don't start that. Don't tell me you haven't had the opportunity."

"But I *haven't*."

"I don't think you've tried. I don't think you ever have. And I want you to, Myra."

"I *am*. I am now."

"I know you are now, and I am, too, and that's wonderful. But this isn't going to last. I'm not going to last. But you are. And I want you

to do something about the way you live, I want you to be with someone. Because you want to be. And you should be."

"It's not as easy as you make it sound, Chip." I sit up, push the pillows behind me. "When you look like me—"

"Bullshit."

"It's *not!*"

He sighs, turns onto his side. "Lie down. Lie down here and look
at me."

I stay sitting up, stare straight ahead.

"Please."

"I can talk from here."

"Myra. I want to look at you. And I don't want to sit up."

I lie down next to him, and he puts his hand to the side of my
face, stares at me. "What, you're not a size four ex-model? You have
real hips?"

I turn away.

"Myra. Look at me."

Reluctantly, I turn back toward him.

"It's not your looks that keep people away. It's you. You need to let
people in. If you'd let them in, they'd see—"

"I know what you're going to say, Chip. But it isn't true. It's not
just the way I look. It's that . . . I just can't get it right with people. I
don't know how to be . . . I don't know how to *be*. Ever since I was
little, I've felt apart from everyone. Maybe that happened because I
was so unattractive. Maybe not. But you have to admit that when you
look like me, you do get sent to the back of the line. You wouldn't
know anything about that, Chip. Whether you choose to admit it or
not, you've used your looks your whole life." I rise up on one elbow,
look at him. "I don't think you understand that I'm all right. I'm *fine*.
I'm not unhappy; I know that, in many respects, I'm really lucky. I
also know I'll never . . . I mean, I can do my work, and I get great joy
from it, but outside of that, I just . . ."

"Do you have any idea how much the people you work with love
you?"

"I'm their *nurse.*"

"And?"

"They don't love me. I mean, I know they appreciate me, but they wouldn't want to . . . *be* with me outside of our visits."

"What about that woman you went to the movies with?"

"Margaret? Oh, that was . . . She was desperate, Chip."

"We're all desperate."

"Look. I know what you're saying. I know. But I'm just not the kind who will ever be able to have a relationship like . . ."

"Like this?"

I look at him. Smile. "Well. But you know why we're doing this."

"Why, Myra? Why are we doing this?"

"Because—"

"Because of who you are. That's why this happened."

"This happened because of terrible, extraordinary circumstances. If you hadn't been sick, we'd never—"

"Don't you know that *most* people who are together never planned it that way?" He turns onto his back and sighs, exasperated. "I don't know how to tell you, Myra. How to show you. But I swear, I'm *going* to."

Saturday morning, he gets up before I do. At nine o'clock, I find him seated at the desk, staring out the window. I walk up behind him, put my hands on his shoulders.

He says nothing.

"Chip? Are you okay?"

"I think . . . You know, I slept badly. I'm not in the best shape this morning. Why don't you go out and get us some bagels, how's that? And I'll just . . . Let me rest a little; and after we eat, we can go somewhere."

"Why don't we get room service?"

"Oh, those bagels are no good. I'd really like a bagel from that place on Newbury Street, do you know where it is?"

"Yes. Okay, I'll get ready and go right away. It won't take me long, twenty minutes, half an hour tops."

"Take your time," he says. "I want you to enjoy being in the city."

When I come out of the shower, he's back in bed, his eyes closed, asleep or pretending to be. I close the door quietly. Out in the hall, two maids chat in Spanish beside their cart, each with one hand on her hip. It doesn't appear that many other guests are up yet; papers lie at all of the doors. I punch the button for the elevator, then stand there, thinking. Something's wrong. I'm the one who slept badly. I awakened many times, at least five or six, and every time I did, he was sleeping soundly. Maybe he just wants some time alone. It occurs to me to think that it's because he regrets what happened between the two of us. But I know he doesn't. I know it.

The bagel shop is crowded; I stand at the end of a long line, and almost immediately three more people join it. I can feel the man behind me watching me. And then he clears his throat and says, "Nice morning."

"Yes," I say, turning slightly, smiling.

"You live here?" he asks.

"Ashton," I say, turning around fully. He's a pleasant-looking sort: nice brown hair, brown eyes behind wire-rimmed glasses. About my age, well dressed in khaki pants and a white linen shirt, sleeves rolled up. In good shape. A nice smile, too—good teeth. "I'm just staying in the city for the weekend," I tell him.

He steps up beside me. "I live here. Right on this street, I come here every morning. Need a bagel recommendation?"

"Well . . ."

"The 'everything' bagel's good," he says. "Everything really is in there."

"Uh-huh."

"Well, they're all good, really." He scans the room, spots a table where two people are leaving. "Hey," he says. "Want to hold my place in line, and I'll get us a table?"

"Oh, I . . . I'll hold your place. But I'm not staying. I'm bringing breakfast back to the hotel."

"Aw, don't do that. Come and sit with me."

"No, I mean . . . I'm with someone. At the hotel. He stayed there."

"Oh!" The man blushes. Endearingly, really. "I'm sorry, I just assumed—"

"It's all right," I say. "I will hold your place, though, if you want to grab that table."

"No, I just thought if you wanted . . . You seem like you'd be nice to talk to."

"Well, thank you."

"You're welcome."

Rather awkwardly, he takes his place behind me again. I think, *Let's see. How many times has* this *happened?* As if I didn't know the answer. I remember once turning on the television and seeing a panel of women talking about frustrations they had with men. One woman was saying, "They're never interested when you're available. But as soon as there's competition, they're all over you."

Is that so, I'd thought, idly licking my finger and running it along the bottom of the bag of Cape Cod potato chips I'd just finished. And then I thought, *I wouldn't know.* Well, now I do.

As I am putting my key into the door, I hear the low sounds of Chip talking to someone. When I walk into the room, I see that he is on the phone. He sees me, says hastily, "Okay, thanks," and hangs up.

He sits on the sofa, smiles. "I've got the whole day planned."

I set the bag of bagels down. I want to ask him who he was talking to, but instead say, "Feeling better?"

"What do you mean?"

"You were so tired."

"Oh. Yeah, I am better. Power nap."

"I see. So. What would you like to do?"

He holds up a list. "First, Harvard Square, some bookstores. Then the science museum, we can sit in the dark and look at the stars. I just got off the phone with them—they have a show starting at three. After that, I don't know, I guess I'll need a damn nap. And then dinner. How's that sound?"

I look down. Nod. Nod again.

I am just getting ready to wake Chip from his nap to get ready for dinner when I hear him quietly swearing. I put down the book of poems we bought and go into the bedroom. He is sitting at the side of the bed, wet sheets gathered around him. He looks up at me.

"It's all right," I say. "I'll just call down and get some clean ones."

"Jesus."

"It's all *right.*"

He won't look at me. I go over to him, kneel at the side of the bed, take his hands between my own. "I know you feel embarrassed, but you don't have to, Chip. It's not your fault. It's no big deal."

He picks up a glass of water from the bedside table, takes a drink. His hands are shaking.

"Chip?"

He puts the glass back, then pulls me to him. "Myra. I'm scared."

"I know you are."

"You're here, right? I mean, really here."

"Yes. I'm here."

He holds me tighter, then lets go. Looks into my face and smiles a smile like nothing I've ever seen, that of someone lost inside himself. And then he says, "Is it time to go to the restaurant?"

"Yes, it's time to get ready. You get in the shower. I'll take care of this."

He stands, steps out of his clothes. I reach out my hand.

When we arrive at the restaurant, we are seated at a luxuriously large table by the window. "Sorry for the rather inconvenient size, it's the only table available," the maître d' says.

"It's fine," I say. I order a martini, Chip a club soda. I spread my napkin on my lap, lean back in my chair, and look out at the beautiful room. Then, coming through the door, I see Mrs. Peters. "Oh, my God," I whisper. "Look who's here!" Chip nods, smiling. Mrs. Peters spots us, waves, and heads directly for us.

"Wait a minute," I say. "What is this? Did you—?"

"Mrs. Peters!" Chip rises to kiss her cheek. His napkin falls, and I pick it up for him, put it on his chair.

"Thank you for inviting me," she tells him. "This is a real honor."

He invited her to dinner?

"Hello, Myra." Mrs. Peters leans down to kiss me. She smells wonderful. She's wearing a midnight blue dress, conservatively cut from some beautiful, crepelike fabric. Diamond-and-sapphire earrings, a matching bracelet. Her hair is styled into an elegant upsweep.

The waiter glides over. "The usual, Mrs. Peters?"

"Yes, Basil, thank you."

After he disappears, she says, "Such a nice man. He's forty, can you believe it? He doesn't look a day over thirty. He's a twin, he and his brother live in the South End. He's an aspiring actor, quite good, really, I've seen him in a few plays around town."

There's a great commotion at the door, and then I see DeWitt coming in, wearing a dark suit, a blindingly white shirt, and an electric blue tie.

Open-mouthed, I stare at Chip, who simply smiles back at me. Who knows what DeWitt was arguing about, but everything seems to have been worked out. He comes to the table, smiles widely at Chip, salutes me, and then, upon being introduced to Mrs. Peters, leans over and pumps her hand enthusiastically. "Very charmed to make your acquaintance, how you doing?"

He sits next to Chip, and when Basil comes over, DeWitt orders a Glenlivet. I am about to ask him what was going on at the door, but then I see Murray and Ethel coming in, followed by Fitz Walters and a beautiful black woman who must be his new wife. Marvelous is there, too, dressed in a white suit and a hat with a feather. They are all beaming, and as they make their way to the table, every person in the restaurant is looking at them. What an assemblage they make: Murray in his lime green summer suit and floral tie, Ethel in a pink chiffon dress, the bodice covered in sequins, a matching scarf draped around her neck, and strappy silver sandals. Fitz is wearing a black turtleneck and trousers, and his wife a simple black sleeveless linen dress. And then I see Grace coming through the door, wearing her blue pantsuit and a white carnation corsage, holding the arm of Rose Banovitz, who is dressed in an ancient trench coat and what I hope is not but certainly appears to be a black slip. And I do not want to do this, I so much do not want to do this, but I burst into tears. After everyone is seated and the introductions are made, I wipe my face with my napkin and start laughing. "I'm sorry," I say. And then, looking around the table, "It's just . . . thank you for coming." Under the table, Chip takes my hand. I don't know the place to put this kind of happiness.

"So what kind of grub they got here?" DeWitt asks, opening the menu.

"Well, I think the tasting menu is always a good idea," Mrs. Peters says. "The variety is marvelous."

"Oh, yes, I always like a tasting menu, too," Ethel says.

Murray frowns. "When did—"

Ethel turns quickly to him, smiles a tight pink smile. "It wasn't with you, darling. It was with my mah-jongg group."

"I ain't tasting *nothing;* I intend to *eat*." DeWitt says.

"Yeah, me too," Murray says. "I'm going to live it up and have steak."

"Or fish," Ethel says. "You could have fish."

"The *ahi* is very nice," Mrs. Peters says, and Ethel says, "Oh, I have *always* loved *ahi!*"

Murray turns to Fitz. "Who's she kidding, the fanciest fish she eats comes frozen in a Gorton's box," he says quietly. And then, "Want I should read the menu to you?"

"Oh, *I'll* read the menu," Rose says. "*I* will!" And, standing, she proceeds to do so. With perfect elocution, if not pronunciation.

Chip and I are lying in bed, having just put DeWitt in a cab to go home. He stayed after the others were taken home by the limo that Chip and Mrs. Peters arranged for, and the three of us went to the Oak Bar in the Copley Plaza for a nightcap. DeWitt and I had martinis, and Chip had a cigar.

"I don't know how to thank you for what you did," I tell Chip.

"I just hope it showed you something."

"I . . . It did."

"All right."

"Did you see Rose eating with her hands?"

"Oh, well. Egyptians always ate with their hands."

"Really?"

"Really." He yawns.

"You must be exhausted, Chip."

"I took a nap this afternoon."

"Still."

"Yeah, I am tired. But I don't want to sleep when there's so little time left."

"There might be more time than you think. You don't know."

"I do know, though."

I turn to him. "What do you mean?"

He sighs. "It's time, Myra. This . . . pissing the bed, and all the other . . . Look, I've thought about this. I knew a few weeks after I was diagnosed that I'd be the one to decide when. I don't want to hang around to see what else will happen. I don't want to be sitting in a car, stuck for five hours."

"But you . . ."

"I'm all set. I have what I need. I just want . . . I would like to not be alone. Will you stay with me when I do it? Can you do that?"

I say nothing. Inside, it feels as though a screw is being tightened, then tightened more.

"I know it's a lot to ask. I have a friend in New York who'll do it if you can't. I made him promise, early on, that if things got bad, he'd help. He said he'd suffocate me, if he had to."

"Oh, Chip."

"No. He's a good friend to agree to it."

"But how are you . . . ?"

"I got some pills."

"From where?"

He says nothing.

"Oh, my God. From DeWitt."

"Well, from a friend of his. A doctor, actually, who buys his marijuana from DeWitt."

"Chip, you can't do that. DeWitt can't be trusted. What if—"

"He *can* be trusted. I know exactly how it'll work. First, you take something to keep you from throwing up. Then, in about twenty minutes, you take the rest."

"The rest of what? What did he give you?"

"He thought it would be better if I didn't know. I think he's right."

I lie quietly for a while. Then, "I'm going with you," I say.

"Don't be ridiculous."

"I *want* to."

He sits up, turns on the light. "Okay. We're going to get this straightened out right now. Get dressed, we're going outside."

"Chip—"

"Myra, you think you love me, right?"

I swallow. "I do love you."

He gets out of bed, reaches for the pants and shirt he left draped on the bench. "Then come with me. I need you to do this. Please come with me, I want to go outside."

I push back the covers, head for the closet.

"Good evening," the doorman says, as we go out the front door of the hotel. "Good morning" would be more appropriate. We go across the street, hand in hand, and sit on a park bench opposite a fountain. Overhead, a dark shape flies by.

"What was *that?*" I ask.

"I don't know," Chip says. "A bat? Are there bats out here?"

"I don't think it was a bat. It was too big."

"Maybe it was a falcon."

"It definitely wasn't that."

"Well, let's say it was. We didn't really see it, and I like falcons."

I look at him, at his fine profile in this dim light. "Why?" I say.

"What?"

"Why do you like falcons?"

"Don't know, really. I have since I was a little kid. I used to call myself 'Falcon,' in fact. My best friend Timmy O'Conner—remember him?—he was 'Eagle.'"

I smile. "How old were you then?"

He leans back against the bench. "Oh, let's see. About thirty-seven, thirty-eight."

I laugh, and he says, "Ten. Ten years old. Falcon Reardon, that was me."

"It does have a nice ring."

"Do you know what falcons do when they court each other?"

"No, what?"

"First, they fly around in the sky together, to determine a certain kind of compatibility. Then they lock talons, and plunge toward the earth."

"Wow," I say. "I assume at some point they reverse the direction."

"Yeah. Just before they crash."

"Where did you read that?"

"I heard it on the radio."

We sit quietly for a while, and then he says, "You know, Myra, I feel like the only good thing that can come out of situation like this is that you have a chance to finally fix some things. Before I left New York, I went to this support group. Diann thought it would be a good idea. It was a group for cancer patients and those who love them, that kind of deal. They met every Wednesday night in some church basement, folding chairs in a circle, you know the deal. It wasn't for me. The group leaders and their glowy-eyed acolytes, offering you trays of terrible cookies. The depressed people, sitting bent over in their chairs, moaning and groaning about loss, loss, loss. The *fear* you saw! And then there were the ones who pretended they weren't afraid, the ones wearing the healing colors and sporting their baldness like it was the latest fad. The ones who *knew* they'd lived before and would again, or the ones who knew they'd 'join with Christ in heaven.' And there was this grim competition for who could live longest. Or maybe it was who could die soonest, I don't know. I didn't want to be in their club, I didn't want to be in any club.

"But I did like one of the things they said. They said that this kind of diagnosis gave you notice. You could resolve some things that might otherwise never get resolved. I thought about that for a long time. It was why I decided to come home. I feel like I've made peace with my mother, and I don't think I ever would have, otherwise. More than that, I feel like I've made peace with something in myself, that there's been a kind of change in me I never thought I'd experience. I didn't plan on that happening, but it did."

"What do you mean?"

"Well, just what I was talking about before. I mean, I spent my whole life walking away from any kind of real commitment. I never learned how to be with just one person. I told myself I didn't want to be, but that was bullshit. I was just afraid." He looks at me. "I know now, though, what can come from loving just one person. From loving, period."

I say nothing. Look away.

"You know what I'm saying, don't you? Myra?"

I swallow, try to speak, cannot.

He takes my hand, kisses it. "I'm glad to know what it's like. I'm glad I get to have it after all."

And now I start crying. "But you don't get to have it! You don't get enough time to have it, it takes *time!*"

"I do have time. It's here. It's happening, and I know it. What else do we get? I'll die, yes, but I'll die knowing I finally did learn how to love one person. You know why? Because you've shown me *what* to love in a person. That'll be the most important thing, what you've given me. I mean, I look at you and I just . . . Oh, Myra, don't you know that you have so much to offer someone? Can't you believe me? Goddamn it, will you just believe me?"

It takes a long time; the water is wide, but finally, in a voice that does not sound like my own, I say, "I believe you."

"Ah. Thank you." He kisses my forehead. "You know what I think? I think we met up with each other again so that we could help each other. If I were going to live, Myra, I would ask you to marry me."

I laugh.

"I *would!*"

"Well, it's easy to say that now."

"It's not that easy, actually. But it's true." He gets up off the bench and kneels before me. "What the hell. Myra Lipinski, I love you. And your little dog, too. Will you marry me?"

I say nothing. My throat aches. "Don't. This isn't funny."

He stops smiling, reaches out, and puts his hand to the side of my face. "Myra," he whispers. "Say yes."

The night air is so soft around us. The trees look like lace. You can hear the water from the fountain, the small irregularities in the flow. I think, Don't ever let me forget one thing about this moment. And then I say yes.

He stands. "All right. And now, as is the custom, I'm going to present you with a big rock."

He starts off down the path.

"Chip."

"Stay there," he says. And then, bending over, "Here's a good one."

He comes back and hands me a rock—a small, round, smooth one. I lay it over my left ring finger. "Beautiful."

He sits on the bench next to me again, puts his arm around me. Pointing up to the sky, he says, "Look at that. Look how bright."

I locate the star he's pointing to. "I wonder how far away it is."

"Well, Arcturus, which is a bright star, is 36 light-years away, if I remember correctly. That's 216 trillion miles. But we can actually see stars that are 10,000 light-years away." He looks over at me, smiles.

I think about a little girl I once had as a patient during my pediatric rotation. She was six years old, in for chemotherapy for some kind of kidney cancer. I was sitting on her bed, coloring with her, and she suddenly laid down her crayon, leaned back, and sighed. "What's up?" I asked. And she said, "I don't know. I was just thinking about how big the sky is."

"Does that scare you?" I asked, and she said, "No. It makes me feel better." I think I understand now why Chip wanted to come outside.

In the distance, we see a man walking toward us. He catches sight of us, pauses, then heads toward us.

"Let's go," I tell Chip.

"Why? It's so nice out."

I look at the man, who is coming closer. Dark hooded sweatshirt. Hands in pockets.

I stand up. "Come on. Hurry."

Chip takes my arm, pulls me back down. "He's just a guy out for a walk. Don't worry."

Except that the guy out for a walk now has a gun pointed toward us. It's fascinating, in a way; I realize I've never seen one quite so close up.

"'Evening, folks," he says. "Guess what this is?"

"I don't have anything," I say. "I don't have my purse." I'm shaking; I can feel my heart beating in my throat.

"You got a watch?"

I take it off and hand it to him. When he leans forward to take it, I see his face a little better. A white man, about fifty or so. Heavy black eyebrows, very thin lips.

"That all the jewelry you got?"

"Yes."

"What's in your hand?"

I open it. "A rock."

He laughs. "That ain't gonna help you much." He gestures with his gun toward Chip. "You got your wallet?"

"I do," Chip's voice is remarkably calm. Friendly, really. I want to look at him, but I'm afraid to turn my head. "But I'll tell you something. I don't feel like giving it to you."

The man snorts, steps closer.

"Chip," I say quietly.

"The reason is, I've had just about enough. If you look at my head, here, you'll see a scar. Surgery for a brain tumor. Didn't work. You're robbing a dying man, pal. You don't want to do that, your karma will be incredibly bad."

The man puts the gun to Chip's temple. "Give me your wallet, you stupid fuck."

Chip reaches in his pocket, hands the man his wallet. Then his watch.

"I'm going to back away," the man says, "and you two are going to sit there. If you move while I can still see you, I'll shoot you both. Don't think I don't mean it. It wouldn't mean shit to me, I've killed lots of people."

We sit still. Cars pass on the road behind us, the wind blows, then stops. Just as the man is nearly out of sight, he starts coming toward us again. "Oh God," I say, and take Chip's hand. The irony, that this is the way we'll die. The absurd thought comes to me that I wish I'd finished my dessert.

When the man is before us again, he asks Chip, "You really got a brain tumor in there?"

"Yes."

He stands there, considering. Then, "What kind?"

"It's called glioblastoma . . . I forget the other part."

"*Multiforme*," I say. "Glioblastoma multiforme." *Let us live, we're being so cooperative.*

"Huh. Sounds like some Italian food or something." He pronounces it "eyetalian," and I have a terrible urge to start laughing.

"I tell you what." The man hands Chip's wallet back to him.

Chip puts it back in his pocket. "Thanks."

The man shrugs. "What the fuck. My mom died of cancer. Of the boobs, that kind." He takes a watch from his pocket, holds it out toward Chip. "Might as well take that back, too." He turns to me. "Yours I gotta keep. Sorry."

"That's all right."

"Uh . . . this isn't my watch," Chip says.

"What's yours?"

"Mine's an Omega."

"What do you got there?"

Chip squints at the face of the watch. "I believe it's a knock-off Rolex."

"Well, which one you like better?"

"Mine."

The man reaches in his pocket, pulls out a watch. "This it?"

"Yes."

"Gimme the other one back."

They make a trade, and then the man straightens. "I expect you to let me walk away. I expect you to sit there for a while after you can't see me anymore, and then walk out of here, you're idiots for being here in the first place."

The man walks backward into the darkness. Finally, we can no longer see him. "Can we leave now?" I ask Chip.

"I guess so."

We start out of the park slowly, then quickly cross the street.

Back in the hotel, I say, "Should we call the police from the desk?"

"Let it go," Chip says.

I turn to him, start to say something, then stop. Together, we wait for the elevator. When it arrives, the *ding* of it sounds so innocent. Preposterous.

On Sunday night, we're back at home, lying in my bed and holding hands. The breeze through the window is enough to make us need a light blanket. "August is almost over," I say.

"It went fast," Chip says. "Well, of course it did."

"Yes."

"I'm thinking about doing it on Friday, Myra. Arrive in heaven for the weekend, they probably have great weekend activities up there."

I say nothing, close my eyes. I feel him turn toward me. But I keep my eyes closed.

"Maybe Janis and Jimi perform on the weekend. And Elvis. Maybe *Liberace*."

I open my eyes, look at him. I don't want to play.

"What's the matter?"

I sit up, turn on the bedside light.

"What?" he says, finally. "Tell me."

"I don't know. Just, maybe you *should* look into some other options. Maybe there's some experimental treatment that really is worth trying."

"Oh, Myra. Please."

"But maybe there *is*."

"There isn't."

For a long time, neither of us says anything. Then I say, "All right. I'm sorry. I said I'll respect your choice, and I will."

"It's better, Myra, believe me. Now, I need to talk to you about some specifics. Are you okay with that?"

"Yes."

"If you've changed your mind about staying with me through this, I understand. In fact, if you change your mind at any time between now and then, I understand."

"I won't change my mind."

"All right. So I want to do it on Friday. That's the day. I thought . . . morning. I thought that might be better for you. I know you have to go to work tomorrow, I'll be fine staying here. I need to see my parents and I want to make some phone calls. But then maybe you could take a few days off."

I nod. Then I turn off the light and stretch out beside him. It's Sunday night. Tomorrow is Monday. Next comes Tuesday. I can't do anything about it, and I never could. I read once about an idea in physics that says time branches out into more than one dimension, so that what doesn't happen in one world may very well take place in another. It's an old habit, using thoughts to comfort me. It's something I don't want to go back to.

The summer I was ten years old, there was a group of kids in my neighborhood who played together every night after dinner. I often watched them from my window; a few times I even joined them in a game of hide-and-seek. Once I hid behind lilac bushes with a boy who stared uncomfortably ahead for a while, then turned to me and whispered, in a not unkind way, "Who *are* you?" But mostly I would watch. I would see them sitting on the grass in a circle, riding bikes around, playing statue and freeze tag, talking and laughing about things I couldn't really hear. There was a time they set off a cherry bomb, and once they had a picnic by moonlight: Kentucky Fried Chicken and lemonade.

Every night around nine-thirty or ten, those kids would get called in, one by one. Mothers would lean around screen doors and call out names, or a brother or sister might come and round someone up. I knew the first ones called were full of resentment. But they needn't have been. Nothing ever happened after they left anyway. Things just sort of ended in a slow motion way, like petals falling off a flower. You couldn't have people leave like that and have anything good happen afterward. Whoever was left couldn't pay much attention to anything other than waiting for their turn to get called in. So it wasn't so bad to go first, to head back toward those deep yellow lights and beds made up with summer linens. It was much better than being last, when you would be left standing there alone, finally going in without anybody calling you.

On Monday, I visit Rose, Ann Peters, and Fitz Walters. Then I go to a convenience store for a tuna sandwich. I eat half of it, then use the pay phone there to call my agency and tell them that as of tomorrow, I'll be taking an indefinite amount of time off. I tell them that they can take DeWitt off my patient list; this will be the last visit he'll need. Then I call DeWitt.

He answers on the first ring, and seems surprised to hear me. But he doesn't start screaming about how I'm calling at the wrong time. Rather, he is extremely cordial. "Yeah, you can come on by now," he says. "I was just about to make lunch, you can have some with me."

"No thanks," I say. "I just ate."

"You ain't ate *this*," he says. "What I got here'll put hair on your chest. Well, maybe you rather have it on your head. But I made me some DeWitt's Chili. It's three alarm, baby. It's five *star*, too. After you do my dressing, we'll have some."

"Twenty mintues," I say, and throw the other half of my sandwich in the trash. I've got a feeling DeWitt's a good cook. And even if he's not, I'm going to tell him he is. I need a favor.

This here bring that cook at the Four Seasons to his knees, right?" DeWitt loads up another bowlful of chili for me.

"It is good," I say. "Where'd you get the recipe?"

"I made it up. First thing you got to do if you want to cook right is throw out the recipes, just listen to your own self. Them cookbooks is all wrote by pussies." He fills another bowl for himself. "You want more cornbread, too?"

"No, thanks."

"Suds?"

"No, I'm fine, thank you."

DeWitt puts the bowls on the kitchen table and pulls up a chair. "How's Chip? How come he ain't here?"

"He . . . had some things to do."

DeWitt looks sharply at me, and I say, "Not that. Not yet."

"When?"

"I . . . don't know."

"I like to see him one more time, will you tell him?"

"Yes."

"I like to tell him good-bye in the proper way."

"I'll tell him. DeWitt . . . speaking of that, I want to ask you something."

185

"I can't tell you what I gave him."

"I wasn't going to ask you that." I put down my spoon, push my chair back from the table. "I wanted to know . . . can you get some more of those drugs? The same combination? Soon?"

His brow furrows. "What for?"

"Well . . ." I was going to say something about Chip wanting to be sure he had enough, but now I find I can't lie. "For me."

"For you? For *what?*"

"I think it's pretty obvious for what, DeWitt."

He stares at me. There's a smear of chili at the side of his mouth and I have a strong urge to wipe it away. But I don't.

"Listen, DeWitt. This is very complicated. I—"

"You can just stop right there, ain't no sense in your beating your gums 'bout this to me. What you think, I'm crazy? You think I'm gon' give you drugs so you can off yourself? Chip know you axin' me this?"

"No."

"That's right. What's the matter with you? I thought you's a smart woman! But this some dumb shit you be laying on me, now. Maybe you cracking up, maybe you need one of them rest cures, go lie around on a lawn chair under a blanket somewhere." He stands up, takes our dishes over to the sink. "Talk 'bout killing your own self," he mutters. Then he spins around, arms crossed, and glares at me. "You think this some kind of soap opera? You think you take them pills and then wake up? Cry some pretty tears and go take a shower?"

"I'm not going to talk to you about why I want to do this. If you don't help me, I'll get the drugs somewhere else."

"The hell you say."

"I will."

"First of all, good luck, it ain't easy. Second, I got connections, remember? I get the word out on the street, and nobody give you shit. Nobody."

"DeWitt. Please. Please don't make me explain this to you. I know what I'm doing. Just give me what you gave him. Please."

He sits down at the table with me. "I can't give you those drugs,

Myra. Don't even have them in the first place. And even if I did, I wouldn't give them to you."

We sit in silence. I hear the call of one bird, the answer of another. Then I say, "Let me ask you something, DeWitt. Have you ever been in love? Have you ever been so much in love with someone that you didn't want to be in the world without them?"

"Sheeeit." He looks out the window.

"Have you?"

"I know what it's like to lose someone you love."

"Yes, but . . . to death?"

"Yeah. As a matter of fact, yeah. I was married once. She died in childbirth. Nineteen years old. Couldn't get the fucking ambulance here fast enough, don't *nobody* want to come here. Bled to death. She be lying on the sofa with her coat on, just waiting. She got her kerchief on her head. I'm kneeling right by her, telling her everything gon' be all right. Baby died, too. They took her out of here with a sheet over her face and I seen that kerchief coming out the top."

"Oh, DeWitt. I'm so sorry. I didn't know."

"Nobody knows. That was a long time ago. And don't be *telling* nobody, neither."

"I won't. But DeWitt, if you loved her like I—"

He stands suddenly, and his chair falls to the floor behind him. He's breathing fast and you can see his pulse throbbing at his temples. "Don't you say another word make it sound like what I felt for that girl any less than what you feel for Chip! Or what anybody feel for anybody!"

"I'm not saying that, DeWitt. I'm not." I start crying, and use one of the paper napkins he laid out for our lunch to wipe my face. "I just . . . God, I just feel like I've lived a long time, you know? And I've been so alone. I found something with Chip that I don't think I can be without anymore, and I know I'm not going to find it again."

DeWitt picks up his chair, sits down again. "You don't know that."

"I will never find it again. And I don't know how to tell you so that you understand, I don't think I could explain it to anyone. But I will not stay here without him. I will not. This is a decision that's only about me. I thought that you of all people would understand the right to make choices, even if they're outside the law. But if you won't give me the drugs, I'll use my father's gun, which is in my basement. I'll just use that."

"How? You tell me that. You tell me exactly how."

"All right. I'll load the gun the night before, and I'll hide it in the linen closet, behind the towels. Right after Chip dies, I'll go and get it. I'll lie down beside him, really close to him. I'll take his hand. With my other hand, I'll put the barrel of the gun to my temple. Then I'll pull the trigger."

He says nothing.

"It doesn't scare me, DeWitt. Telling you this, I don't feel anything except a kind of certainty. One way or another, I'm going to do this."

He looks at me for a long moment, and then he says, "You can pick the drugs up tomorrow. Two o'clock."

I nod. "Thank you."

"Don't you thank me for that. And I don't want you in my house no more, neither." He walks out of the kitchen, goes down the hall to his bedroom, and slams the door. I let myself out quietly.

This is how you do it, when you're standing at the edge of a high place. You just lean a bit more in the right direction. A movement so small. Scarcely measurable. Just a little closer to what once seemed so far away. And then it takes over and moves at its own speed, and you can stop thinking. I've always thought that any fall like that must be so quiet. And that the silence is the sound of relief.

When I come home, I find Chip in the bedroom, sleeping. He is on his side, Frank lying next to him. Frank raises his head and wags his tail, and I whisper, "Stay." Then I close the door quietly and go downstairs to look in the refrigerator for something for dinner. Cheese. Eggs. Salsa. Omelets?

The phone rings, and I pick it up quickly. It's Diann. I can tell by the way she says my name that she's been crying.

"He told you?" I say.

"Yes. And I feel so bad that I didn't stay, that I didn't help more."

"It's okay. We're managing."

"I *know*. He told me about the two of you. And I think it's . . . Well, I think it's good."

"Yes."

"I'll come and be with you if you want."

"No, that's all right," I say, too quickly.

"But it's going to be so hard for you."

"I know. But I think I'll need some time alone right afterward. Maybe after a few days I'll come and visit you."

"I'd love for you to do that. I really would. So . . . tell me. How is he, really?"

I shrug, lean against the kitchen wall. "I don't know, I guess I'd say that he's peacefully resigned. He's really calm. He seems sure of what he's doing."

"Is he hurting?"

"Well, he takes the pain pills and they help. But not as much as they did. His balance is worse, he gets a little confused now and then. He's sleeping a lot more. I think he's actually timed it pretty well, Diann."

"Oh, it's so awful. I keep thinking there's got to be something I can do, but there isn't. We did have a really wonderful conversation, though." She laughs. "Best we ever had."

"Right." I fiddle with the phone cord. I don't have anything else to say. I think from now on I'll let the machine handle calls.

Diann must sense this, because she says, "I'll let you go, Myra. I just want to tell you that if you change your mind and need me to come, call any time. I'll get the next flight out."

"Okay. Thank you."

"And tell Chip . . . I don't know. I don't know what. I told him every-thing. But tell him, just say that I'm thinking of him all the time." She starts crying. "And that I hope it goes peacefully. And that I'm so sorry he had to suffer. And that I love him, tell him I will always love him."

Now I start crying too. "I'll tell him."

A long silence. And then Diann says, "Call me right after it's over, okay? Please call and let me know. Will you?"

That will be hard to do, I think. But I tell her I will.

After dinner—Spanish omelets, a salad—we decide to take Frank for a walk to the video rental store, three blocks away. The man who works there keeps staring at Chip, knowing something's wrong but unable to figure out what it is. Chip's gait is shuffling, uneven. His eyes are affected by his medication; he looks slightly demented. His pants hang low on his hips from the weight he's lost. I've gotten used to these things, I don't really notice anymore, so to see them anew through the eyes of a stranger is unsettling. I want to get out of here.

Chip stands unmoving before the wall of videos. His sense of time has become hampered; after his nap this afternoon, he went into the bathroom to brush his teeth. Fifteen minutes later, I came in to check on him, and he was still brushing away. I wasn't sure what to do, at first. But finally, I put my hand over his and said, "I think it's enough, now."

He nodded and put the toothbrush down. And that was all.

"What do you think?" I say. "Should we go over and look in the comedy section?"

"Or maybe we could get that movie about the woman who takes the bus."

"Who's in it?"

"I don't know, that woman. She's really famous. She takes the bus because she wants to go home."

"*The Trip to Bountiful?*" the clerk says.

I have an impulse to tell him to mind his own business, to stop eavesdropping, and to stop staring, too, but Chip says, "That's it!"

When we start home, I let Frank off his leash and tell him to heel. We've gone a little over a block when Chip stops walking. He stands still, swallowing repeatedly. Then, "Uh oh," he says. He goes to the edge of the sidewalk, sits on the curb, puts his head between his knees and quietly vomits. A middle-aged couple walk by and give us wide berth. "*Disgusting,*" the woman says, just loud enough for us to hear.

"Excuse me," I say, and when the woman turns around, I say, "*Fuck* you!"

"Hey!" her companion says.

"Fuck you, too," I say.

"Myra," Chip says. "Let's just go home." He stands, puts the leash back on Frank. "Come on."

I stand there, staring at the couple, who have turned around and walked away. And then I take Chip's arm. "You okay?"

"Yeah."

"People are so stupid."

"Oh, they probably think I'm drunk. It *is* disgusting."

"No, it isn't."

He laughs. "Okay. We'll call it art."

* * *

Fifteen minutes into the movie, he falls asleep. I watch a few minutes more, then gently awaken him.

"I missed it, didn't I?" he says. "I fell asleep again."

"It's all right."

"Did you watch it, though? I wanted you to watch it."

"Yes. It was wonderful. It was a great idea to rent it."

He sits up. "Is it late?"

"Not so late."

"I'm so tired all the time. I'm sorry."

I move over to sit beside him. "You don't have to be sorry about anything. I'm happy to go upstairs and go to bed with you. I'm happiest there."

He puts his arm around me. "Well, then."

Tuesday afternoon, right after we've finished lunch, I tell him I need to go and drop some papers off at my agency, and then get groceries. "Anything special you want?" I ask.

"Ice cream."

"What kind?"

"I don't care. The cold kind." He looks at me in a kind of puzzled way. "I don't feel good."

"What is it?"

"I don't know. It's . . . you know, like rubber bands."

"I don't know what you mean, Chip."

"Like when they're loose."

I don't know what he means, but I nod my head as if I do. "I'll stay here," I say. "I won't leave."

"No, you don't need to. This isn't new. It's just . . . more. I'll feel better after a nap."

I sit beside him until he falls asleep. I don't want to leave, but I want those pills. If I don't run into any traffic, I can be back in less than an hour. I call Frank to come with me, and we go outside and get into the car.

DeWitt has taped a note with my initials on it to his front door. "Outside the place where we do the dressing," the note says. Nothing else.

I look in the bushes outside his bedroom window and find an large manila envelope, again with my initials on it. Inside are smaller envelopes, marked 1, 2, and 3. I recognize the antiemetic in the first envelope, but not the other pills—a large number of small yellow capsules, a few larger red ones. It doesn't matter what they are. I fold over the envelope, put it in my purse. I ring DeWitt's doorbell, and hear a shuffling movement inside. I wait, but the door does not open. I ring the doorbell again, then finally walk away.

Chip is sitting in the living room when I return. "I couldn't sleep," he says. "So I took a little walk to the library. And I have something startling to report to you."

"Oh?" I hang my purse in my closet, make sure the zipper is closed. Frank goes to his water dish and starts taking one of his marathon drinks. I'm so glad dogs can't talk. *Hey, Chip. We went to see DeWitt, so Myra could get some pills, too!*

"Are you ready to hear this?" Chip asks.

"Yes."

"Okay: Napoleon had hemorrhoids."

I laugh, go and sit on the sofa beside him. "Really!"

"It's true. They bothered him so much he couldn't mount his horse to survey the battle of Waterloo. Call me crazy, but I'd rather be remembered for having a brain tumor."

"I suppose it is more dignified."

"You want to know something else?"

"Sure."

"Hummingbirds can fly backwards, and their wings beat over one hundred times a second."

I smile. "You know, you are the most beautiful man I have ever known. And it's true that I am as foolish as anyone else, and so the way you look is one of the reasons I love you. But the bigger reason is your . . . discrimination. The things you choose to appreciate. Hummingbirds. Mating rituals and stars. Rose Banovitz."

"And *you*," he says. "But you know, you'll do much better than me. You'll find someone who's not so hollow."

"You're not hollow!"

"I am. Macaroni man, all my substance on the outside. I'm better, now, it's true—dying teaches you a lot about how to live; I'm sure you know that as well as anyone. But I lived a pretty shallow life. I kept myself from myself as much as from others. I know you care for me. But what you're in love with, Myra, is the idea of someone loving you. You'll find someone so much better. The truth is, I'm not good enough for you."

I feel as though some hand that holds up my insides has been abruptly pulled away. "That's not true!"

"It is." He leans back, rearranges himself slightly. Something's hurting. "What'd you get at the grocery store?"

"I . . . haven't gone yet. It took longer than I thought at the agency. I had to orient someone to all of my patients."

He nods. And then, carefully, he says, "Myra, is there anything you want to tell me?"

"About what?"

"About anything."

"No."

"Good."

Frank, finally finished with his drink of water, comes over to lay his drenched muzzle in my lap. "Oh, look at this!" I say, jumping up, incredibly grateful for the distraction.

Early Thursday morning, I'm sitting in the living room, drinking a cup of coffee. Chip is sleeping. When he gets up, we're going somewhere. Last night he told me he didn't want to sit around the house anymore, waiting. He wants to take Frank and a basket of food and head out. I'm thinking the ocean, maybe the small town of Rockport. It's only a little over an hour away. There are parks there where he could stretch out and take a nap, nice places to walk that are flat, benches everywhere.

I stare out the front-room window at the cars moving along the road, trying to make out the features of each driver. It's a game I play sometimes. If I can see them clearly enough, I make up a life for them. Here, this red-headed young woman with her hair up in a ponytail, I make her a receptionist at a health club. A gum snapper with a big heart, who dots her *i*'s with an oblique dash. This bald-headed older man, driving along with a scowl on his face: He sells insurance, he's doing poorly, and his gout is acting up. Now comes a woman who looks remarkably like me. Remarkably! I stand, strain to see her more clearly. She's dressed in a white blazer, driving a red Sentra. Amazing resemblance. And what is her life? What *is* her life, I wonder.

The phone rings. I answer it quickly.

"Myra," Chip's mother says. "I hope I didn't wake you."

"No, I've been up for a long time. How are you?"

"Well, I'm . . . You know, this is not like me at all, but I actually called because of a dream I had last night. I dreamed that Chip had died. And I know of course that you'd call me if anything happened. But it was such a strong dream. He died and then he came over to see me and his father. He was just the same, only he was dead. He wanted to go to his room, he said he'd forgotten something."

"He's fine, Mrs. Reardon. He's sleeping."

"Is he?"

"I can wake him up if you'd like to talk to him."

"No, that's not necessary. But would you mind . . . Oh Myra, I know this is silly, but would you please just make sure he's sleeping?"

"Of course. Hold on."

I go upstairs with a chill centered at the base of my spine and starting a slow climb up. What if she's right? I open the bedroom door. He lifts his head, blinks sleepily at me. "Hi."

"Hi. Your mother's on the phone. Want to talk?"

He picks up the extension, says, "Ma?" and I close the door. Then I go downstairs to hang up the phone. I sit beside it, fussing with my bathrobe tie, telling myself that she's better off not knowing.

Late in the afternoon, we are sitting under a tree on the beach, watching Frank play with a black Lab. Their energy seems boundless: for thirty minutes, they've been chasing each other in and out of the waves. Occasionally, one or the other will drop down for a few seconds' rest; then they're back at it.

The beach is crowded today: mothers watching their children; an older couple sitting in beach chairs, reading the newspaper and sharing coffee from a thermos; lots of young people, coupled or with groups of friends. High overhead, gulls circle lazily, watching for food. I lie back, close my eyes, and listen to the sound of the waves. Chip lies down beside me and takes my hand. "I want you to tell me something," he says.

"What."

"I want you to tell me what you'll do on Saturday morning."

I open my eyes, turn to look at him. "Nothing. I won't do anything."

"I want you to. I want you to think of some way you can be with someone."

"All right. I will."

"No, I want you to think of it now. Tell me who it will be."

I feel my eyes start to fill. "I don't want to do this. Let's just be here, okay?"

"Please, Myra. It's important to me."

I look away from him, over toward the group of four teenaged girls who have positioned themselves around the lifeguard's chair. Everything they do is designed for him. So far, he has looked at them once. I take in a breath, turn back toward Chip. "I'll call Diann. I'll go and visit her."

"Diann."

"Yes."

"You'll go on Saturday."

"Yes. I guess so. Yes."

"You haven't thought about it at all, have you, Myra? About what you'll do, either the day after or the weeks after."

"I do have a job, Chip."

"That's not what I mean."

I sit up, dig in the sand with my fingers. "It's getting late," I say. "Do you feel like eating dinner?"

He doesn't answer.

"Do you? I'm really hungry."

"All right." He stands, slowly; and we call Frank, who, after a moment of clear ambivalence, runs toward us. It comes to me in a kind of rush that I've made no provisions for him. I'll leave him with Theresa. He'll wait for me for a while, and then he'll get used to her. I reach down to pet his wet head, then let him run on ahead.

* * *

When we come home, it's eight-thirty. Chip heads upstairs for a soak in the tub. I sit in the kitchen, staring out the window at the sun sinking lower and lower in the sky and thinking about the fact that I don't have a will. I suppose it doesn't matter—there's no one to leave anything to. But I should write a note.

I go into my office, get out a piece of paper, and write, *I am doing this of my own volition.* And then I stop writing, sit back in my chair. This is real. It's real! Someone will have to sort through my things. Is there anything I should throw away? Underwear? Journals I started, then abandoned?

I go into the basement, survey the metal storage shelves I have against one wall. I bought those shelves at Sears, then lugged them home and put them together. I felt so proud when I'd finished—it wasn't nearly as easy to assemble them as the instructions on the box had suggested it would be. I'd wanted to show someone what I'd done, and I remember I spent some time sitting there with a wrench in my hand thinking, *Who?* In the end, I'd cracked open a beer and drank it while I sat there regarding my handiwork.

On the middle shelf I see the basket I use every year to hand out candy to trick-or-treaters, those small heads, those open hands. Inside the basket now is Frank's clown costume, carefully folded. There are the leftover paper napkins from last Thanksgiving; I'd only used two out of the pack of twelve, and they were pretty; I'd liked them a lot. Cornucopias.

There are the Christmas ornaments wrapped one by one in tissue paper and stored in light bulb boxes. Scrapbooks belonging to my mother. What a sad end they will have. I take one down, open it to a picture of me in the sixth grade. I had kept my lips together when I smiled, thinking it would make me less conspicuous. I remember that day so well, the girls behind me excitedly combing their hair, me staring at the floor as the line inched forward. The flatness of the photographer's face when I sat on the little stool, the way he kept telling me look up, look *up*. I'd clenched my fists so hard when I had that picture taken I'd left nail marks in my palm. I flip to the beginning of the scrapbook, find letters from my father to my mother from when he was in the army. Love letters. I close the book, put it back on the shelf.

I wander past the washer and dryer, my sewing machine. I'd been going to make a flannel quilt before this all started, start it this summer so that it would be ready by winter. I look for the fabric I'd been going to use, and lay out the different pieces next to each other. It's a nice combination of colors; it would have been a very pretty quilt.

I go back upstairs into the kitchen and open the cupboards to look at my dishes. There's the creamer with the green stripe that I bought one day at a yard sale, and the mustard yellow plates I got at Filene's because they reminded me of Italy. I'd always meant to go to Italy. And the Loire Valley. And Japan, too; I wanted to see those low mountains. I close my eyes, lean my head against the refrigerator, and feel Frank's head come under my hand. "Okay," I say, smiling. "I see you." I kneel down, pull him to me, bury my face in his neck. He stands so still.

I go to look at the furniture in my living room, my artwork: the print of a barefoot woman clad in a thin white dress sitting outside in the moonlight and playing her flute. An abstract oil I'd splurged on. The books I've bought, so many of which are still unread. I sit on the sofa, thinking. And then I remember that I never paid DeWitt. I never gave him any money for those drugs. I go into my office to call him.

"How come you ain't dead?" he asks.

"I just realized I didn't pay you for what you gave me. I'd like to send you a check."

"You want to pay me."

"Yes."

"Why, you putting your affairs in order?"

"As a matter of fact, yes. So how much, DeWitt?"

"How much? I tell you what, I'll charge you the same thing I charged Chip: nothing. Be my tax-deductible charitable contribution. And now let's cut the bullshit. You didn't call me 'bout no payment. You called 'cause you want me to tell you it's fine what you doing. Say oh, good-bye Myra, boo hoo, don't worry, you doing the right thing. But what you doing is wrong, and you know it the same as me. You just a coward, using Chip as an excuse to back out of what you never got in."

Upstairs, I hear the bathroom door opening. I lower my voice to say, "I have to go. But I just want to say one thing, DeWitt. You don't know anything about my life."

"I know *plenty* 'bout your life! Any fool that meets you can see plenty 'bout your life. Onliest one can't see, be your own sorry self!"

"Well, I'll tell you something. I think you're the one who's a coward, staying in a life so full of despair that you have to numb yourself to it every day!"

"Man, you get stupider and stupider every time I talk to you. We *all* on drugs, baby. Just choose different kinds, is all. Some folks sit in churches with they butts clamped tight. Some spend their whole lives buying shit. But don't you doubt it for a minute, girl, we is all of us in the bidness of numbing ourselves. Now I got a real good idea. Why don't I hang up and save us both more grief?"

"DeWitt," I say. But he is gone.

I hear Chip coming down the stairs and I hang up the phone, go into the living room, flop down on the sofa. "Who were you talking to?" he asks.

"Oh, one of those salesmen. I hate when they call."

"Selling what?"

"Aluminum siding."

"Really."

"Uh-huh."

"I didn't hear the phone ring."

"Oh, really? You must have been running water. He was so hard to get rid of!"

"Last time I got one of those calls I told the guy I had a house made of glass. And I asked if he had any clear siding. Know what he said?"

"What?"

"He said he'd have to check. And he did! He came back and said no, there was no clear siding, but how was I set for windows? In a glass house! I swear it's true."

He sits down beside me, smiles. "God. Good to think of things I *won't* miss, I guess."

"Right. There's plenty of that."

He sighs. "So. The last night. I wish I could stay up until morning. But damn it, I'm tired."

"We can go to bed," I say.

"Let's just stay down here for a while."

I take his hand, lean back against the cushions. "You know, Chip, I feel bad that your parents don't know."

"They do."

I sit up. "How?"

"I told them."

"And they . . ."

"They said for you to call them when it's over." He looks at me. "Amazing, isn't it?"

"Didn't they want to be here?"

"I asked them not to. We . . . talked. I think my mother said good-bye to me the day she gave up pushing treatment. And my dad . . . We understand each other."

So Chip's parents will probably be the ones who will have to figure out what to do with me. I'll add something to the note so that the Reardons are not responsible, the state can decide what to do with me, I don't care who decides. I'll wait until Chip falls asleep tonight, and then I'll figure out exactly what to write. It won't be much. It comes to me that this is the ultimate measure of what your life has been, what you have to say to those you will leave behind. And I don't have anything to say to anyone.

"God, I'm tired," Chip says. "I guess I'm going to have to go to bed."

I go upstairs with him, and we climb into bed. He kisses my forehead, my nose, my eyes, and then, so lightly, my lips. "Thank you," he says.

I nod, my throat aching.

"Ah, Myra. It would only have gotten so bad."

"I know."

"After I go, I want you to get the hell out of here."

"I will." At last, I am not lying to him.

Morning comes. Of course it does. He awakens first—when I open my eyes, I see him sitting up in bed beside me.

I'm amazed I slept. Angry that I did. After Chip fell asleep, I went downstairs to finish my note, then sat in my office for a long time. I came back to bed meaning to lie awake and keep him company. But obviously I didn't.

"I love you," Chip says. "I wanted that to be the first thing you heard today."

I smile, sit up next to him.

"I've been awake a long time. And I'm ready, Myra."

Now?

"I think I'm supposed to eat something. Just a little. Maybe some toast?"

"Okay." *My God, now?* "So . . . should we go downstairs?"

"I would rather just stay here, okay?"

"All right. I'll be right back."

I go downstairs and let Frank out into the yard, then fill his dishes with food and water and bring them out, too. I pet him, but I can't look at him. "You're a good dog," I say.

I go back inside and put water on to boil, then go get my pills out of my purse. Back in the kitchen, I put bread in the toaster, then take out a small baggie into which I dump all the pills. There are five red ones, maybe twenty-five of the yellow. I squint at one of the yellow pills, looking for the name of a drug company. There's nothing on them.

"Myra?" Chip calls down, and I jump, shove the pills in my robe pocket.

"Yes?"

"Don't butter the toast, okay?"

"Okay." I put two mugs on a tray, add tea bags, pour in the hot water. I put the two slices of toast on a plate. My heart feels huge; it knocks in my chest. I start upstairs, then detour to my office, where I read once more the note I wrote last night:

> I am doing this of my own volition. I wish to be cremated, and my remains can be disposed of at the discretion of the state. My dog should be given to my neighbor, Theresa Bartone, of 36 Russell Road. Proceeds from the sale of my house and car should be given to Marvelous Brooks, of 4945 Cedar Street, Number 2, Dorchester.

I look around at my study, think about the rest of my things upstairs. My clothes, some sheets and towels. Cough drops in my nightstand, cold cream in my bathroom drawer. Not so much for a whole life lived. I sit in my desk chair, neaten the pens and pencils in my holder.

One night, I took Frank for a walk around the block, and I was looking in all the living room windows I passed. In one, I saw a child running around a living room in her nightgown, apparently dancing for her parents, and I thought, *I remember that.* I passed a couple reading companionably in their living room and felt the usual longing. Then I passed an old woman sitting out on her porch, and her loneliness was so apparent. She stared out at nothing, her hands folded in her lap. I said hello, but she said nothing back. I thought, *I'll end up like that.*

Turns out I won't. I anchor the note with a clear glass paperweight and go upstairs. *This is the last time I'll climb these steps,* I want to tell myself, but the information remains stubbornly at the door of my brain. No admittance.

Chip is coming out of the bathroom when I reach the top of the stairs. "Got it?" he asks, and I say, "Yes, I've brought breakfast for both of us." I put the tray at the foot of the bed. Then, "Be right back," I tell him.

I go into the bathroom and wash my face, brush my teeth. And then I just stand there, looking into the mirror. I reach my hand out to touch my reflection, then wipe my prints from the glass. I ball up a piece of Kleenex to lay over the bag of pills in my pocket. Then I go into the bedroom to lie next to Chip.

"I took the first one about twenty minutes ago," he says.

When I hear him say these words, I feel like screaming. Instead, I say, "Oh. Okay."

"Now I'm supposed to eat something."

I pour tea for both of us, my hands steady. I think of the elegant composition of water, wire-and-wooden-bead models of atoms, the chemistry class I took one winter and loved. I remember the high, arched windows of that classroom, the smell of heat, the hissing radiators. Once, it began snowing when I was in that class, and it was one of those impossibly gorgeous snowfalls, the flakes so huge they looked fake, they looked like torn-up pieces of paper. And the professor looked out the window and told us all to stop writing and start watching. He was an old guy, with his priorities in the right place. He didn't mind giving up a lecture on chemistry for a ballet of snow.

"Not a great last meal," Chip says, smiling.

I jerk back into the present and look at the remaining piece of bread on the plate, browned evenly. "It *is* good, though," I say, taking one bite, then another. Tea. Toast. It's a perfect meal.

I lean back against my pillow and and feel a sorrowful resignation, a letting go before the letting go. I think of dandelions gone to seed, that fragile whiteness held upright and waiting for the breeze that will both end and begin it. I always loved dandelions in that state. As a child, I frustrated myself by trying to make bouqets from them. Over and over I would try to bring them together, and over and over they would fall apart.

"I'm supposed to take that big bunch of yellow capsules next," Chip says. "And then after just a few minutes, I take the red ones."

"All right." Now I know what to do.

"You'll help me if I . . . if anything happens, right?"

"Yes."

He takes my hand, closes his eyes. And then he starts to cry. "God," he says. "God!"

I move closer, put my arms around him, move his head down onto my chest.

"Tell me something, Myra. Anything. Just talk to me."

"Okay. Okay. You just close your eyes, and you hold on to me. I'm going to tell you something. I'm not afraid. I'm not afraid for you. Where you're going, it's beautiful. I know that. I don't know how, but I know. This won't hurt you, you'll be fine; you'll just float. And then I think . . . you'll fly."

He nods, then holds still, waiting. I clear my throat, keep talking. "Once I met a man out walking in the woods. And we walked together for a long time. He was really happy. He told me he'd been a janitor. He said he'd always worn a lot of keys on his belt and it always made him feel so important, like he could open anything. Said that was the one thing he missed about his job. But you're going to have all the keys now, all the time, Chip."

He sighs. I can feel him relaxing into me.

"Yesterday I saw a cardinal feeding another cardinal. It was the male feeding the female. She could have fed herself; they were both at a feeder. But he gave to her, and she took it."

Outside, I can hear the distant shouting of children, the sound of the cars passing by.

"What else?" Chip asks.

What else? "Well . . . Once I was at an airport, and I saw a man who was in the cab line do a handstand. It was extraordinary—he just all of a sudden stepped back from the line and did a handstand! He stayed in that position for a long time, and he was wearing this brown suit, and the jacket settled over his head, and the pants rode up on his legs, and you could see his nice brown socks. I don't know if his back got a spasm and he was fixing it or what. But when I saw that, I thought, *You know? You just never know.* And I wished . . . I kind of wanted to meet him, someone who would do that."

Chip pulls away from me, sits up straight. "Okay. Okay. Thank you." He takes in a breath. "Okay. I'm ready to do the next part."

He puts a handful of yellow capsules in his mouth, swallows them with some tea, then leans back and closes his eyes. Quickly, I slide the first pill out of my pocket and swallow it. I don't want to be too far behind him.

He takes another handful. Then he sits up suddenly, holds quite still. After a moment, he lies back and says, "I need to wait just a minute before I take the rest."

"Okay."

He takes my hand, looks tenderly at me. "Myra. I'm so sorry. This is too much to ask you."

"No. I want to be here."

"I'm sorry anyway."

"It's all right."

He takes another handful of yellow pills, and he has finished them.

"I'll take the red ones in just a few minutes. Remind me."

"I will."

"God. I'm sleepy already. Can that be?"

"Are you . . . do you want to lie down?"

"After. When I'm all done." He looks out the window. "Look. Look what a beautiful morning it is."

I look out at the sky, cloudless, a pale blue. In my little garden, bees will be crawling into the blossoms on the foxglove. The lilies will open a bit more. In the pond in the woods across the street, minnows will swim like dark clouds from one side to the other.

"Myra? You know, I think . . . I should do the rest alone. I think maybe you should go downstairs, now."

"No."

"It's all right. I'm fine. I'm not scared anymore. I can do it, and then you don't need to be here. Just call my folks when it's done. You go now." He gathers up the five red pills, swallows them. "I'm fine. I'm nearly asleep. Really. " He lies down, crosses his hands over his belly, closes his eyes.

I lie beside him, turn his face gently toward me, and he opens his eyes. "I'm here," I tell him. "And I will not leave you."

"Oh, Myra. I wish . . ."

"I know."

"Tell me what you'll do tomorrow." His speech has slowed; it's slurred now. I tighten my grip on his hand.

"Okay. Here's what I'll do. I'll go over to Hansen's farm. I'll get some eggs from the chicken's nests, the eggs are always warm, and there's a beautiful black-and-white rooster there, he's so proud, got these fierce little yellow eyes. I'll buy some corn and some basil and some green beans. I'll feel the skin of the apricots, they feel just like babies, and I'll pick out a few to bring home and put in a green bowl on the kitchen table. I'll look at the plums and the peaches and all the baskets of red cherries, and I'll get some of those too. And when I come home, I'll sit out in the backyard and I'll feel you all around me, you won't be gone, Chip. You will never be gone from me."

His eyes are closed again and his breathing has become very deep. Cheyne-stoking? Not yet, it's still regular. "I'll talk to you out loud at the end of every day, just like I'm doing now. I'll call you to come back here for a while. And I know you'll come, just like I know you'll be safe. You'll be safe from now on. No pain." I kiss him. "Chip?"

Nothing.

Very slowly, I take my hand from his. Then I reach into my pocket, take out the baggie and pour several yellow capsules into my hand, then into my mouth. *Hurry.* They are somewhat bitter tasting. I sit up slowly, careful not to shake the bed, and reach for the tea. I put the cup up to my lips, take in some liquid, and hold everything in my mouth for a long moment. And then, quietly weeping, I spit it all back into the cup.

I lie back down and pull Chip close to me, say his name. He murmurs something I don't understand, and then he doesn't speak again. I hold him tightly until his breathing stops. It takes a lifetime. It takes one half of one second. Half an hour, maybe; a day or two.

I lay my hand on his chest, then put two fingers to his carotid artery. Nothing. *Call a code,* some old part of my brain says. I kiss his cheek, growing cold already, and then I go downstairs. I sit by the phone for some time, one of my hands holding the other, and then I make the call.

I don't move at all until I hear the cab pull into my driveway. I don't think. But when I let DeWitt in and he wraps his skinny arms around me, I finally let loose. "That's right," he says. "That's the way. Aw, baby, here, here; I got you right here."

I sob and sob and sob until my ribs hurt, my back. But I am not thinking about what you might expect. I am not thinking about Chip at all.

I once took care of a fifty-nine-year-old man who had just moved into a tiny apartment after having been homeless and sleeping on grates for six years. The first time I visited him, I saw a nest of blankets and sheets and pillows in the corner. "Are you sleeping on the floor?" I asked.

"Yeah." He laughed, embarrassed.

"Why?"

He scratched his head, then smoothed down the few strands he still had left up there. "Well, that bed they give me is real nice. But I can't sleep in it. Only way I can get any shut-eye is to sleep on the floor."

"I see."

"It ain't *permanent,*" he said. "I'm working on it. I guess it's about time! In the meantime, you know what I just put up? Curtain rods! I didn't know there even was such a thing!"

He showed me the rods he'd put up, and the curtains he'd hung from them. They were obviously used, but they were lovely, a burgundy-and-cream pattern made more beautiful by their fading, I thought, and I told him so.

Three weeks later, he was sleeping all night in his bed. "It never was the bed's fault," he said. "Bed's just great. But I'll tell you something. Every night, I sit on the edge and think, 'Now, do I want to sleep on the bed or on the floor?' I guess that's just the way it's going to be with me."

"Maybe so," I said. And then I leaned closer to him to say, "But that's all right."

E P I L O G U E

It's late October, a beautiful warm Friday afternoon. I'm out in the woods walking Frank, letting him get some exercise before I leave him alone for several hours. I've got a date. Third one with the same guy. Fred, his name is. A teacher I met when I took care of his mother after her heart surgery. He's kind, and rather nice looking, too. We like a lot of the same things; we have a good time together.

I walk slowly, thinking about a fall day just like this one so many years ago, when Chip had organized a senior skip day. It was almost 100 percent successful—only Thomas Osterhout went to school, saying it would be immoral not to. But the rest of us took a chartered bus we'd all chipped in for and went out to breakfast at McDonald's. Then we went to Dana-Farber Hospital, in Boston. One of our classmates, Danny Christianson, had been admitted there. None of us knew his diagnosis, but we did know he was never coming back to school.

Chip went to the floor and talked to the nurses and they ended up letting all eighty-seven of us come up. Around fifteen at a time went into Danny's room, while the rest waited quietly in the lounge. We all had something for him: books, homemade cookies, stuffed animals, girlie magazines. I brought him a couple of 45's by the Beatles, and Mandy Clark, who sat next to me on the bus, brought him a tin can full of photographs that the yearbook staff had collected. Chip gave Danny—who had tried out spectacularly unsuccessfully for the football team—one of his own jerseys, so that he would have something to wear besides hospital gowns. Danny was wearing it when it was my turn to come in, and I remember being so grateful, because it helped take away from his bald head, his thin wrists, the alien equipment surrounding him.

However briefly, however incompletely, our visit to him that day normalized him, let him turn from isolation and fear to the immeasurable relief of loving companionship. A note our class later received from his mother said that our visit seemed to sustain him until the day he died. He'd kept everything we brought him in a circle around him. She said he died knowing in full measure how much he was cared for. I hope that's true.

I come to a tree so rich with autumn's golds and reds it makes for a mild ache. I lie down under it, close my eyes, and let my mind wander. I think of all that is happening elsewhere, as I lie here. Nearby, I can hear the sounds of a road crew. Somewhere else, monkeys chatter in trees. A male seahorse becomes pregnant. A diamond forms, a bee dances out directions, a windshield shatters. Somewhere a mother spreads peanut butter for her son's lunch, a lover sighs, a knitter binds off the edge of a sleeve. Clouds gather to make rain, corn ripens on the stalk, a cancer cell divides, a little league team scores. Somewhere blossoms open, a man pushes a knife in deeper, a painter darkens her blue. A cashier pours new dimes into an outstretched hand, rainbows form and fade, plates in the earth shift and settle. A woman opens a velvet box, male spiders pluck gently on the females' webs, falcons fall from the sky. Abstracts are real and time is a lie, it cannot be measured when one moment can expand to hold everything. You can want to live and end up choosing death; and you can want to die and end up living. What keeps us here, really? A thread that breaks in a breeze. And yet a thread that cannot be broken.

I open my eyes, look up at leaf-framed pieces of the sky. I do hope Danny knew. I hope Chip knew, too. I hope for everything, now.

I get up, dust off my jeans, and call Frank. It's time to go home and get ready.

NEVER CHANGE

Elizabeth Berg

A Readers Club Guide

ABOUT THIS GUIDE

The suggested questions are intended to
help your reading group find new and interesting
angles and topics for discussion for
Elizabeth Berg's *Never Change*. We hope that
these ideas will enrich your conversation
and increase your enjoyment of the book.

A Conversation with Elizabeth Berg

§

Q: One of the most striking aspects of *Never Change* is your understated depiction of Myra's childhood and how it informs her identity, both as a woman and a nurse. We wonder, initially, how a woman who grew up in such a cold, closed-door type of household could pursue a career as a nurse, of all things, for whom healing, nurturing, and preserving connections are paramount. And then, of course, we see exactly how this could be. What was the germ for Myra's story, and how did it grow? What role did your own previous career in nursing play?

A: First of all, having been a nurse informs virtually everything I write. That profession taught me so many lessons about the fragility of life, the importance of being mindful about the way you live, the need for appreciation of life's beauty and bounty while you are still healthy, and, perhaps most importantly, the worth of "unconditional positive regard," which is the way we were taught to approach our patients.

I never begin a novel with a definite idea of what I want to do. Rather, I start with a vague notion, a feeling, a desire or need to explore some issue. Then I let the book take me where it wants to go. In the case of *Never Change*, I began with wanting to write a kind of love story where two people come together who, under normal circumstances, never would have. Incidentally, when I began the book, I thought the ending would be the opposite of what it turned out to be.

Q: Myra Lipinski is a charming creation: straight-talking, funny, and often achingly insightful. It's always so refreshing to come across a female character like this in contemporary fiction: she's passionate about her work, she's unmistakably self-sufficient, and she's deeply vulnerable—all at once. Did the nuances of Myra's voice come easily?

A: Actually, her voice did come easily. She started talking in my head; I started typing on my computer. This is always the way it is with my characters when they talk. I don't really feel like I'm making up anything—I feel like I'm taking dictation.

Q: We see Myra in the Epilogue beneath a tree, eyes closed, reflecting on the "thread" of life. The change evident in *Never Change*'s heroine here is stirring—and your epigraph by Hemingway speaks directly to this scene. At this point, where would you say Myra is in her healing process? Can we look forward to reading more about Myra in future novels or stories?

A: I would say she was at the beginning. But it's a good, solid beginning—she knows she'll be fine. I don't plan to write about Myra again, but I've learned that I should never say never. So let me just say that it's extremely unlikely.

Q: Answering a question about why she tends to "sing her life" through the memoir form instead of the novel, Mary Karr said, "The truth is that I found it easier to lie in a novel, and what I wanted most of all was to tell the truth." By contrast, E. L. Doctorow has said that the element of truth is never more crucial than it is in the arena of fiction. Do you want to weigh in here? What does "truth" mean in fiction?

A: I am somewhere in the middle of these opinions. There is not literal truth in my novels, but there is certainly emotional truth. Fiction lets you get out of your own way, clearing the way for the unconscious to speak. And the unconscious always shows us the *real* truths; there is nothing to hide behind. For example, Myra is not anyone I know. But her character helped me understand things that are true about myself and what I believe, things I did not necessarily know before. This is not to say, of course, that I believe the same things that all my characters do. Sometimes having a character do or say or think something confirms my belief that it is not anything I would ever want to emulate.

Q: In the world of your novels, the mother-daughter relationship is an emotional minefield, ambivalent and matchlessly complex. *Never Change* is no exception—especially in the backward light of Myra's childhood memories. What is it about this relationship that keeps bringing you back?

A: I am interested in intensity—my idea of a good time is having a really great dinner with one other person, during which each of us reveals remarkably intimate things. I'm drawn to what lives in the truest, deepest places, even (perhaps especially) if they are dark places. I think the mother-daughter relationship is one of the most complex, intense relationships there is. I suppose I explore it so often because I'm both a mother and a daughter, and there are many issues in my life surrounding each role.

Q: Among your writing peers, whose work do you admire and draw inspiration from?

A: These are some of the writers I love: E.B. White, Alice Munro, Jane Hamilton, Anne Tyler, Richard Russo, Richard Ford, Richard Bausch, Haven Kimmel, Anne LaMott, Ellen Gilchrist, Leah Cohen, Mark Slouka, Michael Byers, Pam Houston.

Q: The recent Oprah Winfrey/Jonathan Franzen episode over *The Corrections* raised a lot of tough questions about literary elitism and the subjective lines that separate literary and popular fiction. As both a critically acclaimed author and a handpicked Oprah's Book Club novelist yourself, how do you feel about the Franzen situation and the various reactions it prompted?

A: I love what Oprah Winfrey does for books and reading, and I said that long before she ever picked me to be in her book club. Here's what I think about the Jonathan Franzen episode: If you have concerns about a corporate logo, the time to say it is *before* your book comes out with the cover. Franzen could have said no thanks, when Oprah called. Once having accepted the honor of being in her book club, he should have kept his reservations to himself. Not having done that, he should have had the courage to stand behind his own convictions, rather than doing the kind of vacillating and backpedaling he seemed to do. I think Jonathan Franzen is a remarkably talented writer (with a *great* author photo), and I do sympathize with a writer's desire to keep his book as pure as possible. I suppose having a corporate logo on the cover is tantamount to having advertising on it. But let's put the cards on the table: as soon as you hand your manuscript over to a publishing house, you're in for some compromising, one way or another. If you want to keep the process absolutely pure, you probably should think about publishing your books yourself.

Q: You have a background in nonfiction writing. How and when did you begin writing fiction? To what degree did your parents and teachers play a role in your writing aspirations?

A: I began to write short stories after I'd been writing nonfiction (mostly personal essays) in magazines for several years. The interest in fiction happened organically, gradually—when I first started being published, I *never* thought I would write fiction, especially novels. The word "novel" scared me.

My parents influenced my becoming a writer in very indirect ways. My father said he believed me when I insisted, at nine years old, that someday I would be famous and buy him a red Cadillac. (I did buy him a red Cadillac, too, though it was *many* years later.) It really meant something that he seemed to believe in me, however grandiose my plans. My mother read to me as a child, and she always had a big stack of library books at her bedside. She made it seem like a good idea to read a lot, particularly since she always ate candy bars while she read in bed, propped up on pillows with cases that had been line-dried and ironed. (Usually she ate Heath bars, which still seem exotic to me.)

I was a pretty difficult child—oversensitive, overly dramatic. My parents called me "Sarah" after Sarah Bernhardt, the romantic and tragic French actress of her day. Thank God I found an outlet for that sense of drama.

My teachers were always supportive, telling me from early on that I was a very good writer. Many said I should be a writer, but that was like telling me I should be an astronaut—it just wasn't realistic for me to think I could ever do that.

Q: What is your sense of who your readers are? What do they want from a novel? Describe your ideal reader.

A: I think my readers are mostly women, though more men are coming on board. (A lot of women ask the men in their lives to read certain of my books, especially *The Pull of the Moon*.) I have had people as young as 11 and as old as 80 write to me and come to readings, and the notion that my books appeal to such a wide range of readers is extremely gratifying to me. That having been said, most of my readers, I think, are women about my age. I would guess that they want a novel that makes them think and lets them feel; one that, though it is fiction, tells them something that makes them think and lets them feel; one that, though it is fiction, tells some vital truths. Readers often tell me they feel as if I've been spying on them, or they'll say, "You write what I feel, but can't say." My idea reader is someone who understands and appreciates subtlety, who relishes reading a book where humor and pathos are equally mixed, who agrees with me that it's always the little things that matter most.

Q: What are you working on these days? Tell us about your new novel.

A: The next novel, *True to Form*, features Katie, a character seen in both *Durable Goods* and *Joy School*. The story is about betrayal, about those watershed moments that occur in our lives and mark us forever—*and* point us inexorably in certain directions. It's also about learning to understand and honor your unique self, no matter how it compares with others. Someone at a reading once asked me to write another book about Katie, because "I *have* to know what becomes of her." This book tells you. Katie is my favorite character, so *True to Form* was a pleasure to write.

(I wanted to call it *You Be Connie Francis; I'll Be Sandra Dee*, but I got voted down.)

What I'm working on now are the final edits for a novel called *The Man Who Did Everything Wrong*, which will be out for Christmas 2002. It's written from the man's point of view, a very different kind of thing for me. I read a lot of children's letters to Santa for this book, and I did an extensive interview with "Santa." That was fun, and unexpectedly moving.

After that, I have ideas for three other novels, but they're too new to talk about yet. Suffice it to say that all of them deal with *big* life issues. Still Sarah, after all these years.

Reading Group Questions and Topics for Discussion

❧

1. The Prologue to *Never Change* consists of a detailed, finely
   wrought catalog of vivid images—intimate, precise snatches of
   human activity. Here, Elizabeth Berg employs the painterly
   tools of a poet and manages to capture the invisible rhythms of
   life as they emerge—in the mind of our protagonist Myra
   Lipinski—in the smallest gestures and most incidental occur-
   rences, in situations which seem, at least on the surface, wholly
   unremarkable. Among other things, we see two young girls,
   hand in hand at a traffic intersection, simply "exhilarated by
   their survival." And we see a pair of boys on bicycles possessed
   with what Myra calls a "sweet toughness." What sort of mood
   is being established through the language and style of the
   Prologue? And what are we to take from its final sentence?
   What is the tone of this line in particular?

2. It is in the Prologue, too, that Elizabeth Berg begins subtly to
   lay the framework for certain key themes and concerns that are
   to develop over the course of the novel. What, for example, is
   intimated as early as the first page about Myra's feelings for
   and about children and motherhood? And what sorts of private
   anxieties and fears might be underlying the particular language
   she chooses to describe the solitary woman at the bus stop?
   Even before the first chapter begins, what techniques is Berg
   using to sketch out the initial shadings and dimensions of
   Myra Lipinski, the woman who is about to share with us her
   personal story?

3. What range of emotions did you experience while reading
   Never Change? As you look back through Berg's book, which
   moments and particular scenes do you recall being affected
   by the most? Which were the most compelling, painful,
   frightening, and/or inspiring?

4. All of Elizabeth Berg's novels, from *Durable Goods* on, are
   enjoyed by readers and critics for (among many reasons) the

grace and clarity of Berg's unsentimental writing, and also for the complex, uncompromising ambivalence that marks her characters' lives. Now, with *Never Change*, what additional qualities would you ascribe to her work? Is this novel a significant departure for Elizabeth Berg? Explain. Discuss the notion that, for all of its wry humor and its ultimately hopeful tenor, Berg's latest novel is by no means afraid of the dark. Through the lives of the various characters in this book, the author examines a range of deeply painful human conditions, from chronic isolation to bereavement. What are some others? What roles do they play in the shaping of Myra's narrative?

5. If you had to distill, in a few sentences or so, what the essential themes are that drive the narrative in *Never Change*, what would you say?

6. Is it possible or useful to establish a thematic link between E. M. Forster's famous *Howard's End* trope, "Only connect," and the ideas informing Berg's story? Explain. What is the particular nature of connection in the world of this novel?

7. What other possible literary antecedents—whether thematic, structural, or stylistic—exist for *Never Change*? Talk about Berg's work in relation to that of other novelists, from Jane Austen to Anne Tyler and beyond, who have inhabited with similar intensity and intimacy the lives, quests, and awakenings of strong heroines.

8. In connection with the previous question, discuss what it is about Berg's style that distinguishes it from that of her peers—contemporary novelists. To which novelists would you say Elizabeth Berg bears the closest comparison?

9. "You know people like me," begins Myra. "I'm the one everybody liked but no one wanted to be with." What sorts of narrative clues does Elizabeth Berg thread through her narrative—especially in the first few chapters—in order to clarify and add layers to the exact nature (and provenance) of Myra's personality and character? Discuss, for example, Myra's

apparent lack of self-esteem and her frequent, almost reflexive rush to deride herself—as if she were beating to the punch someone else's potential ridicule. How and where does Berg, in her writing, communicate these and other facets of her protagonist's character without ever explicitly naming them?

10. How would the story change if Elizabeth Berg had chosen to tell it from a more remote, third-person point of view? What would be gained, and what lost?

11. Which aspects of Myra Lipinski do you most and least identify with?

12. Consider the structure of *Never Change*. What sorts of decisions do you imagine Berg had to make in shaping, editing, and essentially fusing two stories—one a death, another a rebirth of sorts—into distinct chapters, passages, and scenes? What narrative spaces and time gaps does Berg inject into her story, and why? What is the first question you would ask Elizabeth Berg about her novel?

13. With the arrival of Chip Reardon into her life, Myra begins cautiously to let herself feel things more deeply than she has in years. And she's profoundly frightened by it. Why?

14. "When he took my arm today, I liked that, I liked so much when he took my arm. I make this thought into a shape, and sleep with it." Discuss all that Berg has packed into these lines, which close the seventh chapter. What is going on here, with Myra's muted recognition of the comfort she is permitting herself to take in Chip's arrival? Is the comfort tangible? And does this matter?

15. Chart the course of the love that blooms between Myra and Chip. How would you characterize their love? [What is the balance between hope, passion, and exhilaration on one hand, and fear, desperation, and loss on the other?]

16. Explain Myra's actions over the last several pages of the novel. What emotions and impulses drive the choice she ultimately makes?

17. Myra's mother is a sort of ghostly presence floating through the present action of the novel. What kind of mother was she? Looking back through the narrative, picking out the fragmented memories and reflections that pepper the story, what can we infer about the nature of Myra's upbringing? And where can we see the legacy of this upbringing coloring and informing Myra's choices and struggles and frustrations as an adult?

18. What is Chip hoping to demonstrate to Myra by organizing the "family" dinner party at the restaurant in Boston? And how do his intentions reveal themselves in their conversations over the remainder of the novel?

19. The final page of the Epilogue is a rich stream of disparate images reflecting life's infinite variety and wonder. Myra asks, in the face of it all, "What keeps us here, really? A thread that breaks in a breeze. And yet a thread cannot be broken." What is meant here? What is the nature of the thread metaphor Berg introduces here, and how does it speak to all that has come before it in *Never Change*?

20. How did your feelings about Myra evolve over the course of the novel? Describe the Myra we meet in the Epilogue. Compare her to the Myra who greeted us early on with the line, "You know people like me." What has happened? And how is the change reflected in Berg's narrative tone and rhythm at the close of the novel? To what degree would you say Myra has healed here? Explain. And from what emotional injuries, beyond Chip's death, might she still be healing?

21. Why is the novel titled *Never Change*? What roles do change/transformation/renewal/rebirth play at different points in the narrative?